Listening for the Crack of Dawn

Listening
for the
Crack of Dawn

Donald D. Davis

August House Publishers, Inc.
L I T T L E   R O C K

Printed in the United States of America

10 9 8 7 6 5 4 3 2 1

LIBRARY OF CONGRESS CATALOGING-IN-PUBLICATION DATA

Davis, Donald D., 1944
Listening for the crack of dawn/by Donald D. Davis.—1st ed.
.p   .cm
ISBN 0-87483-153-9 (alk. paper): $17.95
I. Title
PS3554.A933r7L5   1990
813'.54—dc20   90-40558

First Edition, 1990

Executive in charge: Ted Parkhurst
Project editor: Judith Faust
Design director: Ted Parkhurst
Jacket design and illustration: Ron Bell
Typography: Heritage Publishing Company

This book is printed on archival-quality paper which meets the
guidelines for performance and durability of the Committee on
Production Guidelines for Book Longevity of the
Council on Library Resources.

AUGUST HOUSE, INC.   PUBLISHERS   LITTLE ROCK

For my father

Joseph Simmons Davis

in his ninetieth year

Preface

Most of the stories in this collection were originally created as stories for telling aloud. As their variants grew, and partly because of requests to have them available in written form, I somewhat reluctantly undertook to create written versions of them.

I realized early that in writing I had entered an entirely new medium. The same stories I have told countless times orally here appear in a new medium as stories written to be read. The difference for me is largely the absence of an audience for immediate visual feedback, so that details must be more complete and the stories must be more fully told than is possible when voice, expression and gesture can serve as a storyteller's shortcuts.

As a set, the stories began to take on connections and a sense of wholeness I had not seen in them before. The discovery of this connectedness prompted me to write several new stories—not previously told—to fill what felt like gaps as the whole set began to look like a chronological growing-up cycle. This has been a new and fascinating undertaking. The end product is not a novel, but does seem to have become more than a collection of separate stories. After all, the crack of dawn *is* heard every day.

The end product is finally a set of stories about trying to grow up. The characters live their separate lives, and many are finished in a single story, yet the growing up goes on. The young central characters continue that mysterious educational dynamic that see-saws in all of our lives between clarification and confusion.

My hope is that these stories are about events so ordinary that each reader has, even if living in a totally different world, "been there." The extent to which that identification is achieved v'll be the extent to which the stories succeed, and perhaps, *do* become more than separate tales.

My great debt of appreciation in this work is to the countless audiences of storytelling, who through their laughter, tears, iggles, smiles, and even silence, have affirmed the good and corrected the bad until the stories have become gradually finished.

Specific thanks go to Beth, Doug, Kelly, and Jonathan for their patience and their much-needed encouragement and love.

I am grateful to the board members and staff of the National Association for the Preservation and Perpetuation of Storytelling for being a total support group in my growth as storyteller over many years.

Appreciation and love go to the members of Christ United Methodist Church in High Point, North Carolina, for their constant expressions of love and faith.

Four friends must be mentioned by name: Jimmy Neil Smith, whose unending encouragement is responsible for more than he will ever know; Michael Williams, for the care and feeding off my spirit even at long distance and in scattered doses; Susan Gordon, the most thorough cheerleader in the world; and Merle Smith Creech, for not just reading the manuscript but really "hearing" the stories in a new way so they might get their final tuning and correction.

And to all who read and listen, thank you for believing in stories.

Donald D. Davis

And in the end,
the turtle won the race.

AESOP'S FABLES, PARAPHRASED

Contents

Aunt Laura and
the Crack of Dawn

VERY SHORTLY AFTER I WAS BORN, Aunt Laura came to live with us. She was, in reality, my great-aunt, Daddy's Aunt Laura Henry. She had lived, unmarried, with her sister-in-law, my Grandmother Henry, until Grandmother died the same year I was born. After Grandmother's death, Aunt Laura became what Daddy called "a floater."

She would live in the spare front bedroom at our house for weeks at a time. After her first such visit continued for more than a month, Mother came out of her room one Sunday afternoon and looked harshly up at my Daddy. "It's time," she said, "to take her for a ride!"

We loaded Aunt Laura and her small cardboard suitcase into our old blue Dodge. After a long and scenic ride around Nantahala County, we ended up for a visit at Aunt Hester's house. We returned home alone.

After she had served her month, Aunt Hester "floated" Aunt Laura down to Aunt Marie's house. When that month was past, my brother Joe and I (at least) welcomed her back to our house for another term.

We loved it when she was with us. She was the first adult in my life who kept loving me no matter what I did. In fact, she liked it more the worse I was. She played with us all the time.

Aunt Laura was the oldest living thing I had ever seen. She always wore long dresses which came down to the floor, bonnets on her head, whether indoors or out, and thick rimless glasses, which turned into mirrors when she looked at us. We

13

never knew what color her eyes were; the glasses were impossible to see through.

Her skin, the few places we could see it, was the color and texture of wadded up grocery bags, coarse and rough and wrinkled as it could possibly be. I often thought that if all the wrinkles could be stretched out of her skin, it would be big enough to hold a person at least twice her size. Never, I thought, could there have been such a waste of skin on anyone in the world.

Aunt Laura could get up earlier in the morning than anyone in our house. Joe-brother, as she called him, and I would go to bed at night plotting to wake one another up as soon as either of us awakened. Still we never managed to beat her. As soon as we awakened, we knew we had lost, for even as we rushed down to the kitchen, we already smelled the coffee perked and the fire in the woodstove.

There we found her, frying pan heated and waiting to cook breakfast to order for each of us as we finally got up.

On one of those early mornings I asked her, "Aunt Laura, how do you get up so early?"

She laughed and laughed and finally said, "Why, law, son...I guess I just get up at the crack of dawn!"

I was probably four or five years old and had never heard anyone say that. My next question to her was, "Can you hear the crack of dawn?"

She threw her old head back and laughed even harder this time. "Why, sure, son," she answered. "I hear the crack of dawn and it wakes me up. And I'll tell you what: once I've heard it, nobody else can...and everybody else in the whole countryside just has to get up the best way they can."

I must have looked pretty disappointed at hearing that, and I must have showed it, for she looked down at me and said, "Don't you worry about that. When I'm dead and gone and don't need to get up any more, I'll leave that to you...and you'll be the one who can hear the crack of dawn."

"Don't ever die, Aunt Laura," I said quickly.

"Oh, son, everything in the whole world dies when it gets

old enough. I'm pretty old. Don't you ever worry about that...it's just the natural way things are."

Aunt Laura's job at our house was washing the dishes. We didn't make her do it. She once said my mother didn't do it right. So, with that, we "let" her do it.

Daddy had remodeled the old kitchen in our house when he and Mother got married. When he bought the old house there was no running water in the kitchen. There was a pump on the back porch which brought water that far but not into the kitchen itself.

The decision to remodel changed things. He went to Asheville to Sears-Roebuck and bought a new gigantic sink which was so big he had to borrow Uncle Floyd's pick-up truck to haul it home in.

It was a beautiful (and heavy) white enameled sink, with a rippled white enamel drain board on each side. There were several drawers for knives, and dividers for silverware, and even big doors underneath where you could store pots and pans.

Once the plumber finished, you could turn on the cold water faucet and cold water would come out right there in the house! The faucet which said "hot" just turned around and around and didn't do anything. Joe-brother and I figured it must be a spare.

The most remarkable thing about the entire new sink was that it had a stopper...which really worked! For the first time in her life our mother could make water stay in the sink. She was completely spoiled and started washing dishes right there in the sink itself.

She would, of course, heat the water on the stove, pour it in the sink, add enough cold to make it just right, wash her dishes, and then pull the stopper and smile while she watched the water run out on its own without her having to carry it outside in the cold of winter.

Aunt Laura was shocked. "Everybody knows you're supposed to wash dishes in the dishpan," she said, "so that you can carry the water outside when you're finished and pour it in the flower bed. That's the way we've always done it...washing in

15

the sink is just a big waste of water. That's what dishpans were made for."

Mother gladly turned the dishwashing over to her so she could do it the way she'd always done it.

She was a tiny woman who had to stand on an upside-down Coca-Cola crate in order to reach the sink. She put the cold water in the dishpan, carried it to the stove to heat, then carried it, hot, back to the sink. With the dishpan in the sink, she added cold water and soap and washed the dishes.

Her method was to put the clean dishes in a wire rack on the drainboard, while she boiled more water and scalded them in the end. "A lot more sanitary than drying with a dishtowel," she declared.

Once finished, she was ready to take out the water.

She went to the back door and propped it open with a yellow flint rock she kept there for a door stop. Then it was back up on the Coca-Cola crate. She picked up the heavy dishpan of water, backed up to the opposite wall of the kitchen, and ran for the open back door.

Small steps grew faster and faster as she crossed the kitchen and then sped, now full speed across the back porch.

A railing ran about waist high all the way around the back porch. As she neared the railing, she picked up on the dishpan, and when she ran into the railing, she let loose with one hand and the water went down into the flower bed. Aunt Laura shook the empty pan of its last drops of water, came back into the house, and hung it on the nail behind the stove.

One night she went out the door and didn't come back.

Joe-brother and I looked out into the darkness, and darkness was all we saw. We cried, "Daddy!" By the time he got there, we figured out what had happened. The porch railing hadn't held, and Aunt Laura had gone right through the air, dishpan full of dirty water and all, and landed out in the back yard.

She was very slow in coming back inside, because when she hit the ground she had lost her glasses. Quite some time had been spent there on the wet and soapy ground looking for them. When she re-entered the light at the edge of the porch, she had them back on, but one lens was missing.

Joe-brother got excited. We had never been able to see what color her eyes were! He punched me and said, "Look...look at her eye!" But the side with the missing lens turned out to be the side of her face which had hit the ground hardest, and that eye was swollen shut. We never, ever, knew what color they were.

Often at night, after the dishes were all washed and put away, Aunt Laura would say, "Come on boys, it's a good clear night. Let's go out and look at the stars."

We'd go way down in the pasture, away from the lights of the house. Aunt Laura gave the orders. "Stretch out on the ground now. Put your feet toward the Burgins' house, that's north." The instruction to face north always came in the wintertime when the ground was as cold as it could be, and Aunt Laura never paid attention to whether our cow might have left treasure exactly where we were now sitting.

In the summertime, we were told to "put our feet toward the Mehaffeys' house...that's south."

Beginning with the Big Dipper—unless, as she said, "the old bear's asleep," on those mid-winter nights when the mountains made the dipper's stars too low—we would work our way across the sky until I could find and name dozens of stars and constellations at every season of the year.

My own wintertime favorite was the giant Orion, looking down on us like a great sword-carrying guardian. I thought his head was too small until Aunt Laura told us that the whole full moon would fit into his head, if it were in the right place.

In summer, we watched the parade of the constellations of the zodiac as they marched across the southern sky. My favorite was the scorpion, with his up-stretched pincers and the reddish, pulsing star which looked like his heart. "Antares," Aunt Laura called the red star. "He strives with Mars."

Sometimes Joe-brother and I grew weary of stargazing, especially on those clear, cold nights of winter, and we questioned her. "Aunt Laura, why do we have to learn about all these stars?"

She answered very quietly, like she had said the answer

over and over to herself until she had almost worn it out. "Well, boys, sometimes people grow up and have to go places they don't want to go." The Second World War was going on, but Joe-brother and I knew nothing of that, except that our Uncle William had gone to a place everyone called "Overseas." She must have known all about it, though. "When you have to go places you don't want to go, the same thing always happens to you."

We were far from imagining what she could be talking about, so I just asked her. "What happens to you?"

Her answer came quickly: "You get *homesick*. Boys, if you ever go somewhere and get homesick, just remember this: everybody lives under the same sky! Just wait until it gets dark, then go outside and look up. If you know them, those stars will take you right home."

Then we'd go back inside and check our clothing to see if we had gotten into anything when we stretched out on the pasture ground.

Aunt Laura never got married. It was my observation that she simply had very little use for men as a group, and some of them she seemed to downright dislike. Our attempts to find masculine companionship for her were totally unsuccessful.

There was Mr. William Starker. Mr. Starker came to our house twice each year: once in the spring to plow the garden and once in the fall to clean out the barn and spread the manure from it onto the garden. He was unmarried and had as his sole companion a small mule that he plowed with. It seemed to us he might get along well with Aunt Laura.

Mr. Starker was a tall, thin man who seemed fairly old to me. He had a deeply grooved face, not as wrinkled as Aunt Laura's. He always wore bib overalls and in hot weather neither wore a shirt nor buttoned the overalls on the sides. William Starker smelled like a combination of sweat, chewing tobacco, and alcohol, and Aunt Laura didn't like him.

She said that the reason she didn't like him around was because he sweated and didn't bathe and then sweated some more on top of that. "There's nothing wrong with sweat," she said. "Everyone ought to sweat when he works...you just ought to wash it off between times."

You didn't have to be around William Starker very long to realize that he didn't bother with the "washing off" part.

Mr. Starker would come with his mules to plow and would start in on the corn-and-beans side of the garden. After a few rounds he would come to the back door of the house and knock. I knew what he wanted. Slowly Aunt Laura would go to answer the door and hear his request: "Ma'am...could I please have... Ma'am...a long drink of water?"

Aunt Laura would not answer him; she just turned and did it. But she never gave William Starker one of our glasses to drink out of. Instead, she would reach on the closet shelf for an empty quart canning jar, fill it with water at the sink, and give it to him.

He would drink it all down in one long drink, then wipe his sweaty face with an old dirty handkerchief, say, "Thanks, Ma'am," and return to his work.

Aunt Laura kept the jar set aside for his later requests, but once he had finished work and gone home, she threw the jar in the trash and broke it so that none of us might "get nastified." He was just too dirty for her!

One of the other men Aunt Laura disliked in particular was Mr. Hill Brown. (We jokingly called him "Brown Hill," but he let it be known that he knew about it and hated it when people did that.)

Hill Brown came to do all the dirty little jobs no one else wanted to do. Daddy would call him to clean the chimney or to unstop the septic tank lines (when Mother's favorite weeping willow's roots invaded and clogged them) or even to help deliver a calf.

He drove an old, black, rusty Ford roadster which had no top at all. On the back was a hand-lettered sign that proclaimed, "One more payment, and she's mine!"

The reason Aunt Laura disliked Hill Brown so much was that Daddy hired him to tear down bird nests. English sparrows built nests everywhere. They were in the gables of the house and in the vents below the peak of the roof, in the ends of the garage and, of course, all around the barn.

Hill Brown called them "pests," climbed his wooden ladder, and tore away all remnants of their brushy nests. This made Aunt Laura mad.

"That ignorant man," she would rail about him. "He doesn't know they're not even English sparrows...there's no such thing as an English sparrow...they are weaver finches. You may have to tear their nests down, but I wish he wouldn't smile when he does it."

So Aunt Laura never married. The final reason for her singleness was not that she disliked all men. All her life she knew other men whom she cared for and respected. The real truth was simply that she had a prior commitment, a greater love.

Aunt Laura was absolutely and totally in love with Dental Scotch Snuff, and if getting married meant that she had to give up dipping snuff...well, no man on the face of God's earth was worth that.

She dipped snuff twenty-four hours a day; her lower lip was always full. Joe-brother and I could smell her coming before we could see or hear her. Her snuff-breath turned the air sweet with its heavy brown aroma. As she approached we could see that the tiny wrinkles running from her lower lip to her chin were outlined with escaped trails of brown snuff spittle.

The Dental Scotch Snuff was always bought in big pumpkin-colored boxes which Aunt Laura kept on the dresser in front of the mirror in her bedroom. Normally, she loaded there, but also kept a little tinful of snuff in her apron pocket to be sure she didn't get caught away from the house without a load.

The big boxes were made with small tin spouts which pulled open on the sides. Aunt Laura complained, "Whoever invented these little spouts didn't dip snuff...you can't get enough snuff out of one of those little tin spouts in a half-day to fill your lip full."

Her alternative was to take a kitchen knife and cut the whole top half-off the box, turn back the box top, and now she could get at the snuff when she wanted it!

One day when nobody was at home, I thought, "You really should try that snuff. Why, the way Aunt Laura loves it, it must be good. Looks just like what Mother makes hot chocolate out of."

I checked to be very certain that no one was around, then slipped into Aunt Laura's room. Over to her big dresser I went. There was a good, full box there...she wouldn't miss a thing.

She always loaded in front of the mirror. I had seen her do it a thousand times, watching through the cracked door you could see her in the mirror even if she had her back to the door. I knew exactly what to do!

I picked up the box, pulled out my lower lip with my left hand, tipped the box in the air, and tapped the side of the upturned box with my little finger. "Tap...tap...tap..."

Nothing happened! I tried it again, tapping harder this time, and, when the snuff started sliding out of the box it didn't stop. The whole box full emptied itself at once into my open mouth. The shock was so great that I inhaled—sharply "Huuuh?" before realizing that this was not at all the right thing to do.

In a matter of seconds I was certain that someone had blown up the house. Things which had stayed firmly on the floor all of my life seemed up in the air and the entire world was swirling around and around. I fought the whole world with flailing arms until it settled back into place, then realized a box of snuff will cover a good-sized room.

Aunt Laura saved my life that day. She was the first person back to the house, and she got me breathing again. She also helped me clean up the mess.

In the middle of our cleaning, she looked straight at me. "Son," she said, "if you ever again have to clean up a large volume of snuff, don't use water. If there's anything worse than plain old snuff dust, just look at this snuff mud you've made. Oh, this white chenille bedspread!"

It was midwinter, and very dark at night. Joe-brother and I were sleeping soundly when Daddy came into our room and said:

21

"Get up, boys...go to milk with me."

We always loved to go to milk the cow with him and almost always went in the summertime. In the winter we went in the afternoon, but very seldom in the morning, as morning came too early in winter.

Joe-brother rolled over and went back to sleep while I slipped out of bed in the dark and pulled on my pants. Without ever turning on the light, we felt our way to the kitchen and pulled the milk bucket out from behind the woodstove where it always stayed.

Still in the dark, we stepped out into the freezing winter night of the back porch. The air, carried fast by February wind, cut through our clothes, and as Daddy flipped a light switch on the wall of the porch, the whole world came to light.

The light, which blazed on the side of the barn some fifty yards below the house, revealed to us ice everywhere. A huge winter storm in the night had covered the ground with a sparkling hard carpet of ice. There were yellow-bell bushes bent to the ground, tops of pine trees turned down, and all of the fence wires looked thicker than a man's finger. The world was weighted with ice.

Daddy never said a word. He took the bucket in one hand and grasped my hand in his, and, without really ever picking our feet up, we eased down the steps and scooted out to the barn. The gate was especially hard to open, covered as it was with heavy ice.

Once inside the barn, it was much warmer. Helen, our big guernsey cow, seemed to warm the inside of the barn, and of course, there was no wind. With no light inside the barn, Daddy had to light a kerosene lantern to milk by. I played in the feed room and gave Helen extra dairy mash while I listened to him milk.

It was not necessary to watch what was happening...just to listen. As he started, the heavy squirts of milk rang in the bottom of the big bucket. Along the way the sound flattened from a ringing to a splat, which went on until the squirts grew weak as he stripped the last drops of milk from her udder. Then he was finished.

Daddy patted Helen on the hip, put away his stool, and started for the door. I followed silently. He pushed open the door, stepped up onto the threshold, then turned back and looked, into the dark, at me. I can see him standing there to this very day.

Without any warning in the world he said, "Aunt Laura died." Before I even realized what I had been told, he continued, "But, if anybody says anything about it, you say 'she just passed away.' "

I was not upset hearing that she had died. Even she herself had told me that everything dies when it gets old enough, and she was, after all, the oldest living thing I had ever seen. But I simply could not figure out what "passing away" was.

As we started back to the house I was completely confused. She didn't go to school or drive a car, and those were the only times I had ever heard of anybody "passing" anything. (There was that time when they talked about Uncle Floyd passing a kidney stone, but this didn't sound anything like that, either.)

Was she dead or alive? Would she be there when we got back to the house, or not? Would I ever, ever see her again?

We had just passed my favorite black walnut tree, a split-trunked tree you could climb up in the summer and bounce on the long lower limbs of, when very suddenly, the heavy load of ice from last night's storm became too heavy for the tree.

From right behind us with a deafening *"crack,"* the entire walnut tree split from top to bottom.

When Daddy and I jumped around at the sound, we could just see the edge of the sun peeking over the hill below the Burgins' house.

It was the crack of dawn! And I had heard it! And that hearing answered all my questions at once.

The first thing I knew was that Aunt Laura was really dead. I had heard the crack of dawn...she had left it to me the way she promised.

But the most important thing was, and is to this day, that

now that I hear the crack of dawn, I shall never, not even for one single day, be really very far away from my dear Aunt Laura.

Winning and Losing

FOR SIX YEARS I HAD WAITED for this day to arrive. I was going to school!

Since the time of my earliest memories, Sunday mornings had been spent waiting for Daddy to get up. I waited because Joe-brother and I needed a "reader."

The Sunday Asheville Citizen-Times had arrived with its full-color comic section, and after Joe-brother and I fought over interpreting everything from "Maggie and Jiggs" to "Dick Tracy," we needed someone who could read to clear the whole matter up for us.

After six years of such Sunday mornings, the dream was coming true. I was going—Joe-brother was jealous—to Sulpher Springs School.

My personal plan was to learn to read first thing on the first day. After that, they could go ahead and teach me anything they wanted to.

It was Tuesday, the day after Labor Day. At 6:30 a.m. Mother got me up with orders to take a bath. "What do you mean 'take a bath'?" I asked her. "I take baths on Saturday night."

"Today is the first day of school," was her answer. "You've got to at least start out clean. We don't want any of the teachers at school to get you mixed up with any of those nasty little short-necked Rabbit Creek boys."

So I was scrubbed, then dressed in a brand-new pair of unwashed blue jeans which were so stiff I could barely move my knees. The blue jeans rubbed my skin very harshly at some uncomfortably tender places, and every time I tried to sit down, they were so stiff they tried to stand me up again. The outfit was topped off by a new shirt with a collar which felt like the edge of a tin can.

We all climbed into the blue Dodge, Joe-brother was left with the next neighbor, and Daddy drove Mother and me to Sulpher Springs School as he went on his way to work.

This was a school that looked like a school in a storybook. It was all red brick, with three sets of steps leading up the front to three sets of tall, white columns. The center steps led to the main entrance and on in to the principal's office. The other two sets of steps, I learned later, led to the auditorium and the cafeteria.

Mother and I went in the doors toward the office, but were quickly sent down a long hall of classrooms and into the auditorium for the assembling of new first graders.

I had never been in or even seen such a big room. It was bigger than the inside of our church. There were rows and rows and rows of wooden seats with curved backs and with seat bottoms which folded up and down making a loud "clunk" each time you dared move them. Each row was lettered and every single seat had a little oval-shaped metal plate, bearing the seat number, tacked to the seat back.

Mother and I took seats G-7 and G-8.

"Sounds like 'Bingo,' " I said, trying to make a joke. We were almost exactly in the center of our row, looking straight up at a stage which was closed off by a dark green curtain with "SSS" embroidered in big gold letters at the top.

I pointed to the letters. "What are those gold letters for?" I asked Mother in a whisper.

"Sulpher Springs School," she answered. "Just wait until you can read for yourself."

We were not alone. In the front of an auditorium which must hold the entire school were on this day assembled more than a hundred new first graders. There were also more than another hundred mamas, and, I think, three daddies. Our row was packed. In fact, it seemed that at least the front half of the auditorium was most completely full.

Finally the stage curtain began to open, operated by some

powerful unseen hand. There, standing in the flood of light at center stage, was Mr. Lonnie Underhill. It would be several weeks before I heard that most of the kids at school secretly called him "Loony Lonnie."

With a deliberateness born of years of experience, Mr. Underhill began to welcome us to the first grade and tell us all the things we needed to know for success at Sulpher Springs School.

Mr. Underhill's speech went on and on. It was all about school spirit and behavior rules and school buses and how to pay for lunch in the cafeteria and how to buy school supplies in the office. There were rules about vaccinations and absences and on and on and on. It seemed like we had already been there all day.

At last, he began to introduce the first grade teachers.

First, there was Miss Caldwell. I should have known we were in for trouble when Mr. Underhill began by telling us the life story of Miss Caldwell's mother, who had taught him as a child and had put in years at Sulpher Springs before Miss Caldwell was even born.

"Miss Caldwell," he finally concluded, was just "born with teaching right in her blood." It was a good, long, substantial introduction and the first of four good, long, substantial introductions of first grade teachers we were to hear that day.

About this time I began to slowly make a very frightening discovery: suddenly I began to realize that for the first time in my entire life I was in a place in which I did not know where the bathroom was. Even if I had known, it would have done no good. Trapped in the very center of row G, there was absolutely no way out!

By this time most of us six-year-olds were getting wiggly. There was a growing amount of noise and seat squeaking going on throughout the auditorium.

Mr. Underhill finished his last introduction. I thought, "Maybe we'll get to go now."

"Now children," he looked down at us over his glasses, "we still have a lot of housekeeping to take care of. I see, or rather I *hear,* that some of you are having trouble keeping your seats quiet. Let's stop now and have a few minutes of 'quiet seat drill.' "

For what seemed like the next twenty minutes, we practiced: standing up, folding our seats up so that they didn't make a sound, folding them down again, sitting down. Over and over and over again until we were quiet enough to suit Mr. Underhill. The activity was also somewhat helpful, in that it took my attention off the bathroom emergency for awhile.

"Next, boys and girls," Mr. Underhill began as soon as we were seated quietly again, "we have to call the roll." With every name he called, the bathroom crisis got worse and worse until by the time he was passing "Setzer...Smith...Summey..." I began to realize that I could not possibly be dry by the time we finally got out of this place.

I began to try every trick I could possibly think of to relieve the pain which was steadily increasing in my bladder. I gripped the wooden arms of the auditorium seats until my knuckles turned white and it seemed that the bones might pop through the skin. I took in as much breath as I could hold, then held it as long as possible before quickly letting it all out and even more quickly grabbing another full breath. But, inside, I knew that I would never make it out of this place and to the bathroom in time.

In desperation I tried to think of something good about all this. My mind was blank, until suddenly I got it! "I am wearing brand-new, dark blue, unfaded blue jeans. I won't look nearly as wet in these new dark blue jeans as I would in old, faded jeans!" That thought, helpful as it was, faded itself as the moment of truth closed in.

Mr. Underhill and the four first grade teachers had finished calling the roll. They had tried to find out the whereabouts of those who did not show up. They had added to the list the names of those present who hadn't signed up ahead of time. Finally, they had counted the names and divided by four and determined that "all students from Patricia Abernethy to Thomas Greene will be in Miss Caldwell's room." That's me! If we go now, I can make it!

But it was not to be so. It was time for Mr. Underhill's first-day-of-school principal speech.

"Life," he began. (I was content just to learn to read on this first day...life could wait until later. He went on anyway.) "Life, boys and girls, is made up of two things: WINNING and LOSING." He was right, and I was about to lose right then! "The most important thing that you have to learn in school is that you do a lot more losing than winning. But, once in a while, boys and girls, you do get to win. And when that time finally comes, it is so good that you forget all about all the losing you did to get there."

The closing part of the speech was lost on me as I began my own version of losing—first a drop, then a trickle, then a little squirt. Then I thought, "If you're going to wet your pants, go ahead and do it right!" So I did!

Oh, what a comfort it is to accept defeat *positively*, to sit in the wet warmth of knowing that the crisis is past. I was certain that I would not have to go to the bathroom again for the rest of the week after this.

Besides, the new blue jeans had worked! Seated as I was when the accident happened, I looked completely dry in front. If I could slip out of here sideways, with my back to the wall, no one would ever even know.

The wooden floor of the big auditorium sloped from the back toward the front. I could see kids in front of me jump and punch one another as they looked down and pointed at the mysterious stream of water which was making its way, one row at a time, down the sloping floor and toward the opening in front of the stage.

I could see between the heads of rows A through F well enough to see the growing puddle which was building into a lake on the floor in front of the stage. Just as I was sure Mr. Underhill would step out to the edge of the stage, look down, and demand to know who that came from, he suddenly dismissed us and told our mothers to take us to our rooms.

The crowd was thick in the auditorium, and we were all so

close together that I was sure no one would notice. As soon as we got into the hall, I walked sideways, with my back to the wall. Mother, busy talking with other mothers about "who got the best teachers," didn't even notice.

We were almost to Miss Caldwell's room. I was nearly certain that I was going to make it there and get seated before anyone discovered I was wet. Here, now, was the door to the room, opened outward into the hallway.

It was necessary to turn momentarily to go into Miss Caldwell's door. In that brief unguarded moment when my backside was not protected by the wall, a little ugly nasty six-year-old-girl voice, so loud everyone had to be able to hear her, said, "Look...that little boy wet his pants!"

I really thought I was going to die.

My only hope was, "If I live, I pray that she is not in my room, because she...*knows*...what happened!"

I was without luck. Her name, I was later to learn, was Carrie Boyd, one of the "A through GRs" making up Miss Caldwell's class. After we were all seated alphabetically, that same Carrie Boyd ended up in the next row, right beside me.

It was a long, long time before I ever knew exactly what Carrie Boyd looked like. I could no more have looked at her than I could talk with her. If I looked at her and she looked back at me, I would definitely die. Because...she...knew! I missed out on *everything* that happened on the right side of the room because I just couldn't look toward Carrie Boyd.

We didn't learn to read the first day, or even the first week. It was a great shock to me to gradually realize that the more I learned about reading, the longer it seemed it would take to actually learn.

As the year rolled on, I began to make friends in Miss Caldwell's class. There was Annie Bowen, who lived just outside the fence of the tannery where her father worked. We had to pass by the tannery if we walked from our house into town in Sulpher Springs.

The stink—Mother said we should call it an "odor"—was

horrible. Daddy said nobody who worked at the tannery ever got sick, because germs couldn't live in that smell. In spite of living in such a stinking place, Anna Bowen was a small, sweet, black-haired girl.

(It seems almost strange that I should even *think* of a girl first when most of my time was spent with three particular boys. Perhaps it's because none of these boys were in Miss Caldwell's room, though we all lived on the same side of Sulpher Springs and were together on weekends and in the summer. The three were Freddie Patton, Red McElroy, and Rooster Loftis. Freddie lived closest to me and Rooster lived right next to Red on Maple Creek. We were best friends.)

Miss Caldwell had a paddle. It was a red fly-back paddle, the kind that came from the dime store. It had once had a rubber ball attached to it by a long rubber band. No one I knew could actually ever get the ball to come back and hit the paddle more than once or maybe sometimes twice in a row at the most.

Miss Caldwell had collected the fly-back paddle from a former student along with a collection of marbles, squirt guns and a few broken pocket knives. She loved to wave it in the air and tell the story of Markie Leatherwood, who had dared try to knock a vase of flowers off her desk with the fly-back ball while Miss Caldwell was writing on the blackboard with her back turned.

"Markie hit the vase," the story always went, "but he missed the rubber fly-back ball when its rubber band ran out and it flew straight back toward his face.

"I heard the vase fall," she said, "and turned around just in time to see the red ball smack Markie right in the left eye...hard. While he was hollering about his eye, I lifted the fly-back paddle—ball, rubber band, and all.

"As you can see, I have it to this very day!"

The rubber band and ball had long since disappeared, and now only the paddle remained, a constant threat of corporal punishment, perched on the front edge of her desk.

The paddle was not, however, her favorite punishment. She greatly preferred what she called "a little session of 'ring-nose'."

Convicted of a minor offense, the guilty parties would be marched to the blackboard. Each person to be punished would, in turn, stand in a line on tiptoe. Miss Caldwell would then draw a small chalk circle on the blackboard for each person. The chalk circle would be at the exact height to keep one's nose pressed into if standing on tip-toe. The chalk circle would remain undisturbed only if the guilty party's nose never slipped—any mistakes resulted in a new ring and starting over. One fifteen-minute session of "ring nose" was more miserable than any two or three outright spankings.

As the year wore on, I gradually got to where I could look at Carrie Boyd. By Christmas I could speak to her and just after Easter I actually borrowed a pencil from her. By the time school was out on the last day of May, I was convinced that Carrie Boyd had actually forgotten all about what had happened on that first, terrible day of school—or *perhaps* she had never connected the wet boy with me.

The next year "everybody whose last name starts with A through GR, Patricia Abernethy through Thomas Greene" ended up in Miss Ethel Swinburne's room. No one ever moved to Sulpher Springs, and so the old Caldwell bunch stayed all together for another year.

Miss Swinburne was a portly character, whose girth more than equaled her height. She was one who would never blow over in a hard wind, and she was frighteningly shorter than some second graders. She had a unique voice, that sounded like she was talking through a jar full of marbles rattling under water. All the kids tried to imitate her, but no one ever came close.

She did not seem to walk, but rather, to *flow* around the room. There was absolutely no up-and-down movement about her. We overheard Mr. Underhill one day saying to another teacher (quietly, to be sure) that "when Miss Swinburne comes down the hall, she reminds me of a tugboat, low in the water and full steam ahead."

Seating was again to be alphabetical, and I was again seated next to Carrie Doyd for the year. It wasn't so bad, though. We had actually become fairly good friends by now.

Miss Swinburne also had a fly-back paddle, and she used it. She preferred swift justice to the prolonged agony of "ring nose." In her room, offenders quickly and frequently tasted the nip of the well-worn paddle.

One of the paddle's most frequent customers was Leon Conner. Leon had been educated in general disruption by a long line of older brothers, most of whom had spent significant periods of time at the Stonewall Jackson Training School for delinquent boys. Miss Swinburne had taught all of the Conner boys and so was doubly on the lookout for Leon. He never got away with anything.

The normal procedure for paddling was for four punishment assistants to be chosen. Miss Swinburne jokingly called them her "corporals." Their job was to hold the arms and legs of the offender while he bent over the teacher's desk, rear end in the air.

Girls were never paddled, except once when Nancy Brittain said a word "so ugly that it turned her into a boy."

Leon's mother never thought he got a fair shake. She periodically came to school to have screaming fits in Mr. Underhill's office about "that teacher who beat my baby." Mr. Underhill himself was once overheard after one of the screaming sessions confiding to Miss Swinburne that the boy's mother could use a little taste of fly-back herself!

Leon had learned screaming from his mother. It seemed to be his duty to scream as loudly as he could before, during, and after being paddled. He would yell, "She's killing me...she's killing me..." at the top of his lungs as soon as he was touched.

During one particularly bad week, Leon had been paddled three days in a row. On Thursday he brought a square piece of cornbread back to the room after lunch and crumbled it into Nancy Brittian's hair while Miss Swinburne's back was turned. He told us later he was just trying to get her to "say that word that turned her into a boy" again.

Nancy let out a scream of her own, and in less than a minute the four corporals were assembled at Miss Swinburne's desk as she rolled up her sleeves and picked up the fly-back paddle.

Down went Leon, bent over the desk. Two of the corporals held his arms and the other two held his legs. He was already screaming, before the first blow was ever struck, "She's killing me...she's killing me...!"

Miss Swinburne started paddling. Her normal pattern was five whacks at a time: two slow, followed by three fast. These five-whack sets continued until she decided the punishment was sufficient.

Down came the fly-back paddle on Leon's upturned rear end: "Whack...whack...whackwhackwhack..."

Then, without warning, it happened: on the recoil from the three fast whacks, the fly-back paddle handle slipped out of Miss Swinburne's hand, went flying in an arc above the room, and with a loud crash, broke through a window pane and disappeared.

With this extra excitement, Leon turned up the volume of his screaming, now shrieking, "She's *kiillliiing* me..." at the absolute top of his voice.

This was Leon's fourth paddling of the week, and it happened that his mother, Mrs. Conner, had decided after the third that today would be a good day to come to school to scream at Mr. Underhill.

She was just stepping out of her car, an old rusty low-slung Mercury, when the paddle came crashing through the school window above her head and landed, with a scattering of broken glass, on the sidewalk exactly in front of her.

Through the broken window she could hear "her baby" screaming, *"She's killing me..."* at the top of his voice.

Mrs. Conner's screaming session set a new record that day. Not only did it *last* all through the time all the classes were going to lunch, but also she was so *loud* that all the kids in school got to hear her as they passed through the hall on the way to the lunchroom. No one could, however, understand a word she said.

The next day Leon did not come to school. He was absent the entire next week. When he finally did reappear on the

Monday after that, he was mysteriously in Mrs. Elmer's class. "How did a C get in the GU through M class?" we all wondered. There was no answer.

If life was made up of winning and losing, like Mr. Underhill had said, we figured Leon had lost!

April and May are long months for second graders. The days were getting hotter and hotter, and summer vacation seemed an eternity away. We were getting more and more restless, and Miss Swinburne was having a harder and harder time keeping order in the class.

On one hot day, after a particularly noisy time in the lunchroom, we marched back to our classroom to endure the afternoon. Miss Swinburne got all of us to sit still and be quiet. The she stood up (as tall as she could) in front of the class and made one of her famous "Teacher Speeches."

"Boys and girls," she began in her wet-marble voice, "school is not out yet! We still have four weeks, two days, and if the clock is right, one hour and thirteen minutes to go before school is out.

"You are not animals! The kind of behavior which was displayed in the lunchroom today cannot be repeated. In fact, this entire class is going to have to completely settle down and get under control if we are to come to the end of this year with dignity and order.

"In particular, there has been entirely too much disruption of our classroom routine by an unceasing stream of students claiming to need to visit the restroom when there is absolutely nothing wrong with their bladders except spring fever!

"From now until the end of the year there will be no more of this back-and-forth 'being excused' to run to the restroom during class. Now you will go, on your own, before school, at morning recess, at lunchtime, or wait until after school. No exceptions!" End of speech, amen!

I had never had any problem the entire year until she made that speech. But as soon as she began to make it clear that we couldn't go if we needed to, I started needing to go so badly that

I could see the first day of school beginning to re-create itself all over again. Just as Miss Swinburne said "you can't," something way down inside of me said "yes, you can...*and you will*... SOON!"

There was a big electric clock on the wall, right over the door. The clock was one of those with a red secondhand which went around each minute. I knew that second hand would have to go around seventy-three times (if Miss Swinburne's calculations were correct) before we would get out the door.

I would take a deep breath, look away from the clock, and hold my breath as long as I could. Then I would look back at the clock to see if the red secondhand had gone all the way around once. After about a half-dozen of these big breaths, I knew this method wasn't going to keep me dry. I just wasn't going to make it.

Was there anything good to think about? At first, all I could think about was Mr. Underhill making that old first-day-of-school speech: "Life is made up of winning and losing...and there's a lot more losing than winning." He was right—he knew it, Leon Conner knew it, I knew it, and Miss Swinburne knew it, too!

Then I had a good thought. During the summer before, some of the schoolrooms had been remodeled. In Miss Swinburne's room the old bolted-to-the-floor desks had been removed. After the floors were refinished, new light-colored oak desks were brought in. These new desks, with writing arms on the sides, had sculptured seat bottoms designed to fit second-grade rear ends—they were sort of scooped out.

As I looked at the empty seat beside me, it seemed to me that it would probably hold at least a cup of water. The good thought was this: if my bladder gets any fuller, and if it won't hold, maybe I can let out just enough to ease off the pressure and the part I lose will all stay right there in that scooped out seat! Then I can make it until school's out and no one will ever know what happened.

Miss Swinburne was spending the afternoon of each day in what she called "basic skills review." All during the time I was trying desperately to keep from flooding the room, she was in another world leading us in a phonics review drill.

"Don't forget Mister 'T'," she went on. "Without Mr. 'T', the clock couldn't go 'tic-tock'. Now, all together, let's say the name of the letter, and then review the sound it makes. Here we go: 'T...T...T...T...T'."

As the whole class chanted "T...T...T...T...T...," that is exactly what I did. "T...T...T," a drop at a time until I was almost floating in the scooped out seat of the new oak desk.

Things seemed safe. I looked at the floor. It was all dry. I would just sit in this puddle after the bell rang until all the children were out of the room, then I'd slip out. No one would ever know!

Then, from the row next to me, the same little ugly nasty now-seven-year-old-girl voice, yes, Carrie Boyd, with her volume at its very highest setting, said: "There's water dripping out of your britches leg! HA, HA, HA!"

No conscious thought went into what happened next. The reaction her words inspired was much too fast for thought to have been involved. My right hand clenched itself tightly into a hard little fist and shot out—SMACK!—striking Carrie Boyd full force in the mouth.

The entire room was silent. In the moment before her scream cut the air, we heard a little "plunk," as one of her big front teeth fell out of her ugly mouth and landed, bloody, right in the middle of her desk top.

I never knew what happened next as Miss Swinburne had me by both shoulders, up in the air and dripping. She glided with me all the way down the hall to Mr. Underhill's office.

After a short, private speech, which I didn't hear a single word of, I was deposited in a chair in the outer office where I stayed, stared at by everyone who came and went, until the bell finally rang and we all went home.

Joe-brother and I walked home. If he knew anything about what had happened, he at least had the good sense to be quiet about it.

Mother knew. I could tell the moment that I saw her that she knew. It was written all over her face as she stood there in the door waiting for us to get home.

I did her a favor and saved myself some time by going on to the maple tree in the back yard and breaking off a switch before I even went into the house. Without saying a word, she gave me a pretty good switching right through those wet britches. Then she said, "You ought to be ashamed of yourself. Now change your clothes and wait for your Daddy to get home."

Joe-brother stayed pretty far away from me for the rest of the day. He didn't seem to want any of my trouble to rub off on him merely by association.

Finally I heard the Dodge come in the driveway. Daddy was home. I stayed in the bedroom and thought to myself, "If he wants me, he can just come and get me!"

He did.

"I understand," he began, "that you had trouble at school today."

I nodded my head. "Go ahead and whip me and get it over with."

"I'm not going to whip you," he said. "I guess you've had enough of that. But I'll tell you what you're going to have to do. You're going to have to walk up to Carrie Boyd's house and apologize to her parents for knocking her tooth out."

"No!" I almost cried. "*Please* don't make me do that. Please just whip me and get it over with." I was almost frantic. "Please just whip me...*twice!* Whip me three times...*whip me every day for a week*. Please don't make me go up there."

"No," he said in a tone of voice which had absolutely no room for uncertainty in it. "You have to go up there and apologize."

The Boyds' house was less than a half-mile from ours, up Richland Road and off to the side above Miss Annie Macintosh's house. It took me two hours to walk up there. I would take a few steps, then stop to think about it for awhile. I was trembling, shaking, exuding sweat that felt like cold drops of pure blood popping out one at a time and running slowly down my back. My whole shirt was getting as wet as my pants had been at school earlier in the day.

At last I got to the Boyds' house. I knew exactly where they would be, and it was not in the house.

Mr. Boyd, Carrie's father, had learned to fly in the Second World War and had a yellow Piper Cub airplane which he kept and worked on in Burgie Welch's hay barn in a long field across the road from and below the house. I knew that if he were home, he would be there, working on the airplane. So, as if to prolong the agony even more, I went to the door of the house first.

Sure enough, no one was there. Afraid to go home without my mission accomplished, I started the long walk down and across to the hay barn.

One side of the big sliding door which closed the end of the barn stood pushed partially open. I knew the little airplane was inside and I knew the Boyds would be in there too.

As I started in the door, I saw Carrie's mother helping Mr. Boyd lift the wooden propeller from its shaft on the front of the airplane engine and carry it to a work bench against the wall. Carrie was playing with a kitten. She saw me, picked up the kitten, and disappeared into the back recesses of the barn.

Mr. Boyd was starting to sand the rough edge of the wooden propeller. He stopped when he saw me enter the barn. Both Mr. and Mrs. Boyd just stood there and looked at me as I walked slowly into their presence.

My knees would hardly hold, my chin quivered, my eyes filled with tears which would not quite run over, but made my vision blurry and unreal.

I stood before the Boyds for a long uncomfortable minute while they looked down at me and didn't say a word. I had never talked to either of them before in my entire life.

"I'm sorry," I finally began, almost whimpering. "I'm sorry that I knocked Carrie's tooth out," it all came pouring out as the tears ran over and poured down both cheeks. My nose even bubbled.

The Boyds didn't say a word. They just looked at one another, at me, at one another again.

Then, as if in slow motion, Mr. Boyd reached into his hip

pocket and pulled out his wallet. I did not at all understand what was going on. Slowly he opened the wallet, looked inside, and took out one of the first real five dollar bills I had ever seen close-up in my life.

"That tooth," he was talking to me now, "that tooth was a baby tooth. It's been hanging there by a thread for two months. Carrie wouldn't let either one of us touch it. Thank you for finally getting that thing out!" He handed me the five dollar bill. The Boyds both smiled.

Suddenly I remembered Mr. Underhill's speech, and I knew that he was right. Life *is* made up of winning and losing, and like he said, "When you finally get to win, it's so good, you forget about all the losing you've done to get there."

Miss Annie

MOTHER HAD WORKED HER WAY through teacher's college and then taught school for four years before she and Daddy ran away and got married. I was born the next year, and Joe-brother followed a year later. As soon as we were both old enough to be in school, Mother did what she had been waiting for since marriage: she went back to teaching.

Joe-brother and I both went to Sulpher Springs School, less than a mile from our house, but the only job Mother could get was teaching second grade at East Street School, more than three miles across and on the east side of town.

This created what Daddy described as a "transportation dilemma."

Mother was one of those people who had to be both first and last on the scene. She considered herself a failure if she did not get to school in the morning before the janitor arrived. Neither would she think of leaving until after the principal had gone home in the afternoon.

The "transportation dilemma" was that Mother took us to Sulpher Springs School on her way to East Street in the morning, then picked us up on her way home in the afternoon. Her determination to be first-and-last resulted in our being deposited on the school steps long before our building was unlocked, and in the afternoon, being locked outside to wait for her later arrival.

Joe-brother and I did not consider this a problem in warm weather, we simply played on the schoolyard early and late. But, with the coming of October frost and shorter days, our locked-out times at school grew increasingly uncomfortable.

"Why can't we walk home?" we asked again and again. "We can almost see our house."

"It's not safe for children to go home to an empty house." That was the answer. No more questions should be asked.

Joe-brother asked anyway. "Why is it safe to freeze to death on the school steps when it's not safe to go home where it's warm in the house?" There seemed to be no answer.

The question must have taken its hold, however, for in less than a week Mother gave us a new set of after-school instructions. "As soon as the bell rings this afternoon"—she was using her you-better-listen voice and pointing straight at both of us— "you are both to walk, together, on the left side of the road, as straight as you can go to Miss Annie Macintosh's house. She will take care of you until I get home and pick you up."

So Miss Annie became our after-school baby-sitter.

Her house was only a few hundred yards from ours, on up Richland Road on the side of a small hill that jutted from the base of Plott's Knob Mountain. It was a wonderful house.

Painted white, almost Victorian, the two-story house had five sides, including the bayed-out big windows in the front. There were porches above and below, and the roof, covered with fancy scalloped tin shingles, ran up its five wedge-shaped slopes to a point at the very top. The point was topped by a lightning rod with a blue glass ball in the middle, and a fluted cable which ran from it, off the roof, to a metal stake driven in the ground near the porch.

On the fifth side, a one-story kitchen stuck out, stopping the porches from going all the way around and breaking the symmetry of the whole.

If the outside was lovely, with its soft, grassy lawns and the shade of huge hemlock trees, the inside was just as much fun for six- and seven-year-olds.

There were two sets of stairs: a wide set that curved up the wall near the front door and had a banister you could slide down, if you were careful to stop before hitting the post at the bottom. The back stairs were secretly narrow, with doors at top and bottom, running from the back of the upstairs hall to the kitchen below.

Joe-brother and I loved to go to Miss Annie's house not only after school, but on Saturdays and Sundays. When school was out, we went almost every day throughout the summertime.

The big house had three inhabitants. First, there was Miss Annie. Miss Annie was *old.* She may have been fifty, or she may have been ninety. When you are seven years old, there is little difference. She was probably in her eighties.

She was also not "Miss" but "Mrs." She had been a widow so long, though, that the honorary title of "Miss" had long been returned to her.

She was widowed very early in her life by what she called "the way old McKinley messed up Grover Cleveland's little play war," an allusion to her young husband's death in Cuba in the Spanish-American War. This early widowhood had left her alone with three sons and one daughter to raise.

Miss Annie's father, old Colonel Stewart, had been, in her words, "killed by a bunch of Kirk's scoundrels over about Unicoi, Tennessee, in the Northern Aggression." He had come home, before she was old enough to remember him, in a pine box covered with a Confederate battle flag. She kept the flag, folded, in the bottom drawer of her chest of drawers.

Though the circumstances of her life had made her what Daddy called "a patron saint of lost causes," her severe Calvinism allowed no pity in her life. In spite of what seemed to *us* plenty of contrary evidence, she severely proclaimed, "People get what they deserve."

It was a phrase we heard again and again. "People get what they deserve" seemed to cover all emotions from joy to sorrow. Every possible happening in human life, from birth to death, from success to failure, fell under the leveling gavel of that one phrase: "People get what they deserve."

The second occupant of the Macintosh house was Miss Annie's only daughter, Mary Catherine. Mary Catherine seemed to Joe-brother and me to be about seven years old, for she liked to play all the same things we played. In truth, she was nearly fifty, a perpetually seven-year-old adult whom Daddy said "couldn't quite take care of herself."

If she had been born in a different time, or perhaps in a different place, she surely would have been tested and specially schooled. But in the generation in which she was born, and in Sulpher Springs, it was either conventional public school or no school at all.

Miss Annie had, in fact, enrolled her at Sulpher Springs School at age six, more than forty years before we knew her. Every day for the first week Mary Catherine had been walked to school and then home again by Miss Annie. On Friday of the first week, when Miss Annie came to fetch her, she found Mary Catherine sitting on the playground crying while all the other first-grade girls skipped rope and chanted:

"Mary Catherine Mac-in-tosh...
Got no brains, oh my gosh!"

Mary Catherine never returned to school after that day. Now, more than forty years later, she was still Miss Annie's little girl, and our favorite playmate.

The third resident of Miss Annie's household was Rachel. Her full name was "Rattling Rachel," and she was a gray 1939 Chevrolet sedan, with a sharply-pointed nose and tiny round tail-lights shaped like gray torpedoes. Rachel lived in a wooden garage outside the kitchen door and separate from the rest of the house.

She was a wonderful car. She had two gear shifts. In 1939, Rachel had been built by Chevrolet with a shift on the steering column and one of the first vacuum clutches ever used on one of her kind. Miss Annie said the clutch "burned up," though Joe-brother and I could find no evidence of a fire.

Some unknown dirt-road mechanic had pulled out not only the clutch but the entire transmission and replaced it with a second-hand transmission from a slightly older Chevy. The "new" transmission had a floor shift, which now came through a hole cut in the floorboard. A carpet scrap slipped down over the floor shift made a boot to cover the hole around the base and kept out the dirt and cold air.

The best part of the entire transmission transplant was that the old, disconnected column shift was still there, right on the steering column. When we went to ride, I sat in Miss Annie's lap while she drove, and we each had a gear shift.

I would feel her left knee sink under my bottom as she pushed in the clutch. She would say "Shift!" and I would throw the dead column shift into imaginary second gear while she slipped the floor shift up or down into the right place.

The five of us—Miss Annie, Mary Catherine, Rattling Rachel, Joe-brother, and I—spent afternoons and summer days in adventure around the big house. When things got dull, Miss Annie would say, "Let's shoot some Yankees!"

She'd go to the bottom drawer of her chest of drawers, take out the big Confederate battle flag, and thumb-tack it to a broom stick. Mary Catherine always got to carry the flag. Miss Annie couldn't take a chance on one of us boys letting it drag on the ground.

We would run, led by Miss Annie and followed by Mary Catherine struggling with the flag, up and down hills, through the pastures, in and out of the woods, shooting at Yankees who surely had to be behind every bush and rock. Once we were fully exhausted, we would all drag back to the house, out of breath, to see how many times we had been "wounded."

Wounds were cockleburrs, beggar-lice and whatever other seeds and burrs had clung to our clothes during the battle. A cockleburr counted as a cannonball fragment. Beggar lice and smaller stickers were simple flesh wounds from some sniper's rifle. The winner of the battle was, of course, the one who had collected the greatest number of wounds and still lived!

When we went home each day, Mother would ask, "What did you boys do at Miss Annie's today?"

On this particular day we answered together, "We killed Yankees!"

"The country's safe for awhile," Joe-brother added.

Mother looked at Daddy, pointed her finger at the side of her head, and as she rotated her finger in a gesture indicating lack of all reasonable sense, slowly spelled out to Daddy, "That woman…that woman is C-R-A-Z-Y!" (But we always got to go back because Miss Annie was the only babysitter around.)

One of the biggest reasons we liked to go to Miss Annie's on Saturdays and in the summertime was that, unlike on school days, we could arrive early enough to listen in as she read to Mary Catherine.

We discovered the reading time one day when, on a trip to town, we stopped by the little public library and loaded Rachel's back seat with books. "What are all these books for?" Joe-brother asked Miss Annie.

"Oh, I like to read them to Mary Catherine," was the answer.

What we learned was that each day, right after lunch, Miss Annie read aloud to Mary Catherine. The reading went on for at least an hour, sometimes much longer. As often as possible, Joe-brother and I joined the party.

The first book I remember hearing her read was a small Dickens novel called *Dombey and Son,* a tragic story of failed possibilities, and a book I have difficulty finding even on library shelves to this day.

Miss Annie's favorites included Thomas Nelson Page's stories of the South. I remember especially *Two Little Confederates.*

My all-time favorite was a thick, squarish red book entitled *Beautiful Joe.* It was the tearful story of a dog who had been abused by its cruel owner. But finally, even with ears and tail cut off, poor Joe found a new home where he was deemed "beautiful."

We loved reading time.

There was a small farm pond in Miss Annie's pasture that she called the "cow pond." It was half-way between Rachel's garage and the Caldwell's barn, and though no fish lived there, it was a good place to throw rocks and sail boats.

After hearing Miss Annie read *Huckleberry Finn,* Joe-brother and I decided it would be a great thing to have a raft to ride around on the cow pond.

When we told Miss Annie about our idea, she said, "Go to it, boys! What do you need to build a raft?"

"Logs. Trees, I guess," I replied. Joe-brother agreed.

"How about those right there," she said, pointing to a stand of rough-barked black pine trees just below the garage.

Miss Annie hunted around in the back of Rachel's garage until she came up with an old double-bitted axe, a hatchet, and a hand saw. All three looked more like early-American antiques than usable tools.

So armed, Joe-brother and I set to work. In two days we had managed to cut down a tall pine tree with a substantial, sappy trunk. After trimming off all the limbs, we sawed the trunk into two sections, each half about twelve feet long.

The plan had been (following Miss Annie's suggestion) to cut the trees and then assemble the raft in Rachel's garage, but now we discovered we could not budge even half of the first log. Discouraged, we told Miss Annie.

"Rachel will do it," she replied. We watched as she tied one end of a long, thick rope to the pine log, ran the rope around a pole in the back of the garage, then tied the other end to Rachel's bumper. After it was all hooked up, she drove Rachel down the driveway until we yelled "Stop!" One more hook-up and both pieces of the pine log were neatly in the garage.

Over the next two weeks Joe-brother and I managed to cut down enough black pine trees to end up with nine good-sized logs in Rachel's garage.

We levered them into place side by side, and then nailed a platform of boards across the top. The whole structure was completed with Coca-Cola crates for seats and a flag staff on the front. The finished raft must have weighed in at close to a ton.

This time Joe-brother and I went to Miss Annie and asked for help. "The raft's all finished," we reported. "Now we need you and Rachel to help us get it down to the cow pond."

Miss Annie backed Rachel up to the garage and tied the raft to the back bumper. After considerable wheel spinning and our observation that Miss Annie could handle a car better than we had thought she could, the raft began to emerge from the garage and travel in a cloud of dust toward the cow pond.

Miss Annie drove as close to the cow pond as she could. Still, we could not begin to budge the raft the last couple of feet to the water.

"Wait right here," she ordered. Again we watched as she drove Rachel to the other side of the cow pond then pulled the long rope through the water as she walked back around to where we were. Once the rope was tied to the raft, she returned to the car.

"Stand back!" she ordered. The rope tightened, the wheels spun momentarily, and then the huge raft moved forward, launched on its maiden voyage in the cow pond.

As soon as the sappy pine logs touched the water, the entire contraption sank straight to the bottom. All you could see was the tip of the flagstaff sticking up into the air. Rachel stopped abruptly and Miss Annie, realizing what had happened, got out.

"Don't worry, boys," she shouted as she untied the rope from Rachel's bumper. "It'll float to the top as soon as the logs dry out!"

Joe-brother and I just looked at one another. We were both thinking the same thing. Is she really C-R-A-Z-Y the way Mother says? Or is this another mysterious case in which, somehow, "people get what they deserve?" I guessed we weren't old enough to know.

Whenever Miss Annie was not babysitting us, her favorite pastime was growing flowers, summer and winter, indoors and out.

During the warm months, she dug and planted outside. There were wild flowers: jack-in-the-pulpit, trillium, ferns of various kinds, at the edge of the yard and under the big hemlock trees. Wide beds of annuals served as a source of cut flowers throughout summer and into fall. There was a rose garden, and my favorite, a wide band of dahlias with blooms so big the plants had to be staked to hold them upright.

Mother said that in spite of being C-R-A-Z-Y, Miss Annie surely did have a "green thumb."

When the outdoor growing season was past, Miss Annie continued to grow flowers indoors...with needle and thread.

Her finished products were beautiful pieces of crewel embroidery, cross-stitch "samplers" which looked like the front of candy boxes, with rows of ABCs running around the outside and flower arrangements in the center.

Sometimes she created needlepoint pillow covers and chair cushions, all done in flowers.

Of all her needle-and-thread creations, the thing Joe-brother and I loved most were what she called her "applied work" quilt tops. She would save scraps of every sort to get ready. Then she would lay out a huge solid-colored background, usually green for the earth with an occasional strip of blue for the sky.

The saved scraps were cut into the shapes of animals and trees and houses and flowers. There were calico cows and gingham mountains—whatever Miss Annie thought of at the moment. The pieces were hemmed, placed, and sewn to the background, making a beautiful, primitive scene of rural life (as she saw it).

Joe-brother and I could watch her do "applied work" for hours.

Joe-brother and I never fought at Miss Annie's house but once. On that one occasion, we tried to have a little fight which we were both determined to finish as soon as it was started. Miss Annie, however, caught us before we got stopped.

"You want to fight?" she said.

"Oh, no," we answered in chorus. "We don't want to fight. We were just playing."

"No," she replied, "you were fighting. I saw you. If you want to fight, then we'll just find out about fighting. Hit him again, Joe."

She made us fight through most of the afternoon. Her instructions were, "Hit him again. No, hit him hard enough that I can see a red place where you hit him. Now you scratch him back, and I want to see the fingernail marks where you scratched. Now pull hair, and pull it *out* while you're at it—now *bite,* and I'd better see tooth marks where you bite, or you'll just have to do it again..."

On and on we fought, wounded and exhausted, not allowed

by Miss Annie to stop. All the while she gave the orders, she watched with tears running down her face, saying finally, "If old KcKinley had only known...if old McKinley had only known what happens when you really fight, maybe things wouldn't have turned out the way they did."

After that, if we wanted to fight, we did it at home where it was safe. Mother always stopped us! We wouldn't take a chance on another fight at Miss Annie's house.

One afternoon Miss Annie said, "Come on boys, let's shoot down airplanes!"

The "Sulpher Springs Air Force" was made up of two J-3 Piper Cubs and a yellow Stearman biplane flown in and out of Burgie Welch's hay field by a half-dozen local heroes, Carrie Boyd's father included, who had learned to fly in the war. The hay field curved slightly, which made landings especially exciting, and the hanger was an old hay barn with an orange windsock on top.

Miss Annie took us to the top of a long hill which overlooked most of the length of the hay field, and we got ready.

We had come armed with an old .410 shotgun which Miss Annie always kept in the front closet loaded with rat-shot. The loaded gun was kept, in her words, "to protect us from the roving element." She did occasionally fire it out the door when strange noises came in the night, and the noises usually stopped immediately.

It was years later that I realized we were at least a hundred yards from the landing strip, and no real danger to airplanes—or anything else there, for that matter. The realization came when I tried to shoot a squirrel with the rat-shotted .410. I did knock the squirrel off the limb it was on, but it jumped up and ran away, hardly injured, before I could get to where it had hit the ground.

On top of the hill that day, though, we were deadly and dangerous.

We'd take turns loading the little single-shot gun with the rat-shot. Then when one of the airplanes (they were all painted the same color of yellow) came in for a landing, we would shoot—*Blam!*—just as the wheels touched the ground. Miraculously, the airplane would stop after being "shot," and Miss Annie would shout, "You got it!" We laid rows of sticks on the ground to keep score about how many we had each shot down.

We were doing so well that Joe-brother and I had both been declared "aces" when I said, "Miss Annie, I want to shoot one as it takes off."

"They're hard to hit when they take off," she said, "but you can try."

I reloaded the little shotgun and waited. Soon one of the yellow Piper Cubs taxied to the far end of the runway, turned around, and with a whooshing roar came down the field from right to left below us, tail off the ground and building speed fast.

When the wheels were about ten feet off the ground, I pulled the trigger. *Blam,* went the shotgun. At nearly the same time the Piper Cub's engine coughed, and the wooden propeller seemed to jump backwards and stop.

Silently the Piper Cub sank to the ground and bounced twice on its front wheels as the end of the hay field ran out. On the third bounce the landing gear caught the top of the hedgerow between the hayfield and Daddy's garden, and as if in slow motion, the tail of the Cub came up and over until the whole yellow airplane landed flat upside-down in the middle of Daddy's corn and beans patch.

I looked at Miss Annie. She looked pale. All three of us started running down the hill toward the airplane.

We stopped when we saw the doors pop open as Willie Parker came out one side and Mr. Boyd (Carrie's daddy) came out the other. They began to walk around in the corn and examine the almost-undamaged airplane.

As soon as she realized that no one was hurt, Miss Annie looked at me and said, "You got it!" Then we headed back to her house—fast.

That afternoon Mary Catherine walked home with Joe-brother and me. Mother was standing in the door waiting for us when we got there. When we got close enough to hear, she was already talking, "Do you know what happened? They were trying to take off in one of those crazy awful airplanes, you know they scare me to death, and the engine just cut off and it ended up upside down…"

She never got to finish her story because Joe-brother and I answered together, "We know."

"Miss Annie and I shot it down!" I said.

She turned quickly toward Daddy, finger pointed toward her head and already moving. "I told you," she said, "that woman is C-R-A-Z-Y!"

Mary Catherine was standing there watching the whole scene. Daddy hushed Mother quickly. "Don't say that in front of Mary Catherine, Mama."

"Oh, she doesn't know what that means. You know she can't read or write or anything." We thanked Mary Catherine for walking home with us and she left, heading home more quickly than usual.

Whenever we stayed all day at Miss Annie's, she always put us down for a nap in the afternoon. She would take us upstairs to one of several bedrooms. There was a big, high four-poster bed with a thick feather mattress on it. She'd put us on top of the bedspread and cover us both with a quilt. One of us would always say, "Show us where the clock hands have to point before we can get up." She would go to the loud-ticking clock on the dresser and answer, "The short hand has to point to the four and the long hand has to point to the twelve."

Joe-brother and I would both agree.

As soon as Miss Annie's footsteps faded down the stairs, Joe-brother and I would jump up, turn the knobs on the back of the alarm clock until, indeed, the short hand was on the four and the long hand exactly on the twelve. Then we would get up.

Miss Annie didn't care. All she needed was to be able to answer with an honest "yes" if Mother happened to ask her, "Did you put the boys down for a nap today?"

On one long summer afternoon, Miss Annie put us down for a nap just as a thunderstorm came across Plott's Knob mountain. Almost as soon as she left the room, Joe-brother and I jumped up and changed the clock.

Because the thunder and the rain made so much noise, we couldn't tell where in the big house Miss Annie might be. So, we stayed in the bedroom and raised the shades to watch the rain and the lightning.

When we looked out the window we saw Miss Annie outside. She was walking around in the yard, in the rain, wearing only her normal cotton print dress. She had on no hat, no coat, had not even an umbrella, but she seemed to invite—to even *enjoy*—the soaking the summer rain gave her as it drenched down, underlined by lightning and thunderclaps. She'd look up and stretch out her arms toward the falling rain.

I thought the rain streaming down her face looked like rivers of tears. Then, with a second thought, I realized there could *be* tears there as well, but with the rain, no one would ever see them.

"Maybe she is C-R-A-Z-Y," Joe-brother whispered.

We quietly decided not to tell our Mother what we had seen on this particular day. We might not get to come back any more.

Later in the afternoon Miss Annie came to the bedroom, dry and in a fresh dress, to tell us it was time to get up.

The years rolled past. Joe-brother and I did get older. Gradually the need for a babysitter was outgrown, and the growth seemed to dull our earlier fascination with going to Miss Annie's house. We seldom went there on our own anymore.

Miss Annie and Mary Catherine also got older, though, in part, Mary Catherine still seemed a seven-year-old. More than once we overheard our parents talking about the two of them. "I wonder what poor Mary Catherine will do when Miss Annie's not there to take care of her anymore?"

Finally Daddy would say, "You better check on them tomorrow, Mama."

Rattling Rachel was dead. Miss Annie told about her sudden death. "She was perfectly fine when we went to town on Tuesday, and then on Wednesday morning, when I turned her on and pushed the starter button, she was completely dead. Oh, well, I guess she's run long enough—and I guess maybe I've driven long enough. Rachel deserves a rest."

With that, she washed and dried the gray car, swept out the inside, covered it with clean sheets, and locked it in the garage by padlocking the door shut. It was something we had never seen her do before.

Then she took Rachel's keys, put them in an envelope with her oldest grandson's name on it, and placed it on the mantel in the living room. "He'll probably want to bring her back to life someday."

Mother now became chauffeur for Miss Annie and Mary Catherine.

"Could you take me to see Dr. York?" The call would come in mid-morning. Joe-brother and I rode along, as did Mary Catherine (it was almost like old times) as we went to town and waited for Miss Annie to finish at Dr. York's office.

It was never straight home, though, as she asked—one at a time—to stop at the church, the library, the circle president's house, the home of the secretary of the D.A.R., the drug store, and finally "just a minute at the grocery store."

It would be well after dark before we returned home, and Mother would be furious. Our supper was still to be fixed before we could even begin to go to bed.

Daddy would try to calm her down. "You have to take her places, Mama. After all, she helped us raise the boys."

Miss Annie didn't die all at once. She simply faded from action one part at a time.

First her legs failed, and she could no longer work in the yard or maintain the flower beds. The wild flowers didn't care... they just got wilder and wilder, and gradually there was less and less lawn to mow as they took it over very well.

Still, she grew her needlework flowers and assembled her applied-work worlds until her eyes failed. She tried to do it by touch, but the stems came out in one place while the blooms were in another, and she gradually gave it up.

Most of her days were spent in bed, and occasionally Joe-brother and I would go to her house. Now we'd read to her.

Again and again she asked for *Two Little Confederates* and *Beautiful Joe*. Tears ran down all our faces, Mary Catherine's as well, as we read about the poor, earless dog until the book fell apart.

People who had for years worried about Mary Catherine gradually began to realize that she had become the mother even as Miss Annie had become the child, and that she could, in fact, take care of herself very well.

Finally, when she was ninety-seven years old, Miss Annie's heart stopped, and as suddenly as Rachel had died, she was gone.

The day after Miss Annie was buried in Cedar Hill Cemetery, Mary Catherine called our mother. "All of you come up here." It was an order not to be ignored. "Mother left something she said I was supposed to give you if she ever died."

We got in the blue Dodge and drove up to the old, now failing, house. Rachel's road was badly washed out, the yard had gone long unmowed, the porch was rotten in spots, paint was badly peeled. "I didn't realize what bad shape this place was in," Daddy said as we knocked on the door.

Mary Catherine let us in and led us into the dining room.

There above the dining room table was a chandelier which held seven light bulbs. Miss Annie had always kept all but one unscrewed. When Mary Catherine reached up and screwed in all seven until the room blazed with light, we knew we had come for something important.

"Stay here," she ordered as she retreated into Miss Annie's bedroom. Joe-brother and I saw her fumbling in the bottom drawer of the dresser. We knew the Confederate flag stayed there—maybe that was going to be for us. We had always wanted it.

Mary Catherine ignored the flag and removed a huge package wrapped in brown paper. She carried it to the dining room table and began to unwrap the contents with great and deliberate care.

There on the table in front of us began to unfold the biggest applied-work quilt we had ever seen.

The background was earth and sky and mountains. There was a big ridiculous-looking white Victorian house in the center, with a pointed roof and a lightning rod (blue glass ball and all) on the peak.

On the porch was the figure of a girl holding a Confederate flag on what looked for all the world like a broomstick. There was a gray car at the side, a yellow airplane overhead, and flowers everywhere.

Through the yard in front of the house raced two little boys. Between them was an old lady, gray-haired, with her hands reached out—not to hold, but with fingers just touching the tops of their heads.

At the bottom of it all, in big block letters, we read the words "MY BOYS."

Mother began to cry. "Why did she do it?" she asked. "How did she do it...with those old fingers? Why, she has grandchildren of her own. Why did she do this for us?"

Daddy tried to save the day. "Oh, Mama, you know why she did it. She said it herself. 'People get what they deserve.' Nobody could have deserved this more than you did. You took her to the doctor, you drove her to the store, you looked after her...you deserved it. That's why she did it. 'People get what they deserve,' isn't that right, Mary Catherine?"

Mary Catherine did not hesitate even for a moment, but very quickly and firmly said, "No! That isn't why she did it at all. She did it because she was C-R-A-Z-Y!"

The Last Butler
in Sulpher Springs

SULPHER SPRINGS CAME AS close to having two main streets as any small town possibly could.

First there was what everybody called "Old Main Street," the official and originally named "Main Street" of the town. From the time Sulpher Springs was founded, this original main street had been not only the center of all business, but, in fact, the only street developed at all for many years.

Along its sides grew general merchandise stores, the bank and post office, and later a drug store, hardware store, and a variety of other offices and businesses. This street dominated Sulpher Springs for nearly a hundred years...until the railroad came.

It was old Colonel Halford Butler who brought the railroad to town and made his fortune in doing so. Though the Civil War had relieved him of everything generations of Butlers had accumulated, there were chances to be taken by men of daring, and one of those chances involved putting together a group of investors to extend the railroad line from Asheville to Sulpher Springs. The purpose was largely for removing a vast fortune in hardwood cheaply acquired on high mountain land. Since the town was already there, the railroad was not its center, as in those towns built after the rails were already in place. It paralleled the *back* of Main Street, then came to its end (for years) at a big hand-turned turntable where an engine could be unhooked, reversed, and shunted past the cars to rehook at the other end.

Everyone in Sulpher Springs was so fascinated by the railroad that new building began to gravitate to it instead of to Main Street. The result was that in twenty years this second street (officially named "Railroad Street") had become the "New Main Street" of the town.

When the hardwood was all gone, the railroad faded from its days of glory, though the line went on to Chattanooga now. From then on, building continued to be fairly well divided between the two streets until, as we were growing up, there was a real choice about which seemed to be more important.

In spite of stores and offices, the central structure—as far as *interest* goes—on "New Main," or Railroad Street, was the big house built by Colonel Butler after his family fortune was restored by the railroad.

It occupied the only raised plot of land along the street, and though only two stories high, its sheer mass dominated later structures.

The house was purely square, and constructed of brick hauled almost to the site by the railroad. Long porches ran the length of the structure upstairs and downstairs, and visitors to Sulpher Springs in later years thought it had surely been built as a hotel rather than a private dwelling.

There were strange tales that even after the war Colonel Butler had kept slaves impressed there, though no one really knew whether the Butlers had ever even owned slaves or not.

In my childhood the house had a single occupant. Miss Martha Anne Butler, called by my Daddy "the last surviving member of a failed Southern family," lived there, totally alone.

As the railroad ran down, the Butlers' money ran out, and Miss Martha Anne lived in the aristocratic poverty of one whose former wealth is trapped in vast possessions with no redeemable value on the market at all.

Though we knew better, we called her a witch and called the house haunted as a running battle grew between the old woman and every mischief-dealing Sulpher Springs boy. "Daring Miss Butler" was an often-played game we all participated in.

Her nearest neighbors were the Wrights and the Campbells, both of whom had malicious boys. Bobby and Robbie Wright, sixth graders, and older by several years than Joe-brother and me, were her chief sources of irritation. They were aided in their endeavors by Hayden Campbell, himself a year older than either of them, and a source of simple terror for the whole neighborhood.

The boys could not stay away from Miss Martha Anne's house.

There were old apple trees in the back yard which, though twisted and broken, still produced a huge yield of unused apples each year. In the fall, these three neighbors would slip into the yard and toss apples on the roof of the Butler house, then watch as the apples rolled down the slope of the roof and into the big gutters. The game was to see whether it was possible to toss up so many apples that the weight would pull the gutters off the house before Miss Martha Anne heard them and screamed the boys away.

On some of these occasions Miss Martha Anne called her cousin, Sheriff Roy Parks, and sought his help. He never came.

In truth, Miss Martha Anne was a closet alcoholic. She spent her lonely days (and probably nights as well) slowly sipping her way into perpetual, partial oblivion, a state in which she had existed for as long as most adults in Sulpher Springs could remember. Knowing nothing of such adult habits, Joe-brother and I persisted in our simple conviction that she was just a witch.

It was raining one day as we rode in the blue Dodge past the house. As we went by, we saw Miss Martha Anne standing at a front window. She held the curtain aside, and her face was pressed against the glass as she stood and stared, alone, out into the rain.

Joe-brother asked Daddy, "Why does Miss Martha Anne live in that big old house all by herself?" The answer did not come all at once. He had to think about it, it seemed.

Daddy finally said, "Well, son, that is the Butler home, and she lives there because she is the only Butler left in Sulpher Springs." We simply accepted his answer without understanding.

We did not realize it at the time, but what he had said was not exactly true. There was another Butler in town, but no one would ever have thought of him as having the same last name as Miss Martha Anne.

Abraham Lincoln Butler was black, and drove the only taxi in Sulpher Springs. He operated from and lived in a little shack which everyone called "Abraham Lincoln's Taxi Stand." It was next door to Welch's Cash Grocery at the far end of "Old Main Street," about as far from Miss Martha Anne's as you could go in town.

Abraham Lincoln's taxi was a black 1930 Buick sedan. The huge car, with twin spare tires sunk into the front fenders on both sides, and heavy chrome bumpers, had, ironically, belonged to Miss Martha Anne's father, Halford Butler II, until, in some unclear way, Abraham Lincoln had obtained it upon Mr. Butler's death in 1945. Now the car was more than twenty years old, and still Abraham Lincoln changed the oil once a week and polished it almost every day. It seemed to look better and better with age, and it was his very pride and joy.

Very few people in Sulpher Springs ever rode in the taxi, but still, Abraham Lincoln did a thriving business. His obvious source of income was from delivering groceries directly to people's homes from Welch's cash grocery. Many older people in Sulpher Springs did not drive. They often either telephoned or sent grocery lists to Welch's. Little Burgie Welch (whose father owned the hayfield airstrip) ran the store. Except for Harley Conner, the meat cutter (and Leon's father), Burgie had a one-man operation.

He would fill the sent-in grocery orders, then call on Abraham Lincoln to deliver them to the proper house. In town, he got twenty-five cents for each full bag of groceries delivered to a house, and the bags were *very* full, since Little Burgie did the paying. (The store advertised "free delivery.")

Abraham Lincoln's *main* source of income, however, was from another kind of delivery. He was the town's leading and most discreet bootlegger of store-bought whiskey.

"When Mr. Roosevelt ended the prohibition," Abraham Lincoln explained, "the higher class of white folks in Sulpher Springs got to thinking they were too good for home-made drinking. They got to thinking they had to have store-bought whiskey, but they weren't going to be seen going to Asheville and buying it for themselves. Seemed like the helpfullest thing I could do was to kind of help 'em out."

Every Saturday after he changed the oil in the Buick, he drove an hour and a half to the A.B.C. store in Asheville where the manager, who knew exactly what Abraham Lincoln was doing, let him buy all he had the cash money to pay for.

He only bought pints. In a seller's market, they brought as much as fifths, and ran out much more often.

Abraham Lincoln had a telephone at the taxi stand, and after discreet telephone calls, he made special deliveries to the finest old homes in Sulpher Springs.

One of the homes was Miss Martha Anne Butler's house.

Abraham Lincoln made one regular grocery delivery to the big Butler house each week, always on Monday. It was obvious to anyone who cared to watch that in addition to groceries he delivered two pints of gin to her back porch. The groceries lasted the week; the gin did not.

Most of the kids in the neighborhood knew that if the black Buick stopped at the house at any other time during the week, an additional pint of gin was soon to be found just inside the screen door of the back porch.

Miss Martha Anne never came to the door either on the grocery Mondays or when supplemental deliveries were made. She stayed completely out of sight for twenty minutes after Abraham Lincoln had completed his task and left. We had all watched this ritual and could anticipate her appearance almost to the exact minute. She loudly turned the big key in the back door and casually walked out on the screened back porch. She glanced around, never really seeing or expecting to see anyone, picked up the delivery, and disappeared back into the house. We could hear the key turn loudly again. Other than seeing her arm reach out to empty the front-porch mailbox of its few contents, these moments on the back porch were about the most we had ever really seen of her.

It was Hayden Campbell who, as usual, came up with the

idea. It was an idea which was very easily sold to the "Wright brothers," Robbie and Bobby.

The plan was to stay on the lookout for Abraham Lincoln's Buick to come to the Butler house. The Monday grocery delivery was ruled out as too dangerous to mess with, so the lookout got serious on about Thursday, when the supplementary delivery had not yet come.

Thursday turned out to be the right day. It was almost four-thirty in the afternoon when Abraham Lincoln pulled way up into the driveway, slid from behind the wheel of the Buick, and slipped a package inside the screen door of Miss Martha Anne's back porch.

As soon as the Buick was out of sight, Hayden ran across the yard. Without opening the door more than the few necessary inches, he reached inside and came running back with a brown paper bag.

Safely out in the woods, Hayden and the Wright brothers opened the bag. There they discovered to their complete and amazed pleasure not one but *two* pints of gin. The party was going to be wonderful.

In spite of all of his thirteen-year-old malice, Hayden had had absolutely no prior experience with alcohol. He had smelled empty beer bottles and even sniffed a whisky bottle or two, but the reality of the liquid spirit had never touched his lips.

All three boys decided they better think about this for a while. So the two bottles of gin were hidden, in their original brown paper bag, in a culvert under the railroad track about two-hundred yards from Miss Martha Anne's back porch. The agreement was to split up, go home to supper, then meet as soon as it was "good and dark."

It was July, and "good and dark" didn't come until nearly nine o'clock. It was fully nine when Robbie and Bobby Wright met Hayden Campbell at the railroad culvert. They pulled out the brown paper bag and climbed up on the railroad tracks with it. They sat there side by side on the rail, and tried to figure out what to do next.

"Well, open the stuff up," Robbie dared Hayden. "It was your idea to do this to start with."

Hayden pulled one of the pints of clear liquid from the bag, twisted the cap hard until the tax-paid seal broke, then slowly unscrewed it the rest of the way. He took a sniff.

"What does it smell like?" Bobby asked.

"Kind of funny," Hayden answered. "A little bit like when you take pine needles and rub them in your hands, or when you scratch a green pine cone with your fingernails."

"Let us smell," Bobby reached out for the bottle.

"No smelling unless you take a drink." Hayden held back at the bottle.

"Of course I'm going to take a drink," smarted Bobby. "What do you think we've gone to all this trouble for?"

Bobby Wright tipped up the offered bottle, and before he realized what had happened, swallowed a good ounce of the gin. His face flushed and his ears absolutely glowed as his breath first stopped, then came out with a wail which was some kind of mixture of anguish and discovery.

About five minutes later, he pushed the bottle back to Hayden and said, "That's real stuff."

What the three boys began to do was use the bottle cap as a shot glass, each two daring the third to empty the cap, straight, faster than the one before. After the first few breath-stopping rounds, the gin seemed to go right down, being felt now not in the throat so much as up against the inside of the skull above the eyes and in some vague wanderings of the entire stomach. It seemed no time (actually it took more than an hour) until the pint was empty and the second bottle was opened (with difficulty).

It was well after ten o'clock at night now, and as efforts to dispel the contents of pint-number-two slowed to a near halt, the rail on which the boys were sitting began to buzz and then to vibrate. It was the 10:20 freight on its end-of-the-day trip from Chattanooga back to Asheville.

Realizing the train was coming, Robbie, Bobby and Hayden took the bottle with them as they ran up into the woods above the track and waited for it.

The track came so nearly through downtown—"New Main Street" being what it was—that all trains coming through had to slow down to fifteen miles-per-hour once inside the city-limit yard. We had often observed that it looked like it might be possible to outrun one of those slow trains, at least for a hundred yards or so.

As Hayden and the Wright brothers, totally drunk on gin, watched the big Baldwin locomotive slow down (no diesels on these tracks for another year or so), they all thought the same thing.

Hayden said, "I could outrun that train all the way through town."

Bobby Wright responded to the challenge. "Why, I could run right alongside that thing and jump on it before it speeds up at the other end of town."

With all of the good common sense available to two twelve-year-olds and a thirteen-year-old who have just consumed more than a pint of gin—their first, straight down—all three boys decided to hop the 10:20 freight and ride it "all the way to Asheville." Concerns about the how and when of getting home had long ago been antiseptically removed from their heads.

Hayden tossed the last remnants of the gin bottle into the brush and headed toward the train. It was just beginning to pass by. Bobby and Robbie were running close behind.

Though he had never done it before, things like hopping freight trains came to Hayden by instinct. He ran alongside the train, sprinting until he almost matched speed with it, then grabbed the next freight-car ladder as it passed, actually letting the train pull him into the air before his feet found the bottom rung. He was on his way to Asheville.

Bobby was to be next. He had watched Hayden and did almost as well, though for a moment he feared losing his grip until his feet were solidly in place.

Things did not go as well after that. Robbie, the least adventuresome of the three, had watched the other boys with secret hopes that they would back out at the last minute. When he saw that they did not, he had no choice but to follow their lead.

By this time, the big locomotive had cleared the yard and was beginning to speed up. Robbie ran as hard as he absolutely could, trying to catch an accelerating freight train. The cars were coming past faster and faster, and though the sound blocked out all hearing, he was sure that he could hear Bobby and Hayden hollering, "Come on, jump for it!"

The train was running out, the time had to be now. Robbie grabbed desperately for a freight-car ladder and jumped toward the train at the same time.

It was impossible for anyone to describe exactly what happened, for no one saw it, and Robbie had absolutely no memory at all of anything that happened. Whether Hayden and Bobby heard his scream, or in some other way perceived that he had missed, was also uncertain, but they both dropped from the speeding train and harshly tumbled along the dark ground until the freight disappeared in the distance. The two of them made their way back up the track, sobered by the fear of what they knew they were to find.

When they got to Robbie, he was not screaming. His mouth was open and his face was turning blue, but all of the breath had gone out of him in that first, long, horrible shriek, and it was not until he passed out that his limp body began breathing again, on its own.

Hayden and Bobby looked at him there in the dark, while that same darkness protected them somewhat from the full impact of seeing. His right foot was completely gone, and the lower part of the same leg was horribly mangled into blood-soaked blue jeans.

The sound of the offending freight train had almost faded completely from hearing, and were it not for this terrible evidence, no one would have ever known the train had even passed through.

The silence was suddenly broken by the dragging crunch of someone else, there in the dark, walking along the gravel of the railroad bed. In the faintest of light, Hayden looked up to see Abraham Lincoln Butler coming from the end of town where his taxi-stand house was. He walked straight toward them, looking at where he stepped, until he saw the inert form of Robbie Wright, passed out cold and limp, and bleeding profusely, there on the track.

"Oh, Lord God Almighty!" Abraham Lincoln stopped, then looked at Hayden and Bobby as he seemed instantly to understand everything that had happened to bring them all to this time and place, strangely together in the night.

"Is he dead?" Bobby finally dared ask.

"He's just passed out," Abraham Lincoln said, "but he's bleeding so fast he'll be dead purty soon if we don't get it stopped."

Abraham Lincoln took off his belt. It was old and of worn, soft leather. He slipped it under the thigh of Robbie's mangled right leg and tightened it until circulation was compressed.

"You've got to help me boys. I just can't carry him all by myself." Working together, the three, Abraham Lincoln bloodied by holding Robbie under the knees, Hayden and Bobby holding one shoulder each, made their way toward the first house they could come to. It was dark and closed up for the night. It was Miss Martha Anne Butler's house.

They approached the screened back porch. ("This is where it all started," Hayden thought.)

Abraham Lincoln did not even knock. He simply shouldered the door open as he carried his end of Robbie, then crossed to the back door where he let go with one hand long enough to reach up, seeming to know the exact place to find the switch for the porch light. He switched it on.

Holding his end of Robbie Wright in the crook of his big left arm, Abraham Lincoln fished in his right-hand pants pocket for a few moments before coming up with a key-ring containing the keys to the black Buick.

He flipped out one of the keys on the ring. It was not a car key. He inserted it into the lock in the back door, it turned, and in an instant, he was leading the two boys in carrying Robbie inside. Once inside, he again seemed to know where the light switch was, and reached to turn it on, flooding the kitchen with light.

Still Miss Martha Anne was nowhere to be seen.

Robbie was coming to and beginning to moan as he was placed on the kitchen table. The two boys looked away as Abraham Lincoln began to try to see exactly what shape the leg was in.

Suddenly a door opened, and Miss Martha Anne entered the room. She took in the entire scene, but never said a word.

"We have a problem," Abraham Lincoln began. "Tried to hop the 10:20 freight. You can see he didn't make it."

"What should we do?" Miss Martha Anne asked. She didn't look very drunk to either Bobby or Hayden.

"Get on the phone and call your cousin," Abraham Lincoln answered.

"My cousin?" Miss Martha Anne looked puzzled.

"Your cousin Roy Parks, the sheriff. Tell him to pick up Dr. York and to get over here as fast as he can. This boy's about to bleed to death on us."

"I forgot all about Roy being my cousin," Miss Martha Anne muttered as she got on the phone and made the call. Her speech was clear as a bell as she gave unmistakable orders over the telephone.

It took a few minutes for Sheriff Roy and Dr. York to arrive, and in those few minutes Robbie Wright really roused up and started wailing.

"He needs a good drink," Abraham Lincoln said. "You got anything that's not drunk up?"

Miss Martha Anne reached into a kitchen cabinet and took out three glasses. She poured about two ounces of gin into each one.

"All three of them could use a drink from the smell of things."

Abraham Lincoln coaxed the gin into Robbie Wright while Miss Martha Anne plied Bobby and Hayden. "Drink this, boys, so that when the Sheriff smells gin on your breath I can tell him I made you drink it...to calm you down."

About that time, Sheriff Roy arrived with Dr. York in tow. They took one look at Robbie, and asked no questions. Dr. York filled a syringe with morphine.

"We've got to get him on to Asheville to see if any of that leg can be saved," he said as he cut away the remnants of the blood-soaked blue jeans. "Let's be sure the bleeding is stopped, and I'll try to clean him up and do as much disinfecting as I can. Time is the most important thing. I'll call Mission Hospital and we'll take him on in the Sheriff's car." He was telling Sheriff Parks, not asking.

"That'll be the fastest way we can get him there."

When Dr. York looked to see if Sheriff Parks was in agreement, he discovered that the Sheriff was not listening to a word he said. There Roy Parks stood, frozen in place, his eyes suddenly glued in a cold, hard stare at Abraham Lincoln.

"How'd the nigger get in here?" he asked Miss Martha Anne. "Did he break in?"

"No he didn't break in, Roy, he has a key," she calmly answered.

Roy Parks face took on a look which could neither then nor now be described in any understandable way whatsoever.

"The 'nigger,' as you call him, Roy, is my cousin…yours, too, since you and I are first cousins. He shares as much blood with you as I do. And he lives here. Has since we were both born…all his life. Walks down here in the dark every night from the taxi stand."

Roy Parks's face was more unbelievable than ever.

"You see, Roy, our grandfather, Colonel Halford Butler, was also *his* grandfather. He owned Abraham Lincoln's grandmother, and he fathered not only my father and your mother, but Abraham's own mother as well. We're all first cousins."

Dr. York had finished his telephone call and was pushing to get on the way. Sheriff Roy wasn't sure he could drive.

He didn't have to. Abraham Lincoln had disappeared in the middle of Miss Martha Anne's genealogy lesson, and suddenly there was in the driveway the huge black Buick taxi, ready to go.

Bobbie and Hayden helped Dr. York and Miss Martha Anne ease Robbie out and into the back seat of the Buick. The Buick sped out the driveway, leaving Sheriff Roy and Miss Martha Anne to finish a conversation never to be heard by anyone else.

By mid-morning the next day, everyone in Sulpher Springs seemed to know what had happened. How Robbie Wright was in Mission Hospital, leg surgically amputated below his right knee, but otherwise expected to recover very well. How that drunken Miss Martha Anne Butler had given the three boys a drink of gin to "calm them down," to hear her tell it. How Abraham Lincoln Butler had rescued Robbie to begin with, and then had driven him to Asheville in just over an hour. All these things were talked about up and down both "Main Streets" of Sulpher Springs.

As time passed, other things were known, accepted, and talked about, but only behind closed doors. How Miss Martha Anne, Sheriff Roy, and Abraham Lincoln were all first cousins. How Abraham Lincoln no longer pretended to deliver groceries to the Butler house, and no longer pretended to live in the taxi stand, but now parked the Buick right in the driveway and entered with his own key, and lived openly for the first time in the house he had lived in all of his life.

Four years later, Miss Martha Anne (who never touched another drop of gin after the drinks she poured for the three boys) died in her sleep. For the remaining years of his life, Abraham Lincoln Butler lived alone in the big, square brick house on "New Main Street."

And for all those years, when children in Sulpher Springs rode by with their parents and asked, "Why does that old black man live in that big house all by himself?" the answer came quickly.

"Well, boys," (I had heard my Daddy say it when Joe-brother asked a very similar question), "that's the Butler home, and he's the only Butler left in Sulpher Springs."

Christmas in Sulpher Springs

CHRISTMAS IN SULPHER SPRINGS was a strangely fascinating combination of two worlds, old and new. Traditional mountain customs and ancient observances formed the heart and soul of the season. At the same time, the new power of advertising and the proliferation of newspapers and radios had made us part of the "modern" world of commercialized holidays.

There were gift-making traditions of generations which still lived on all over Nantahala County. But many homemade crafts had to come to town to be sold side-by-side with the "made in Japan" junk toys so highly prized by children of all ages. Winning and losing took place even on Christmas, and even in that idyllic world.

Our family began to gather as soon as school was out. Sulpher Springs was still "home" to more than a dozen aunts and uncles who had left the mountains to seek their fortunes from Chicago to Florida—but who always planned to come home...some day.

Christmas, like summertime, was a brief season of homecoming. This whole extended family came pouring in, with more and more new little cousins each year tumbling from cars with strange license tags to push us from our own beds for two weeks and eat everything Mother had put up at the cannery last summer.

It was a wonderful time of holiday smells and special food, of staying up late and listening to the old people talk. It was a time for telling stories and feeling the world all in its proper place.

On Christmas mornings we loaded up in the blue Dodge and went to Grandmother's house.

Grandmother and Grandaddy Wilson lived nearly twenty miles out of Sulpher Springs up on Cedar Fork Mountain. It took almost an hour to get there on the curving roads out through Bowlegged Valley and past Crabtree Creek, even though an eight-foot wide strip of the road was paved nearly all the way to their house.

It was an exciting ride. In early years Mother had not learned to drive and Daddy took advantage of that fact by driving fast enough to scare her all the way. Joe-brother and I played in the floor of the back seat, trying to get away from Daddy's ever-present cigar smoke which was much worse in the winter when the windows were rolled up and the heater was turned on.

The last part of the drive was a two-mile climb up and over the gap in Cedar Fork Mountain. Daddy had a special little game he played with himself (and with the Dodge) on this part of the trip. The game was to see how far up Cedar Fork he could get before he had to shift the Dodge down into second gear.

As soon as we passed the saw mill below Crabtree Creek, it was time for the game to begin. The road ran straight from here up and over Sutton Farm Hill, then down through a long dip and then right up the mountain toward Cedar Fork Gap.

Daddy poured on the gas and puffed the cigar at the same time. Mother always protested, but weakly. "Don't go too fast..." she'd say, which always just made him stick the accelerator right to the floor.

We topped Sutton Farm Hill at forty-five miles an hour and started down the last dip before climbing the big mountain. Daddy kept it on the floor. Joe-brother and I peeped over the seat so that we could see the speedometer. The needle climbed to fifty...fifty-five...

If you should meet another car on the narrow strip of pavement, you had to each put two wheels off in the gravel to pass safely. At this speed, that would have been totally out of the question. But here the road was straight, and Daddy could well see that nothing was coming.

"Please slow down!" Mother pleaded.

71

Now we were pulling the mountain, and even with the gas pedal on the floor, the Dodge was slowing down. Up, up, up the steep hill we went. Joe-brother and I could see the speedometer needle dropping. Fifty...forty-five...forty...thirty-five...

It was coming. The time we were waiting for.

Up ahead was "Second Gear Curve." That's where it always happened: the Dodge went into second gear, and more importantly, Daddy gave his interpretation of the event for the day. Joe-brother and I were ready for it.

The Dodge approached "Second Gear Curve," the speedometer dropped to thirty then twenty-five. We entered the curve. It was time.

Daddy bit down on the cigar, pushed in the clutch, and threw the gearshift of the Dodge into second gear. At the same time he grinned, looked at Mother, and this time said, "This six-cylinder Dodge wouldn't pull a wet booger out of a baby's nose...with the baby blowing, to boot!"

Mother only turned a little bit red this time. Some of his worst interpretations in the past had included terms like "greasy strings" and "tom cats' rear ends." A baby's booger wasn't very bad at all.

By the time all the blush had left Mother's face, we were over the top of Cedar Fork and almost to Grandmother's house.

There was a mile-long unpaved farm road that led through the woods to Grandmother Wilson's house, but we seldom drove down it to the house, especially in wintertime. Grandaddy Wilson was of that suspicious breed who regarded having company as something between a bother and an outright danger. To be sure that no wandering tourist accidentally drove down the road to his house, he simply refused to maintain it, so that it was not only allowed to erode, but even dug out at times and encouraged to wash. Only *he* knew exactly how you had to drive at any given time to keep your wheels on the high spots, avoid the rocks, and keep from cracking an oil pan, or worse. The road served better than a mine field as a deterrent to unwanted company.

Sometimes we tried the road in the summer when the

weather was dry. But now, as on most occasions, we drove on down the highway parallel to the unpaved road, until we were through the woods and below Grandmother's house near the mailbox.

There, Daddy pulled the Dodge off onto the grassy side of the road where it would soon be joined by the cars of aunts, uncles and loads of cousins. We opened the trunk, decided who would carry what bundles of food and presents, and walked through a stand of hemlocks up the worn trail from the mailbox to the house.

"I hope Grandaddy sees that it's relatives before he starts shooting at us," cousin George would always joke.

His mother would reassure him. "Grandmother unloads all his guns on Christmas Day."

Finally, at the house, we entered another world.

Grandmother and Grandaddy Wilson lived in a big, two-story T-shaped log house. It was two-rooms wide in the front, a living room and a bedroom, with a hall running back through the middle. The kitchen was the one room on the back, and had been added on to the log house later. It even had a root cellar dug beneath it for potatoes, turnips, carrots and the like.

The upstairs of the house, reached by small, narrow stairs from the hall beside the kitchen, was really a huge two-part bedroom, with a variety of straw-tick and feather-mattress beds.

Mother and her five brothers and five sisters had all been born and raised in that house and had all slept upstairs while Grandmother and Grandaddy slept down in the big front bedroom, as they still did to this very day.

The house had no electricity and no running water. There were kerosene lamps everywhere and a few brilliant Aladdin gas lamps in the main living areas. Water was carried in from a spring about a hundred feet around the slope of the hill from the kitchen door.

The log house was always warm. There was a big wood cookstove in the kitchen. It held a reservoir of water which the fire heated. In the living room there was a big "Warm Morning" wood heater. It had adjustable chrome-plated drafts on the front which no one but Grandaddy was allowed to open or close.

The first job of the day was to find a Christmas tree. Grandaddy Wilson, tempered as he was, never took care of this task ahead of time. We were instructed by Grandmother to "get a big one. Not a floppy cedar tree like all the neighbors get, but a white-pine tree with good, strong limbs."

There was a particular reason that a white-pine tree was on order rather than a cedar tree. The reason was to be found in a wooden box of unknown origin that was kept hidden in the back recesses of a wardrobe in Grandmother's bedroom. The box contained her only Christmas tree decorations: a set of twenty-three (had there once been an even two dozen?) wooden candle holders, mounted on clips like short clothes pins. These could be clipped to the Christmas tree...if the limbs were strong and well spaced.

The candle holders were varnished, unpainted natural wood. No one knew where they came from, whether they were homemade or bought. Grandmother had simply inherited them from her mother. The reason for the white pine was clear: a cedar, with its limber branches and close-spaced foliage would never work. The limbs wouldn't support the weight, and the candles would set the tree on fire. White pine was perfect. It had stiff, strong limbs, spaced far enough apart and graduated so that the candles were stable and safe.

Each year Mother would bring two dozen fresh white candles to go on the tree. While we were tramping after Daddy and the uncles in search of the proper tree, Mother and the aunts would clean off the old wax and fit the new candles into the holders.

As soon as we found a tree everyone agreed on (it never took very long), one of the uncles would cut it down with a handsaw, flush with the ground, after which we would drag it back to the house and another Uncle would nail crossed pieces of plank to the bottom to make it stand up.

Now it was time to decorate. The adults clipped on the candle holders. Each person got to put one on the tree after which they fussed like children over who got to put on the extras. Everyone had a different memory about "who did it last year."

While this was going on, Grandmother was in the kitchen with the children. She would get out an eggbeater, a big crockery mixing bowl, and a box of Ivory Snow flakes bought especially for this occasion. We would put a tiny bit of water into the mixing bowl, add some Ivory Snow flakes, and watch her beat it into mountains of whipped "snow." Then we children would frost the white pine tree with several bowls of this bubbly snow, which, when it dried, actually looked like a frosting of dry, midwinter snowflakes.

The finished tree was all green and white. The grownups would light the candles, under Grandmother's direction, a few minutes at a time, then blow them out for fear that, unwatched, they would set the tree (and that meant the whole log house!) on fire. Even Grandaddy Wilson had to "allow as how it was a purty tree."

We would finally eat Christmas dinner about two o'clock in the afternoon, and some time after that, return home to take up what Santa Claus had brought, which gifts we had briefly checked out and left behind earlier in order to go to Grandmother's house.

In later years, after Grandaddy died and Grandmother moved in with her sister Irene, things seemed to fall apart. Sometimes everyone would come to our house, but for most of the time, the growing cousins wanted to stay at home for Christmas and the number of out-of-state cars in the driveway seemed to get smaller each year.

One Christmas Joe-brother and I lost our Christmas presents. Joe-brother was seven years old and I was eight.

Very often both of us wanted the same things for Christmas, and this was one of those years. The newest toy—which all the kids we knew wanted—was Lincoln Logs. Some of our friends already had them, and we were fascinated by the notched-end building logs in various lengths and the green-slat roof-pieces from which whole farmsteads of houses, barns, and fences could be built. The logs were especially fascinating in that there were still a lot of log houses in Nantahala County at the time, and we had a lot of full-sized models we wanted to duplicate.

Joe-brother and I thought that with two sets of the logs we would have enough to really build something, so we each asked Santa Claus for the biggest possible set of Lincoln Logs.

On Christmas morning, our wishes came true. There, under the Christmas tree, were two big sets of dark brown Lincoln Logs. We built a house and a barn and still had enough logs left to build a fence around both of them to boot.

Daddy always got a lot of Christmas gifts from salesmen who called on him at the hardware store. Since he was a known tobacco chewer and cigar smoker, a lot of his Christmas gifts consisted of plugs of Penn's Natural Leaf Chewing Tobacco (his favorite) and Tampa Nugget Cigars (again his favorite).

This year was no exception. He came home with enough tobacco and cigars to last through the coming year, and over Mother's objections, he put all of them in the refrigerator, "where they will stay nice and fresh."

One gift this year was, however, different. In the midst of all the Tampa Nugget boxes was a strange cigar box. Someone who had not known about Daddy's brand preferences had given him a big box of long, almost black, Marsh-Wheeling cigars. The mouth end of the long cigars ended in a twist of tobacco which had to be either clipped or broken off before air would come through and the cigar could be smoked.

Daddy smoked one of these monsters about half-way through. Mother coughed and complained with every breath of smoke he exhaled.

"Those cigars," he finally declared, "will take the hair off your tonsils." He ground the cigar out in his ash tray, then closed the box and put the remainder in his underwear drawer instead of the refrigerator.

"Maybe I'll give them to Brown Hill next time he comes to tear down bird's nests."

Later in the day, as he watched us building with the Lincoln Logs, it occurred to him that the big cigars looked a lot like our

Lincoln Logs (which were, he declared, probably easier to smoke). He suggested that we just add the cigars to the Lincoln Log sets and use them for building zig-zag rail fences and such. We gladly accepted the gift, and the cigar-logs worked very well.

After Christmas dinner, we returned to the Lincoln Logs and built a whole mountain farmstead of buildings, complete with a little pig-pen built out of cigar logs.

By mid-afternoon the dinner-time relatives had left, all the dishes were washed, and Daddy had settled in his chair to sleep and snore for a while. Joe-brother and I were beginning to get tired of our initial building projects. We needed some excitement.

Finally I said to Joe-brother, "Would you like to learn how to smoke one of these cigars?"

"Do you know how?" he asked.

"I can show you how," I answered, with as much self-assurance as possible. "We'd better just take one of them, so Daddy won't notice in case he counts them."

We went through the kitchen, where I picked up a handful of "strike anywhere" matches from the shelf above the woodstove.

We slipped out the back door and across the yard toward the garage.

The garage was a wooden building with a peaked roof. It was just big enough to hold one car and a few storage shelves in the back. There was a woodshed built onto the rear of the garage, and it had an almost-flat tin roof that butted against the garage just below the end gable. Since the woodshed was behind the garage, and its flat tin roof was hidden from the house by the peak of the garage, it made a good hideout. I had used it often.

We climbed the wooden fence (almost as good as a ladder) that ran to the corner of the woodshed, then swung up onto the tin roof, out of sight of anyone who might be watching from the house. It never occurred to me that anyone might see the smoke rising from our hiding place. No one did.

Together we unwrapped the cellophane from the big cigar. "I'll do the hard part," I said, taking the cigar and breaking off the twisted tip, then opening a bigger hole in the end with the stick-end of the wooden match. I did this as much as possible just as I had seen Daddy do it on the one he had smoked. The hole I made looked plenty big for the air to come through.

"What do I do?" Joe-brother asked with innocent eagerness.

"Just put the cigar in your mouth," I instructed. Joe-brother did as he was told. "When I light the match and hold it up to the cigar, take a big, deep breath, then blow it out. Suck in, take the cigar out of your mouth, and blow out. Just do that over and over again, and you're smoking! But...don't dare stop and let it go out. Keep it going!"

I struck the match, and Joe-brother did exactly what I had told him. For the next twenty minutes, every breath of air he drew came into his lungs through the now-diminishing black cigar.

As the cigar burned down, all the color began to drain out of Joe-brother. It was replaced by a strange, unnatural color—a green not at all like the healthy green of Christmas, but one with a pale yellowish tint.

About the time the cigar burned down to where Joe-brother couldn't hold it anymore, he slumped against the end of the garage and dropped the cigar butt. It rolled down the slope of the tin roof and disappeared off the edge out of sight.

Just then the back door of the house opened, and Mother called us to come to supper. I took one look at Joe-brother and decided it was time for me to abandon him right then and there.

When I got to the back door, Mother was waiting and holding it open as she looked for us. "Come in," she said, "Where's Joe-brother?"

I shrugged my shoulders in an I-don't-know kind of shrug, passed her by, and never said a word.

We both saw Joe-brother at the same time. He was running as fast as he could across the back yard toward us. I couldn't figure out how he had gotten off the roof so quickly, unless he had flopped over and rolled off the slope the same way the cigar butt had.

As he ran, he was vomiting—fast and hard. I thought that it

was a good thing Mother was calling us to supper, because he was going to need food. He was losing everything he had had to eat since *way* before Christmas.

Joe-brother got to the door.

Our house had been built without a bathroom, but in more recent years a part of the back porch had been enclosed to make one.

Mother grabbed Joe-brother by the back of his overalls and hoisted him straight from the porch up into the bathroom. Once there, she dropped him, slimy clothes and all, straight into the big claw-footed bathtub.

On one of our trips to town, Mother had bought a hair-washing contraption at Jones' Drug Store. It was a rubber hose with a fitting you could push on over the tub faucet and a sprayer at the other end to create a nice hair-rinsing spray. Mother pushed the fitting onto the faucet and turned the water on full force. She quickly adjusted the temperature, and then she sprayed Joe-brother, face, clothes, and all, over and over again, every time he was sick.

I did hope that Joe-brother would live, but I was not at all looking forward to his recovering enough to explain what had happened there behind the garage.

Finally Joe-brother fell over in the bottom of the big bathtub like a limp washed-out rag, and the vomiting was over.

From the smell of things, Mother somehow seemed to know what had happened before Joe-brother even began to tell her about it. Still, she asked, and Joe-brother told her every single detail of the story. She didn't look at him, but stared at me with fire in her eyes while she listened.

When Joe-brother was finished, Mother said, "Go get a switch."

I did—a good one, to keep from her from sending me back if it didn't pass her inspection. She wore it out on my legs. I now knew Joe-brother would live, because the grin on his face got bigger and bigger with every blow of the switch.

Later in the day, when we looked for them to play with, the Lincoln Logs had disappeared. Joe-brother asked Daddy where they were. "They've been repossessed," was his answer. Neither of us knew what that meant.

The Lincoln Logs reappeared sometime after the Fourth of July, but we never did see the Marsh-Wheeling Cigars again.

The next Christmas I was in my first Christmas play at church.

The Methodist church in Sulpher Springs was a brick building right in the middle of town on "Old Main Street" at the corner of Oak. It faced Main straight across from the Post Office, and right across Oak Street to the side was our Daddy's hardware store, also an "Old Main Street" business.

The main part of the church building was the sanctuary, built a half-story above ground level so that a wide set of ten steps led up to the door. You were supposed to go up steps, I assumed, to go to church.

Under the sanctuary floor was a basement, only half-underground, with Sunday School rooms for adults. There was also a kitchen and a big room the adults called the "fellowship hall." On the back side of the church was the "new Sunday School building," with two floors of classrooms, mostly for children.

This was the "town church," as opposed to the many white frame "country churches," some Methodist, more Baptist (of every possible variety), which centered every community and marked most crossroads in Nantahala County.

"Our church" was dark red brick and had a dome on the top instead of a steeple. It had an organ and stained glass windows with pictures of Jesus, angels, and Moses on them. Under each of these windows were the names of the dead people whose families had paid for the windows. At least, that's what Hayden Campbell told Joe-brother.

Inside the front door, in what Daddy called the "vestibule," near where the coat and hat racks were, was a sign board with the names of all those who were in "Our Country's Service." There were gold stars beside some of the names, and Daddy told us those were the men who had been killed in the war.

Mrs. Minnie Yarborough was in charge of the Children's Department.

Mrs. Minnie's husband, Mr. Leonard Yarborough, ran the Esso station, another block on down Oak Street at the corner of Railroad Street. The Esso station was not an "Old Main Street" business. He also taught the Old Men's Regular Bible Class in Sunday School.

On the Sunday after Thanksgiving, Mrs. Minnie came into Sunday School and asked: "Now, who would like to be in this year's Christmas play? It will be at six o'clock on Christmas eve and will be over in plenty of time for Santa Claus to come."

Joe-brother and I both raised our hands, and that very afternoon at four o'clock Daddy took us back to the church to start Christmas play practice.

Mrs. Minnie explained the play. We were going to act out her version of the Christmas story.

A big manger-scene set was being built by Mr. Yarborough. It would go right where the pulpit in the church was. Mary and Joseph and the baby Jesus would be in the manger scene from the start. Then all of the people and animals who came to visit the baby Jesus would come in, one at a time, singing their own special Christmas songs.

At the very end, Santa Claus would arrive and give every-body candy (even the baby Jesus, we guessed).

She went through the parts and had us hold up our hands to show which parts we would like to have. Everybody held up their hands for all the parts, so Mrs. Minnie was the one who had to decide.

"Joey and Laura Ray Smith will be Mary and Joseph. They're the tallest," said Mrs. Minnie while we giggled for some unknown reason about Mary and Joseph being played by a brother and sister. (We could all see that they didn't like the idea very much either.)

"Who gets to be the baby Jesus?" we all asked.

"The baby Jesus," Mrs. Minnie explained, "will by symbol-ized by a flashlight shining out of the top of the manger." None of us got the symbolism, but nobody said anything; maybe we just weren't old enough to understand.

Finally Mrs. Minnie got down to Joe-brother and me. Joe-brother was to be a shepherd, and I was to be one of the Wise Men.

For the next two Sunday afternoons we practiced, with Mrs. Minnie playing the piano while we sang. Joe-brother and the other shepherds had it hard. They had to sing a song called "While Shepherds Watched Their Flocks by Night," a song we had never heard of, and so one that had to be learned from the start.

The three of us Wise Men were much luckier. We were to sing "We Three Kings," and I already knew that.

It was going to be wonderful. We Three Kings—Red McElroy, Freddie Patton, and myself—would come down the aisle singing the first verse together. Then we would turn around, face the congregation, and each sing his own solo verse in front of the whole church.

I was the third and last Wise Man. My gift was myrrh, and I would sing my verse about it before presenting it at the manger of the baby Jesus.

We were each responsible for our own costumes.

On the Saturday before Christmas eve, Mother and Daddy helped Joe-brother and me get our costumes together.

I had already picked out Daddy's blue-striped bathrobe for myself, but Joe-brother got to it first. Mother said to let him keep it, because Wise Men could do better than that.

She put the bathrobe on Joe-brother, turned it under, and pinned it up at the bottom so it would be short enough for him. His headgear was a towel pulled tightly over his head, with a necktie tied as a headband around his forehead so the excess towel hung down in the back. He looked like an Arab in the comic strips.

Me being a wealthy Wise Man, Mother had another idea. I got to wear her good nylon robe. It seemed like silk to me, with a paisley print mostly in reds and purples...what could be finer? It came to below my knees but not all the way to the floor, so it didn't need to be pinned up. My turban was made from a dark red silk scarf wrapped around my head with a costume-jewelled pin of Mother's holding it together on my forehead.

Joe-brother and I both looked wonderful.

Daddy helped us with our props. He had thought ahead of time and had taken a limber maple limb, soaked it in hot water in the bathtub, and gradually bent and tied the end into a shepherd's crook for Joe-brother. Now it was dry and stiff. He untied the string and it looked perfect.

The only thing I needed was myrrh.

There was not a lot of myrrh used by people in Sulpher Springs, and Mother and Daddy had quite a time just figuring out what myrrh was, anyway. Finally Daddy disappeared. He came back in the room with a pretty glass bottle he had taken from the cedar chest.

Mother said, "He can't take that to church. That's a whiskey decanter. You can't let him use that!" Daddy just laughed and said of course we could.

None of us could figure out what myrrh ought to look like in the bottle. My verse of the song called it a "bitter perfume." We finally decided to fill the bottle with coffee, as everyone agreed that a bright color wouldn't look very bitter.

Now we were ready, except for the shoes. Mother dug in the closet and brought out our summertime sandals. We had to carry them to church in a paper bag because it was so cold. We wore our regular shoes and socks on the way, but we would change into the sandals before the play started.

We were ready.

On Christmas eve we all went to the church at four o'clock in the afternoon. Mrs. Minnie was waiting for us. We put on our costumes for a "dress rehearsal." Everything went very well. We were all excited and ready for the real show.

While we were down in the church basement waiting for the people to come in and watching the clock inch toward six o'clock, Mrs. Minnie called me over to the side.

"Honey," (she called everybody 'Honey') "you sure do look nice, but your pants are showing between your robe and your sandals. Now you just slip off your pants so you'll look more like you're supposed to...real Wise Men didn't have any pants."

I didn't like that idea, but I did what Mrs. Minnie told me to do. After all, she was the director. Once my blue jeans were safely in the paper sack with my shoes and socks, Miss Minnie re-tied the knot in the sash around the robe's waist that Mother had so carefully knotted before we had left home.

At last it was six o'clock. Time for the big show to begin. The churchbell rang. The organ began to play "O Come All Ye Faithful," and Mrs. Minnie herded all of us up and into the vestibule so that we could begin.

Mary and Joseph came in while the rest of us, from the back, sang "Gentle Mary Laid Her Child." Laura Ray knelt at the end of the manger, not so much out of reverence as so she could switch on the flashlight that stood for the baby Jesus.

First all the angels came in singing. Their song was, "Hark the Herald Angels Sing." Some of the smallest angels wandered all over the church, forgetting the words and finally hollering "Mama!" until they were at last all herded in the right direction and lined up in the front.

Next came the shepherds. They had finally learned their song, and so they proudly sang "While Shepherds Watched Their Flocks By Night." Some carried crooks and others carried stuffed animals of several varieties, all covered with drug-store cotton to make them look like sheep.

Now it was our turn.

"We three kings of orient are…" we began. In practice, Red McElroy had always sung the next line as "trying to smoke a loaded cigar…BANG!" Even tonight, we all had the giggles until we got past that part. We kept singing.

"…bearing gifts we traverse afar; field and fountain, moor and mountain; following yonder star…" By now the three of us had sung our way side by side clear down the church aisle. Now we turned around, faced the congregation, and got ready for our solo verses.

Red McElroy was first. He sang "Born a king on Bethlehem's plain…" and presented the baby with a big, gold-painted brick.

Freddie Patton was next. He sang about frankincense, put a perfume bottle full of green colored water beside the manger, and bowed deeply to the congregation. There was a bit of laughter following the deep bow.

Now it was really my turn.

As I stepped to the center, I sensed a giggle run through the congregation. I thought that they had not yet settled down from Freddie's bow. The music was playing, so I had to start singing: "Myrrh is mine, its bitter perfume…" I held up the whiskey decanter filled with coffee. Some of the big kids on the front row actually laughed out loud.

"…breathes a life of gathering gloom," The laughter grew and so I put on my loudest and most dramatic voice. "…sorrowing, sighing, bleeding, dying…" They were actually pointing at me now as they laughed out loud, and I sang, at the top of my voice, "…sealed in a stone-cold tomb."

Suddenly I became aware of where everyone was pointing. I looked down. Then and there I saw that the knot Mrs. Minnie had re-tied in my sash had come untied, and that there I stood, in front of the entire congregation, in the *spotlights,* singing at the top of my voice, with Mother's nylon robe hanging completely open in front. I had no pants on.

Those final words, *sealed in a stone-cold tomb* seemed to ring through the air, and I dropped the myrrh.

Red and Freddie sang "Star of wonder, star of light…" just like nothing had happened, and the congregation laughed as I ran out of the sanctuary with the robe streaming out behind me.

For many years, there was a huge coffee stain on the carpet at the front of the church, and I never again so much as even *participated* in another children's program.

The next year the adult choir sang on Christmas eve, and no one ever mentioned what had happened the year before.

The most memorable and important Christmas Joe-brother and I ever had came on us by surprise. It was not the Christmas when Miss Swinburne ate the cookies that had soaked up fumes from the airplane glue mother had used to glue decorations inside the tin box the cookies were in. Neither was it the year when Freddie Patton had tried to stop Joe-brother's basketball-induced nosebleed with his new bicycle pump. It was, instead, the year we learned all about Santa Claus.

I was ten years old and Joe-brother was nine.

For the past couple of years, I had been hearing ugly rumors about the reality of Santa Claus. They were not to be taken seriously, because they seemed to be always whispered by those children whom any Santa Claus of justice would have given up on years before. Most of the no-necked Rabbit Creek kids came in this bunch, and I figured Santa Claus probably didn't even know where Rabbit Creek was.

This year, poor Joe-brother had begun to hear the same rumors. One day around Thanksgiving time he came home to say that as he was walking home from school, a car loaded with big kids had slowed down as they passed by. One of the big kids had stuck his head out of the window and yelled, "There ain't no Santy Claus!" before the car sped away amid sounds of laughter.

Joe-brother told me about this with tears in his eyes, but neither one of us would dare tell Mother or Daddy.

The next time we saw Santa Claus we looked at one another, but decided not to take any chances. We carefully told Santa what we wanted every time we saw him.

This year Joe-brother and I both wanted red scooters for Christmas. Red scooters, metal with hard rubber wheels, the kind you put one foot on while you push with the other foot. (There was no pavement anywhere around our house so we never would know it was possible to actually get your speed up and coast with both feet off the ground.) The scooters we wanted had little brake levers you could step on that pushed against the rear wheel and skidded it to a stop.

We showed Mother and Daddy the kind of scooters we wanted. Daddy said, "They're awful big." Mostly, though, we told Santa Claus every chance we got.

Mother would take us to town shopping on Saturday. We'd go in the back door of Belk's Department Store and climb the stairs.

At Belk's, the North Pole was on the second floor in the middle of Ladies Ready-to-wear. There was cotton everywhere, and inside a little fence sat Santa Claus. I waited in line until it was finally my turn, and then I talked for both of us.

Joe-brother would not talk to Santa Claus for himself this year. Last year, on this very spot, Santa Claus had talked too long to Joe-brother, and in the end they were both wet. This year Joe-brother hid behind the ladies woolen pants and waited for me to communicate for us both.

"What's your name, little boy?" Santa would say once I was firmly in his lap. "And what do you want for Christmas?"

I would tell him politely and also point out Joe-brother, who would be out of sight in the ladies pants.

"We both want red scooters for Christmas," I would say. With an extra big "ho-ho-ho," Santa would put me down with two pieces of peppermint candy, one for me and one for Joe-brother.

Finished at Belk's, Mother would lead us across the street and into Harris's Department Store. Santa Claus was fast! He was already there. We had just left him at Belk's not five minutes before, and here he was again! It also looked like he had had a difficult trip: his suit and beard were not quite as clean as they had been over at Belk's.

Joe-brother and I still weren't taking any chances. I got into line again while he hid in the men's shoe department and played with the shoe horns scattered there.

When I finally worked my way up to Santa Claus, I came to understand why it was important to talk to him several times. His memory was extremely bad. The first thing he said to me was, "What's your name, little boy? And what do you want for Christmas?"

I thought, "I just told you that—you tell me! Maybe you're getting too old for this job." But what I did was tell him my name, very politely, and then point out Joe-brother and remind him again that he had us down for red scooters for Christmas.

Before the season was over, I had talked to Santa Claus while Joe-brother watched between twenty-five and thirty times. He never *once* remembered the scooters before I had to remind him.

The last day of school before Christmas was a Wednesday. We went to town to finish our shopping as soon as Mother got home from school. After the shopping was done, we ended at Daddy's hardware store just before closing time. The four of us got in the Dodge and started home in the dark.

On the way home we passed Jimmy's Drive-In Restaurant. Mother suggested, "Let's pick some food up at Jimmy's so I won't have to cook supper when we get home."

Daddy agreed and we pulled into the curb-service side of the parking lot. Out came Jimmy himself to get our orders. Daddy ordered "four special cheeseburgers, four orders of fried potatoes, and four Co-colas."

In less than five minutes, Jimmy was coming back with the food. The cheeseburgers and potatoes were in a brown paper sack, and he carried the four unopened Cokes in one hand with the bottle necks between his fingers. As he handed the order in the window and Daddy got his money out to pay, Jimmy said to Daddy, "You-all got any bottles to swap?" If we didn't have any empty Coke bottles, Daddy would have to pay a two-cent deposit on each bottle we took.

We always had empty bottles. I knew we did. There were always some in the trunk of the car. As I said, "I know where some bottles are," I was already out the car door and on my way back to the trunk.

You didn't need a key to open the trunk of the old blue Dodge. Just turn the handle and lift. I did, and there before my eyes were two brand-new red scooters!

I slammed the trunk as fast as I could. "No bottles!" I said, as I climbed back into the car, flushed, looking only at the floor mat in the back seat floor. Neither Daddy nor Mother said a word as we went home. We ate our supper quickly and went to bed.

Christmas morning finally came. Joe-brother got a wind-up toy train and I got a tool set from Santa Claus. We spent the whole morning playing and opening other presents.

A few of the cousins were with us for Christmas dinner, and we played together, compared and defended our several presents, until they all finally left in the middle of the afternoon.

Joe-brother and I were playing quietly when Daddy came into the living room. "How was Christmas?" he asked. "Did both of you get what you wanted?"

"Oh, yes!" we both insisted. "This is about the best Christmas we ever had! Santa Claus sure did a good job."

"Well, I'm glad," Daddy said. "Your Mother and I were awful worried. You see, we knew you had been asking Santa Claus for scooters for Christmas. When we saw some scooters at the store, they were so big that we were just afraid that Santa Claus would never get down the chimney with them.

"So..." he was speaking softly now, almost a whispered secret, "your Mother and I got scooters for you for Christmas. We've had them hidden in the trunk of the car! You can go out there and get them now if you want to."

Later that night, Joe-brother and I talked. We decided that after this year it didn't matter what little kids said at school or even what big kids yelled out of car windows, because, at best, the real Santa Claus only came around once a year anyway. We had found out a lot about our Mother and Daddy, and we had them *all* the time.

Miss Daisy

IN THE FOURTH GRADE ALL THE A-through-GRs (still Patricia Abernethy through Thomas Greene, though Leon Connor had gone to Jackson Training School for good by now) ended up in Miss Daisy Rose Boring's class.

Miss Daisy was one of the six daughters of Mr. Robert Boring. Mr. Boring had started Boring's Hardware in 1909, and having no son to take over the business, had hired Daddy to work for him in 1924.

Sixteen years later Mr. Boring died, and the six sisters sold the store to Daddy, who still ran it as Boring's Hardware. That same year he married Mother, having waited, properly, until he could adequately support a wife and family.

Instead of entering the hardware business the six daughters had years before become school teachers...for life!

I had not had Miss Lily, who taught second grade at Sulpher Springs School. She taught the GU-through-M class.

Anyone who had one of the Boring sisters for any grade in school usually spent the next year wondering, "Will I get the next one?" They taught all the even-numbered grades (2, 4, 6, 8, 10, and senior English) at Sulpher Springs school. If your name fell just right in the alphabet, it was possible to receive half of your entire public education from the Boring sisters.

Mr. Robert, their father (we never heard anything about their mother), tried to give all of them botanical names. He did well through Miss Lily, Miss Pansy and Miss Violet. He must have thought Miss Daisy Rose would be the last, for he used two flowers in naming her. (Perhaps he was convinced a boy would come next.) When two more girls appeared, he started on gemstones. The youngest were Miss Opal and Miss Pearl.

Miss Daisy had taught fourth grade for forty-one years. She was a tiny, frail-looking woman in her early sixties. Her bird-like appearance prompted all of us to begin our first day of school wondering whether that little old woman could really handle us. We had, after all, been at this for three years already. The A-through-GRs were a tough bunch!

As we were whispering and wondering, Miss Daisy was giving what she called "housekeeping" instructions to the class. This consisted of instructions on everything from how to use the pencil sharpener to where to hang your coat.

The door of the classroom was standing open to the hall, and a mouse, who had had the entire school to himself all summer and was now trying innocently to escape this first-day invasion of wild children, came into our room in search of a safe place of retreat.

The mouse, scared to death, made its way a few cautious steps and sniffs at a time along the base of the blackboard wall just behind Miss Daisy.

No one was watching Miss Daisy. Every eye in the classroom was on the mouse. All of us secretly knew that very soon Miss Daisy would realize that we were not watching her. "This will be the test," I thought. "As soon as she turns to see what we're watching, we'll see what she's made of!"

In a few moments Miss Daisy caught on. She turned to see what we were staring at, and spotted the brown mouse just as it reached the corner of the room. She didn't make a sound.

Very quietly she opened the side drawer of her desk and took out two brown paper towels. We all watched, rapt, as the tiny woman slipped quietly toward the corner where the mouse was, squatted slowly to the floor, reached out, and caught the mouse in the brown paper towels.

She carried the mouse back to her desk (still in the towels), held it up in front of us. With one hand—*crrrunch*—crushed it to death and dropped it in the trash can!

Not a sound came from anyone in the room. ("Quiet as a mouse," I thought later.) After that, no one ever had any doubts about Miss Daisy's power; we listened to every word she said.

The whole course of the year was going to be great fun. As she described her plan to us, Miss Daisy was going to take us, without our ever leaving our room at Sulpher Springs School, on an imaginary trip around the world.

It was going to be a year of play. Each day we'd get out our maps and plan our travels. Then, with Miss Daisy's help, we'd go on our travels for the day.

She didn't pass out the spelling books. She didn't even pass out the arithmetic books. We were just going to play all year.

Our imaginary plan was this: we would get some of our parents to pretend to drive us to Atlanta in their cars. I was not sure about whether Daddy would take the blue Dodge. He didn't usually like to travel very far from home.

Once in Atlanta, our plan was to board the train. Miss Daisy told us all about it. It was "the wonderful Southern Crescent," with a dining car that had fresh-cut flowers and real sterling silver on the tables. We were all to ride the train to New Orleans.

After a day or two in New Orleans, we would load up on what Miss Daisy called a "tramp steamer," and steam away for South America.

The real truth was that Miss Daisy had never actually been out of Nantahala County in her life except for four brief years some forty-one years in the past when she had ridden the train less than a hundred miles to Asheville Normal to learn to teach fourth grade. But for forty-one years she had sent away by mail and had ordered thousands and thousands and thousands of picture postcards. It was not possible for us to go anywhere on our imaginary travels, from a small town in Alabama to a temple garden in Japan, without Miss Daisy being able to dig down through her files of shoe-boxes to finally come up with a post-card to show us what that place looked like.

Some of the cards were very old, with black-and-white pictures and ragged edges. We were fascinated by the old ones most of all.

As we went on our travels, we had to write down the names of all the places we visited and the things we saw: states, towns, geographical and historical sites, even crops and industries. We made long lists of famous people who had lived everywhere we went. We learned about all the things they had done.

All year long we worked at this without ever figuring out that Miss Daisy had us making up our own lists of spelling words. They were words which were much harder than those in the slender fourth-grade spelling books she had never bothered to pass out.

We also never figured out (or was it because we didn't want to admit it) that as we calculated how far we had traveled each day, how much money we spent for gasoline or food or tickets, how to change money from one country to another, and how to calculate latitude and longitude, we were doing arithmetic. Miss Daisy never called it that. We were just doing what you have to do to make your way around the world.

The class was divided into four "travel teams." Most of each morning was spent in planning each day's travels. Each team was given certain parts of the journey to take the class on. Miss Daisy would flit from team to team as we planned. She was informer, guide, questioner, always insisting that no matter how much we learned, she could always learn more in a day than we could!

Each afternoon, on a strictly alternating schedule, two of the four "travel teams" would take the class on their assigned part of the journey.

Miss Daisy explained it this way: "It takes twice as long to plan anything as it does to do it, so you get two days to plan before you present. 'Plan-plan-present, plan-plan-present,' that's the pattern we work on."

She called the first day of planning "rounding up" and the second day "closing in on it."

On Fridays Miss Daisy did all the presenting herself, filling in our gaps and giving us what felt like a day off. This did help to make up for the tests, which also always came on Fridays.

We worked our way to Atlanta, then on to New Orleans, where we finally boarded a steamer named the "Aurelia" for our trip to South America.

The first day of sailing was very rough! One of the "travel teams" was charged with teaching us all about the ship we were sailing on. They decided it would be a good idea to list all the parts of the ship, and learning to spell those awful words with their apostrophes and unpronounced extra letters nearly made some of us seasick.

On Friday of that week we came to school very excited, wondering what Miss Daisy might have in store for us on her day to present. As we gathered in the room a boy named Lucius Grasty, one of the last of the GRs, came running into the room.

His head was stooped and he wore a wool knit toboggan. The home-made hat was pulled way down over his ears. He wouldn't take it off though it was still September, and not even beginning to get cold yet.

Lucius went straight to the back of the room, squatted in a corner, and refused to come out.

Miss Daisy came breezing into the room, took little notice of Lucius, and began the day.

"Today, children," she started in a hurry, "we cross the equator!"

"That was fast," I thought.

"Have any of you ever crossed the equator?" she asked. We met the question with blank stares. We didn't even understand what she was talking about.

"Good," she went on, "because when we cross the equator we must have a big party for Neptune, King of the Deep."

As she kept talking about King Neptune, she went back into the cloak closet and started bringing out things that had been left there by kids at the end of school for forty-one years. Out she came with old coats, abandoned caps and hats, odd galoshes, umbrellas with broken ribs, even brooms and mops.

"On a ship, we have to work with what we have," she said as she began to dress us up for the party. Mop-heads became wigs and we took off our shoes and socks like sailors. She pulled the shades way out from the windows and twisted them at an angle to make sails for the ship. We found a rope and took turns throwing one another overboard out the first floor window, and pulling each other back onto the ship again. She came up with a shaving mug from somewhere, lathered the boys up, and shaved them with a sword made from a yardstick.

"Some sailors even have their clothes run up the mast," she said. No one volunteered for that one!

"And some," she said, as she eased back through the room to where Lucius was still squatting in the floor (he had taken part in nothing), "...some *special* sailors, like the captain's son on his first voyage, even have their heads shaved!"

As she spoke those words, she lifted Lucius's toboggan. There we saw it: he was the sailor whose head was shaved! We were all jealous. How did *Lucius* get to be the special one?

It was a long time later that I overheard Mother telling a friend about that day and learned that when Lucius had gone home the day before, his mother had found lice in his hair. She had shaved his head and washed it in kerosene to get rid of the lice. Miss Daisy had taken that little boy with the blistered head, and in a moment had transformed him into the hero of crossing the equator.

At last we made land in South America. After leaving the steamer, we visited our first city, Belim, where we discovered that everyone spoke not Spanish but Portuguese. Then we hired small boats and guides to take us up the Amazon River.

Miss Daisy would stand in front of the classroom and say, "The Amazon is the longest river in the Americas. There are giant ferns there, ferns as big as trees. And butterflies—there are butterflies so big you could ride them...if you could catch one!"

Some of us who thought we were pretty smart would try to argue with her about the "longest river" idea. We would gather the maps and say, "Miss Daisy, what about the Mississippi and the Missouri put together? That's really just one river. They just got two names on it a long time ago. If you put all of it together, it's longer than the Amazon, isn't it?"

"Two names, two rivers," she replied. "The Amazon is the longest. Remember that—it will be on the test!"

No matter where we went after that (all the way down to the tip of South America, on an imaginary ice-breaker to the South

Pole, up the Congo and down the Nile), the Amazon was always my favorite place.

That was because my big art project for the year was making a butterfly "so big you could ride on it."

Several months earlier my Uncle Floyd had tried to invent a flying machine. He had made a two-part framework out of copper tubing and the flat sides of orange crates. It was joined in the middle by a long piano hinge so that the wings could flap.

Once the basic construction was finished, he had glued what looked like two million white-leghorn feathers to both sides of the "wings." Finally he rigged a harness to the underside so that the wings could be strapped on his back and he could flap them with his arms.

When the glue was all dry, he carried the huge wings up a ladder to the roof of the front porch of his house.

He told us all about it later. "I was going to try a little test flight from the house out to that red maple tree," he said, "but a downdraft got me!"

He sprained his ankle crash-landing. He was lucky he hadn't broken his neck.

The lucky thing for *me* was that the crash didn't tear up the wings. As soon as the Friday after the art project assignments came, I started begging Daddy to take me to Uncle Floyd's. Once there, I started begging Uncle Floyd for the wings.

After taking off the harness straps to be sure that I couldn't try to fly with them, he gave me the wings for the foundation of my butterfly. We folded them by the piano hinge and took them home in the blue Dodge.

I went to work. The body was made out of some big mailing tubes with the ends stopped up. The head was a rubber ball, with pieces of coat hanger bent to the shape of antennae.

The big job was painting the wings. It took nearly all day Saturday. Yellow and green, blue and red, purple and orange, swirls and patterns, matching on both sides of both wings, until by the end of the day I had created a butterfly so big you could really ride on it.

The only problem was that with the body and all the paint I

had used, the wings wouldn't flap by the piano hinge anymore. It took all day Sunday for the paint to dry.

On Monday morning Daddy said he would take Joe-brother and me to school in the blue Dodge. "I don't think that thing will go through the door of the school bus," was his excuse.

Now that the paint was dry and the wings were stiff, it wouldn't fit through the door of the Dodge either. So Daddy drove us to school very slowly, with the window rolled down, holding the big butterfly outside the window. Several times he pulled to the side of the road to let the cars pass which had backed up behind us as he drove slowly enough to keep the butterfly from taking off.

When I got to the classroom with the butterfly, Miss Daisy was thrilled! She fastened a wire to the butterfly's back, climbed on top of a desk in the middle of the room, and suspended the butterfly from one of the light fixtures.

For the remainder of the year it hung there, multicolored and beautiful, decorating the room and reminding us of the Amazon.

We traveled overland from the headwaters of the Amazon to the very tip of Cape Horn, took an icebreaker for a brief visit to a scientific research station on "that frozen, southernmost continent," then sailed to Cape Good Hope and up the west coast of Africa to the mouth of the Congo.

We hired small boats and guides to travel up the Congo. Miss Daisy showed us a postcard picture of logs being burned out to build dug-out canoes, and we were sure they were ours.

To our surprise, the Congo was not like the Amazon at all. Here we met shining black tribes ranging from Pygmies to Zulus, and we saw sharp-nosed crocodiles instead of alligators.

At the head of the Congo, we joined a safari which took us by Jeep and then on foot all the way to Victoria Falls, and on to the very beginning waters of the Nile.

As soon as the Nile was navigable, we built huge rafts, supplied them, and floated for days and days until we landed at last beside the pyramids.

After a short time of sailing on the Mediterranean, we

landed for a visit to the brand-new country of Israel. It could have been an old country as far as our visit was concerned, because all the things we visited were, in Miss Daisy's words, "nearly two thousand important years old."

If the United States Supreme Court (the "Nine Old Men in Washington," Uncle Floyd called them) ever happened to come down to Sulpher Springs School to be sure that the separation of church and state was being properly maintained, they would have found Miss Daisy dutifully teaching us to spell the names of the leaders of the new nation of Israel, and other important fourth-grade facts such as the distance from Jerusalem to Cairo.

They never came, though, and so when school let out for Christmas holidays, Miss Daisy told us we could stay over in Bethlehem while school was out. In spite of what the Supreme Court may or may not have seen had they been there, none of us was at all uncertain about why it was important to her that we go home for Christmas thinking of Bethlehem.

After Christmas, we again set sail on the Mediterranean, this time bound for Greece and then on to Europe.

While we were in Greece, one of the four "travel teams" was assigned to take us to the ancient Olympic games. This group decided that we really should have Olympic games of our own. Miss Daisy thought the idea was great.

"There is only one thing I must warn you about, boys and girls. In the old Olympic games the athletes competed with no clothes on." We all looked around the room and stared at one another.

Miss Daisy went on. "But since it's wintertime, I suppose we will have to wear clothing for our Olympics. Does anyone mind that?" It was as quiet in the room as when the mouse died.

On Friday (no tests this week) we all came to school with sheets to wrap over our clothes. It looked more like a ninth-grade Latin banquet than the Olympics, but we didn't care. Miss Daisy had even made laurel wreaths for the winners.

It was a day of great competition. Relays were run back and forth from one end of the playground to another, passing a baton made from an empty paper-towel roller.

There was shot-put with wooden croquet balls, javelin throwing with sharp wooden tobacco sticks, and finally a marathon which went from the school yard out and all the way down Railroad Street, around a big oak tree at the post office, back behind the stores on Main Street, ending at a finish line on the school ground just across the creek from where we had begun.

Running wrapped in a sheet was going to be difficult. We did as well as we could to tie the sheets up between the legs of our blue jeans so we could move more freely.

I wasn't much of a competitor in either the shot-put or the javelin contests. Not being able to throw straight made it all but impossible to figure out just how far you could throw when a straight line was the object. Pauletta Donaldson won both these contests, but then she was the biggest kid in the fourth grade, boy or girl, and had longer arms than all the rest of us.

The relays were more even. Our team of four came in in second place and could have won if the baton hadn't been dropped twice (the winning team only dropped theirs once). At the very end of the day came the marathon.

The fastest down-and-out runner in the class was a tiny boy named Hallie Curtis. Everyone was pretty sure that Hallie could take the marathon with no competition.

Hallie was very small and had two cow-licks in his hair. One was over his right eye and the other near the crown of his head. His hair insisted on standing up in these two places, and Hallie couldn't stand it. It was hard enough being teased about being little. The cow-licks were too much.

Hallie would put lard on his hair in a futile attempt to make the wild spots lie down. It never worked for very long. The lard, however, vulnerable as it was to Hallie's body temperature, gradually ran down his face and neck. His shirt collar was always dark and greasy with melted hair-lard.

Hallie had the longest arms for his body of anyone we had ever seen. His hands seemed to dangle alongside his knees as he walked along. Hallic's special trick was that he could bend just a bit and run on all fours, just like a greyhound or a whippet—

though he looked more like a greasy, escaped, dressed-up ba-
boon. It was simply true: Hallie Curtis, running on all four legs,
could completely outrun any boy or girl in any grade at Sulpher
Springs School.

Before the marathon started, everyone complained to Miss
Daisy that Hallie's four-legged running was not fair. So, to be fair,
Miss Daisy warned him, "Now, Hallie, no running on your
hands. You have to run on two feet like everybody else does.
Those old Greeks didn't run on four legs!"

Miss Daisy lined us up. "One for the money, two for the
show, three to get ready, and four...to...*GO!*"

Off we went, sheets flapping, girls screaming, across the
playground, then spread out a little now, through the schoolyard
gate and down the side of the empty street which ran behind
Main Street and along by the railroad tracks.

The first half of the race told nothing. The sprinters rushed
ahead, then started to wear out as the whole column began the
mid-point turn around the oak tree at the post office.

On the way back the race really settled down. There was
one good solid group of runners in the middle, with a slowly
growing assortment of stragglers stringing out behind.

Out in front of everybody else, the real race was between
Hallie Curtis and Pauletta Donaldson. She was nearly a foot
taller and ran with flailing arms and long, gangling paces. Hallie's little legs seemed to spin like eggbeaters. His individual
short strides couldn't even be seen as separate steps at all.

When they entered the gate to the school-yard and poured
on the heat for the finish line, Pauletta began to pull farther and
farther ahead.

Hallie couldn't stand the thought of losing to a girl. He didn't
care if Miss Daisy had said that he had to run on two legs. He
dropped to all-fours, and looking like a greasy-headed dog
wrapped in a sheet, began to close the gap as the two of them
outran everyone else toward the finish line.

· A little creek ran down the middle of the schoolyard and the
finish line was across this little creek from where we were
coming back onto the playground from the post office. The last

thing all the runners had to do before crossing the finish line was to jump the creek.

It wasn't a hard creek to jump. We jumped it every day during recess as a regular part of most games, but I had never seen Hallie jump it while running on all fours like a dog.

As Hallie and Pauletta approached the creek, Hallie took the lead. He was nearly twenty feet ahead of her when, with a great push of his hind legs, he took to the air, arms reaching out in front of him, then coming back to touch the ground as his legs moved forward for the next step.

Something happened. Hallie's legs seemed to tangle in midair so that he couldn't pull his knees up. Instead of sailing across the creek, he fell like a rock, flat on his belly, in the middle of the water.

Pauletta never missed a step. She jumped right across him, and with a look of certain pride on her face, crossed the finish line alone.

Later we learned what had happened. Hallie's nose was itching as he came across the playground field on all fours. He tried to hold back a sneeze as long as he could, but just as he started to leave the ground for his great leap across the creek, the long-saved-up sneeze burst loose. The great escape of the held-back sneeze snapped Hallie's belt right in two, and his blue jeans fell down to his knees, where they tangled hopelessly with the sheet which was tied up between his knees.

The sheet did protect his modesty, but the tangle had brought him down in great agony of defeat. He had lost to a girl.

Pauletta was simply disgusting as she wore her laurel wreath for the rest of the entire day.

When we finished with Greece, we made a great circle through Europe and spent the rest of the springtime crossing Asia: China, Japan, down to New Zealand and Australia, then over the Pacific, past Pearl Harbor and on to Los Angeles.

The last month of the school year was a long imaginary train ride, not across the United States, but across *North America,* Canada to Mexico, until on the last day of May, there we were, right back in our classroom at Sulpher Springs School.

The next year the A-through-GRs got Mrs. Kinney for the fifth grade. Mother said Mrs. Kinney was very smart, that we were lucky to have her, but it seemed like a long year as she tried to teach us how interesting the Greeks and Romans were, straight out of the book.

I had none of Miss Daisy's sisters in later years, and gradually I forgot about her as the importance of growing up made the fourth grade unreal, unimportant, and further and further behind.

At least ten years passed. I had graduated from Sulpher Springs High School and been away from home and college for a couple of years when I came home to work for the summer.

My job for this particular summer was working as bus boy in the dining room of the Mountain Vale Inn. The Mountain Vale Inn was an old hotel which topped the hill above "Old Main Street." It was the kind of place where retired Floridians spent the entire summer, while residents of Sulpher Springs had still not learned to charge them Florida prices.

It was a place with a dining room, a place where local residents went out for evening meals and after church on Sunday.

We served supper each evening from five until eight o'clock.

One afternoon about four-thirty I was outside sweeping off the steps and the sidewalk to the dining room when an old two-tone brown LaSalle sedan pulled up into the parking side of the yard.

Though I had not seen it in years, I knew the ancient car well. With its double-spares on the back and its landau trim, there was not another car like it anywhere in Nantahala County.

The LaSalle belonged to the Boring sisters. It had been their father's last car, new when he died, and they had carefully kept it. More than twenty years later, they were still keeping it—and driving it, it seemed, all over Nantahala County.

Miss Lily was driving that day. She opened her door and got out. As she walked around the long nose of the LaSalle, the other front door opened, and Miss Opal got out. The two of them opened the back door, lifted something from the back seat, and began to walk side by side up the sidewalk to the dining room.

I looked more closely and saw that they had between them all that was left of my old Miss Daisy.

A tiny skin-and-bones figure, less than half, it seemed, of the tiny thing she had been more than a decade earlier when I was in the fourth grade. She was between them, with each holding an arm as they brought her up the walk, little toes barely touching the ground. They were taking her out to supper.

As soon as I recognized them, I hurried down the walk to meet them. Miss Lily recognized me at once and spoke to me. Then she turned to Miss Daisy and said, "Look, Daisy. Look! It's one of your little boys...all grown up."

Miss Daisy lifted her head and it did turn toward me, but her eyes were colorless and blank and empty. Nobody in there. After a long moment, her head dropped back to her chest.

My curiosity asked for a response. It came from Miss Lily. "Daisy has had a stroke," she offered.

While I was thinking that perhaps they were pushing things a bit having her out too soon in this condition I asked, "When did she have it?"

In unison they replied, "She's had it six years." Miss Lily continued, "She got it when she retired."

I stood aside and watched as they partly led, partly carried, Miss Daisy up the steps and into the dining room for her supper.

Once inside, I tried to do my work without staring, but from time to time did glance to see Miss Lily and Miss Opal cutting up tiny bites on Miss Daisy's plate. They mashed green beans and bits of potato, then helped her swallow it with drinks from a small glass of milk.

Part of my job was to clear the dishes from tables as soon as people were finished with their meals so that the dessert tray could be brought to the table.

It looked like they were finished, so I rolled my dish cart to their table and began clearing things away as quickly as I could.

Suddenly, in the midst of my doing this job, I was paralyzed by the strange feeling of someone staring at me. I looked toward the feeling, and it was Miss Daisy.

She was staring straight at me, and her eyes were sparkling and clear. They were alive, and as blue as they had ever been.

Her lips began to quiver and then move as from somewhere way down inside of her tiny body a thin, wispy ghost-of-a-voice came to life and softly said, straight to me, "The Amazon is the longest...there are butterflies here we can ride on..."

Then her eyes went blank and her head dropped back to her chest.

I grabbed my dish cart and ran for the kitchen.

Mr. Gibbons, the old cook, was looking out of the kitchen door and muttering to himself, "Isn't it sad about poor Miss Daisy...isn't it sad."

"No, it's not!" I thought, but only to myself. "No, it's not sad." Until a few moments ago I had thought the same thing, but now I felt as if I had made the greatest discovery in the world and had to find some way to explain it to Mr. Gibbons.

Then I remembered. "Mr. Gibbons," I said, "way back in Miss Daisy's room in the fourth grade sometimes we would get so full of learning new things and so tired of that traveling that we would look at her and say, 'Miss Daisy, why do we have to learn all these things?' " In memory, I could still see Miss Daisy holding her mouse-crushing fist high in the air, clenched, as she answered the question.

"She would say, 'Because, boys and girls...*because!* One of these days, when you grow up, you'll be able to go anywhere you want to. When that day comes, you simply must know where you are going!'

"You see, it's not sad, Mr. Gibbons," I pleaded, returning to the present, "because I have seen that Miss Daisy is in a world in which she can go anywhere she wants to go, and she knows where she's going. Why, she can even ride the butterflies."

We looked back into the dining room, but they had finished and were gone. We heard the LaSalle whining from the driveway. I never saw Miss Daisy again.

Dr. York

DR. YORK DROVE A STUDEBAKER. Daddy said that made him a good doctor.

"Why does driving a Studebaker make him a good doctor?" I asked.

"Well," Daddy answered, "It shows that when he makes up his mind he sticks to what he believes in, even if it's a whole lot of trouble to do it."

"I still don't understand," I complained.

"It's like this," he continued, "You can buy a Ford or a Chevrolet or even a Plymouth right here in Sulpher Springs. But you have to go all the way to Asheville to buy a Studebaker!"

I was still not sure of the logic of it all, but I did know that Dr. York owned not one Studebaker but two.

He himself drove a two-door 1949 "business coupe," with a multi-sectioned rear window that wrapped all the way around the back. There was no back seat, just a flat cargo area (normally used for salesmen's samples) where he carried his medical bag and other assorted medical devices.

Mrs. York, a tall, broad-shouldered woman a full head taller than the slender doctor, drove a 1950 four-door Studebaker "Commander" sedan. Like the doctor's coupe, it had a pointed nose that looked more like it belonged on an airplane than on a car—but it *did* have a back seat.

These two cars were the only Studebakers which actually belonged to people who lived in Sulpher Springs.

A frail, balding man who wore wire-rim spectacles, Dr. York was the family doctor, and that meant the *whole* family. In addition to taking care of Mother, Daddy, Joe-brother and me, he never hesitated to look at any veterinary problems which might be encountered along the way.

Part of the collection of equipment he carried in the back of the Studebaker included calf-pullers, hypodermic syringes you could shoot a horse or cow with, and an oversized set of fisherman's waders he would step into to protect his suit when he was called on to go to the barnyard. He was willing to give rabies shots or deliver a calf as he made his rounds.

Anytime Dr. York came to our house, Daddy gave him a bucket of sorghum molasses made by Grandaddy Wilson. Having grown up in Baltimore, Maryland, Dr. York always sounded like a Yankee to us until he got the molasses. Then, sounding like he was born and raised in Nantahala County, he'd lean back and say, "Them sorghum molasses is the best medicine they is...they'll cure anything." The miraculous cure-all molasses would always be an even swap for whatever medical services had been rendered.

Dr. York's office was in a white frame house which stood one street back from "Old Main Street" in down-town Sulpher Springs. It was next door to the white frame house which housed the first public library in town.

The doctor and Mrs. York lived upstairs in the house. Downstairs, the front part of the house was his waiting room and office, while in the back rooms of the same level lived Miss Winnie O'Sullivan, his plump, ancient, spinster, twenty-four-hour nurse.

In the mornings Dr. York "kept clinic" in his office. There were no appointments. People came to the office, signed in with Miss Winnie, and were taken in turn. Many of the most routine cases were examined and prescribed for by Miss Winnie, who even signed the doctor's name to her prescriptions, leaving the more unusual cases for the doctor himself.

This was a system of medical care readily agreed to by everyone in Sulpher Springs. We were all certain that Miss Winnie really knew as much about medicine as Dr. York.

Through the course of the morning, phone calls and hand-delivered messages (not everyone in Sulpher Springs had a telephone) came in from people too sick to come to the office. It was not considered acceptable for someone with something "catching" to come to the clinic and take a chance on spreading it around. From these requests, Dr. York set up his house-call schedule for the afternoon.

Some of the callers were sent medicine, but others were visited by Dr. York personally as he made his rounds in the Studebaker business coupe.

The doctor came to our house any time we needed him. If one of us was throwing up or running a high fever, the protocol was to "call for the doctor," never to go to the office if you're really sick. We went to the office for routine check-ups and for terrible, terrible things like SHOTS.

I hated shots.

Wednesday was shot day at Dr. York's office. On each Wednesday afternoon, usually after Dr. York had left for his house calls, Miss Winnie opened up the "vaccination clinic."

Mothers with babies, older kids getting ready for school or the summer vacation, people who needed tetanus or typhoid boosters—they all lined up in the office to get their shots from Miss Winnie.

One of the horrors of springtime was that each year Joe-brother and I had to go to Dr. York's office on shot day to get our typhoid boosters. With most water sources in Nantahala County being untreated, this was viewed as an absolute necessity by responsible parents.

As soon as the weather began to warm, I knew that each Wednesday afternoon was potentially disaster day. By the time I was in the fifth grade, I had learned to completely disappear on Wednesday afternoons.

Normally Joe-brother and I would walk from school to Miss Annie Macintosh's house. Then we would tell her that since it was springtime and the weather was getting pretty, we wanted to go up on the mountain to play. She would agree, and we'd walk so long and so far that I was sure we wouldn't get back to the big house before the five o'clock closing time of the shot clinic.

Mother would be sitting in the blue Dodge, honking the horn, angry, when we got back to the house. But we had made it! It was too late to get to the clinic today. All was safe until the next Wednesday.

After a few Wednesdays like this one, Mother began to catch on. The next week as we were riding to school she said, "This afternoon we have to get our typhoid shots. Don't walk to Miss Annie's today. Wait at school and as soon as I get out, I'll come straight there and pick you up. Remember, if you want to play in the creek and go barefoot in the summer, you have to get your typhoid shots."

The entire day at school was wasted and miserable for me as I could pay no attention at all to anything we were supposed to be learning. All I could do was think of the giant, sharp, long, cold-steel typhoid needle, held poised in the air by Miss Winnie, who, smiling, wanted to stab it deeply and painfully into my precious, tender, fifth-grade arm.

When the bell finally rang, I headed as fast as I could across the school yard to the softball field, where I hid in the dugout and planned to act like I was playing instead of hiding when Mother finally found me, hopefully after five o'clock.

Joe-brother found me first. He had missed me as he waited for Mother, so he looked around until he found me in the softball dugout.

"You better come on," he said, "Mother's going to be here soon." Joe-brother wasn't scared of getting shots, but after all, he was only nine years old and didn't know what ten-year-olds knew.

"Go away," I said. "I'll be there in a minute. Now GET OUT OF HERE!" He hesitated and I screamed it again, "GET ON OUT OF HERE!"

He left, but as soon as Mother arrived, he brought her straight to the dugout, where she got hold of me by the loose skin on the back of my arm and marched me straight to the blue Dodge. Then we drove directly to Dr. York's house.

I had already decided that I would NOT get a shot today no matter what it took to escape the needle.

All the way to the doctor's house I tried to get sick. I held my head, I held my stomach, I gagged, I tried to throw up, I held my head out the car window. Mother ignored me. Joe-brother laughed at me. We pulled up into the gravel driveway at Dr. York's house.

As we went in the door to the living-room-waiting-room, I could hear a child screaming. Some poor defenseless baby was being murdered, stabbed to death by Miss Winnie, who was probably saying "that doesn't hurt" in her soft little voice while she did it.

There were two children ahead of us. They disappeared through the door, and in what seemed like just a moment, they emerged whimpering and left the office.

Miss Winnie called, "Next!" Joe-brother led the way on his own while Mother dragged me through the door and into the examination room. Miss Winnie closed the door behind us. I suddenly realized that I, at ten years of age, was nearly as tall as she was.

At some time in the house's past, the examination room had been the dining room. Here it was, examination table in place of the dining room table, an added sink (looking very out of place), and assorted white cabinets around the walls. I had been here before.

The lower panes of the large dining room windows had been painted beige for privacy and there was a small refrigerator against one wall.

Miss Winnie opened the refrigerator and took out the glass bottle of typhoid shot serum. The very thought of COLD serum coming into my arm through that steel needle gave me the clammy shivers.

She held the bottle aloft and inverted it in the light while she stuck the needle through the rubber center of the lid and carefully drew just the right amount of cold serum into the glass syringe.

After withdrawing the needle, she carefully pushed the plunger just enough for a drop of serum to bead up at the tip of the needle. Then she asked, "Who's first?"

I sat still, like maybe no one would see me, while Joe-brother volunteered. "I want to be first and get it over with," he said, though I knew that nobody who knew what they were doing would ever volunteer for this abuse for any sensible reason.

I could not look. Miss Winnie shot Joe-brother, who didn't even whimper, then unsnapped the separate parts of the syringe and dropped them into the sterilizer pans on the table next to the refrigerator.

She assembled and loaded a second syringe. I did not watch, but hearing the refrigerator door open, then close, I knew well what was happening.

"Now," Miss Winnie said as she came toward me, "roll up your sleeve."

My mind was made up. In a small, quiet voice I said it. "I'm not going to have a shot today."

Miss Winnie stopped in her tracks and looked at Mother. Mother focused her eyes, looked at me, then said, firmly, "What did you say?"

All control was lost. Trembling, voice now high-pitched and as loud as it had been soft before, I said, "YOU HEARD ME...BOTH OF YOU...I'M NOT GOING TO GET A SHOT TO-DAY...CAN'T YOU UNDERSTAND PLAIN ENGLISH?"

Mother's look said it all. I had said too much, especially the part about plain English.

She turned to Joe-brother and said quietly, "Go back out into the waiting room and stay until we get through." Joe-brother left. Then she turned to me with both hands reaching out to grab and hold. Miss Winnie was poised and ready with the loaded needle.

I was too fast for either of them. As fast as lightning, I had already scooted between the two of them and around the examination table on the far side of the room. When they came after me, both of them came around the table in the same direction, and for a few seconds we went around and around the table.

When they finally split up, they found out how fast I *really* was as I went up and over the examination table between the two of them and headed straight through a swinging door which went I-knew-not-where but was the only visible route of escape.

Once through the swinging door, I found myself in Miss Winnie's little kitchen. There was a door to the outside, but it was closed, and probably locked, while there was an invitingly open door on the other side of the room.

I headed for the open door and found myself in Miss Winnie's bedroom as Mother and Miss Winnie, needle held high like a jousting knight's lance, came through the swinging door.

The bedroom was dark and smelled of Cloverine salve. Hand-washed white nurse's stockings, ribbed girdles, and a brassiere of gigantic proportions hung on a folding wooden drying rack under which layers of newspaper had been spread to catch the drips. The rack of undergarments stood in front of the only way out of that room, the only other door, standing open, obviously led to a black-and-white tiled bathroom. I flung the drying-rack aside, and burst through the door only to find myself back in the examination room again.

The new chase which now began was simply a larger version of our earlier race around the examination table. This time we were going with me in the lead screaming, "I'm not going to have a shot!" followed by Mother shrieking, "Stop...stop...I'm going to kill you," followed by Miss Winnie trotting with needle in hand, yelling, "It won't hurt...it won't hurt!" Around and around we went, from the examination room, through the kitchen, through Miss Winnie's bedroom, and then around again.

Mother's heel had caught in one of Miss Winnie's white stockings and now the stocking was dragging along with us. On one round, Joe-brother stood with his head stuck through the door from the waiting room. He surely just wanted to see what was going on in there. I heard Mother yell "Go back!" as she passed him, and the next time I came through, he was gone.

I kept wondering why one of them didn't turn back the other way and just head me off. It would have been easy enough. Perhaps the pure insult of being run from and then outrun by a child interfered so with their thought processes that neither of them ever figured it out.

None of us heard the sound of the Studebaker coupe as it drove into the gravel driveway and stopped behind the house. None of us heard Dr. York slam the car door and come in the kitchen door, home from the afternoon's house calls. Suddenly he was just there.

As I passed through the swinging door and into the kitchen, there he stood. He held his black bag in one hand and his wire frame glasses in the other, as if he wanted to look with his naked eyes to see if he believed what was happening here. He stood and watched as I disappeared into the bedroom followed quickly by Mother and Miss Winnie.

As we went around the next time, I heard him say, "I've just delivered one little bull calf, I guess it's time for me to rope this one!" The next time I went through the kitchen door he grabbed me.

I screamed as loudly and kicked as hard as I could, but he held me from behind in a calf-roping grip around the waist that I couldn't begin to break loose from.

"Winnie," he said, "we'd better try to give it to him in the hip. The way his arms are flailing, it wouldn't be safe to try to hit an arm."

He told Mother to unbuckle my pants and slip them down. Once that was done, he swung me up onto the examination table, face down.

The next thing I knew, Dr. York had let me loose!

"That wasn't so bad, now, was it?" Miss Winnie asked.

"Aren't you going to give me the shot now that you've caught me?" I asked.

"She just gave it to you," Mother answered this time. "See, silly, you didn't even feel it."

When we got home and Mother told Daddy all about what had happened, he got me in the blue Dodge and we drove all the way back to Dr. York's house. Then he had me go up to the kitchen door with two buckets of molasses, one for Dr. York and one for Miss Winnie.

Dr. York smiled when he took his. He never said a word to

me about what has taken place that day. He just thanked me and said, "Them molasses is the best medicine they is. You ought to try some. They'll cure anything. Now, be sure to thank your Daddy."

I wondered why he hadn't just given me some molasses instead of the typhoid shot. When I got home, I ate a big spoon just full of straight molasses syrup. It didn't seem to help any, though, because the next day, I was as sore as I could be all over.

All summer long, I played in the creek. I wanted to take full advantage of the typhoid shot as long as I could. When school started and we had to start wearing shoes again, creek-playing time was over, and so was the summer for another year.

In spite of school, the fall of the year was a fine season in the mountains.

The trees changed colors beautifully through October. There was wood to split, and we started building wonderful wood-smoke-smelling fires in the kitchen stove just to keep warm.

Best of all, it was the time of year when we spent several Saturdays at Grandaddy Wilson's house helping him make molasses.

It was the second week of October and the prime time for making molasses. Grandaddy Wilson had recruited Mother, Joe-brother and me (Daddy had to keep the hardware store open on Saturday and couldn't come), to help for a good long day of molasses making on Saturday.

As soon as school was out on Friday, we got in the blue Dodge and went out to their house on Cedar Fork to spend the night.

Grandaddy Wilson, and his brother, Uncle Willie, had been crushing sorghum cane all day on Friday to be sure they had plenty of raw juice to start out with on Saturday.

They had a small roller mill into which they fed the freshly-cut sorghum stalks a few at a time. Grandaddy's work horse, old Pat, was harnessed to a long pole, and as she walked around and around, the mill crushed the sorghum stalks flat and the juice ran out the bottom into a wooden bucket.

One bucketful at a time, a whole barrel of raw juice was finally crushed out and ready.

When we arrived on Friday afternoon, the wooden barrel was full and ready, perched as it was at the end of the cooking furnace, so the juice could be let out a spigot at the bottom and into the big cooking pan.

We went straight in the log house for supper, and then did the last job to be done before starting in to make molasses the next day. It was one of our favorite jobs. It consisted of unpacking the tin buckets which were to hold the molasses and putting Grandaddy's labels on them. Joe-brother and I tore the cardboard boxes open and took out the gallon galvanized tin buckets. Then we all licked printed labels and stuck them to the sides of the buckets. The labels read: "Genuine Sorghum Molasses... 100 per cent pure...George Wilson, Cedar Fork, North Carolina."

When the buckets were labelled and stacked, we were ready for tomorrow.

Long before Joe-brother and I were awake, Grandaddy and Uncle Willie had gotten up to build the fire in the molasses furnace. The furnace, under an open shed of its own, was made of two long low rock walls. The fire was built between these walls and the cooking pan sat on top of them. As raw syrup was let into the sectioned pan at one end, it was moved along with stirring paddles until it came out, cooked just right, at the other end. Then it was put into the tin buckets and allowed to cool.

The grown-ups had eaten breakfast and started cooking the first run of syrup before Joe-brother and I even woke up. (The longer we stayed in bed and out of the way the better.)

When I finally did wake up, I knew I was sick. I had a terrible sore throat and a headache and my whole head was stopped up. If it had been a school day, I would have called for Mother and begged to stay in bed, but making molasses was such fun that I got up in spite of the way I felt and put on my clothes.

Joe-brother and I went into the kitchen to get breakfast.

"You seem stopped up," Grandmother said, after she listened to me sniffle for a few minutes.

"Do you feel ok?" Mother asked. She felt my head, but said that she didn't think I had a fever.

"I do have a little sore throat," I answered, "but I'll be fine in a little while."

Mother frowned, but in the end she bundled me up and she, Joe-brother, Grandmother, and I all went down into the field where the sorghum cooker was so we could do our part with the cooking.

It was a cold, bright October day, and a little sharp wind was blowing around the mountain side. Grandaddy had taken a big tarpaulin and hung it from the roof to the ground on the windy side of the molasses cooker to keep the wind off everyone. Mother put me inside, between the tarp and the furnace. It was snug and warm there, and it felt good being out of the wind.

Everyone had a job. Joe-brother and I were yellow-jacket skimmers. Yellow-jackets, attracted by the smell of the sweet cooking syrup, would fly over the cooking pan. When the steam from the hot syrup hit their wings, they fell in and drowned.

Joe-brother and I each had a "skimmer," a long stick with a tin scoop on the end of it. Our job was to scoop up dead yellow-jackets as soon as they fell in the syrup and dump them into a little bucket each of us had. It was a contest to see who could collect the most.

It was a wonderful day, clear and blue, with beautifully colored autumn trees above us on the mountainside. I even got to sip some hot, sweetened coffee to make my throat feel better.

Late in the afternoon, the last run was finished and the cooking pan was scrubbed out and covered up until next Saturday.

When we were ready to go home, Mother said, "I'd better take a bucket of fresh molasses home to give to Dr. York. He knows this is the time of year to be on the lookout for a fresh supply."

"Take this last bucketful," Grandaddy replied. "The only thing is, it's hot. I don't want to put the lid on tight or you won't get it off when it cools down. I'll tell you what: let's just put the bucket on the floorboard and set the lid loose on top. It ought to be all right there, and you can push the lid down tight when you get home."

We all got in the blue Dodge. Joe-brother got in the front seat, and I begged to lie down on the back seat because by now my throat and head were killing me.

Mother rolled up her coat and made a pillow for me. Then she told me to "sort of look out for the molasses on the way home."

Everything went well for about half the ride home. Then Joe-brother started to get bored. Every time Mother would look away from him, he would look back at me and stick out his tongue.

I knew how to get him back. I sat up and stuck my toes under his seat. Then I pushed up under where he was sitting. I had long ago accidentally discovered that he couldn't stand for me to do this and had since annoyed him many times this way.

He told Mother. She glanced around and told me to stop. "Lie back down. You have a sore throat," she said. I did it again anyway. Joe-brother yelled again. Mother glanced around and said, "Stop it!"

When she looked back toward the front, she had almost run out of a curve in the road. She jerked the wheel to bring the blue Dodge back into its place. When she did, I lost my balance and my foot kicked over the tin bucket of fresh molasses.

Hot and runny, the molasses ran under the front seat and all the way into the floorboard of the front seat. They got on Joe-brother's shoes and he really hollered.

I knew I was in bad trouble. When we came to a wide place in the road, Mother pulled off. She broke a switch off a wild cherry tree and blistered my legs, sore throat or not.

When we got home she got a big dishpan full of hot, soapy water and started the impossible task of cleaning up. She would clean for a while and cry for a while, clean for a while and cry for a while.

Soon the telephone rang. Grandmother had been worried about my sore throat and had made Grandaddy walk to Burnett's Store, where there was a telephone, to call to be sure I was going to be all right. Since Mother was crying and cleaning, I answered the telephone and talked to Grandaddy.

"Where have you been?" he asked. "I've been calling for nearly an hour and you weren't home."

I told him what happened. There was silence on the other end of the telephone.

The first sound I heard was a fine, high-pitched, "Hee... hee...heee..." Grandaddy was laughing so hard he couldn't get his breath. It was the first time in my life I had ever heard him laugh.

As soon as he could talk he said, "Will you tell me about that again?" Later he said, "That's one bucket of sorghum that little doctor's not going to get."

By bedtime I was really sick, and now that Mother was at home where she had a thermometer, she found that my temperature was 103 degrees. She said to Daddy, "I know it's late, but you better call Dr. York."

It was nearly ten o'clock when I heard the tires of Dr. York's Studebaker crunching the cinders of the driveway. Though part of me dreaded his coming, the rest of me actually felt better knowing that he had come. Now the entire situation, after all Mother's fretting, was under control at last.

Mother ushered him in.

I was in the front bedroom, now the "sick room," the same room in which Aunt Laura used to live. Mother liked to call it the "guest bedroom."

Dr. York put his bag on the foot of the big, double bed, opened it, and took out his thermometer, flashlight, and stethoscope.

The thermometer, tasting of the alcohol it had been cleaned with, was stuck in my mouth while the stethoscope roamed, pausing for a few seconds at a time, over my chest and then my back. Once Dr. York said, "Cough!" as he listened to my back.

As he turned the thermometer to catch the light on the mercury, he reported to Mother. "His lungs are clear, but his temp is one-oh-three-point-two." Then, after shining his flashlight down my throat and gagging me twice with a tongue depressor, he finished the diagnosis. "My best guess is a pretty bad case of strep throat."

Strep throat! I knew what that meant: penicillin. Thick, cold penicillin and a huge, sharp needle you could vaccinate a cow with. My throat and head hurt so bad. I whimpered and pulled the cover tightly under my chin.

"A good shot of penicillin would probably take care of it," Dr. York said to Mother. Daddy, who had been standing silent until now (speculative medicine was not his field, as it was Mother's), grunted in agreement.

"But," Dr. York went on, "I remember the last time we had to give this one a shot." (So did we all!) "I'd like to try something new."

I did not have any idea in this world what he was talking about, but I was ready to vote for it, sight unseen.

The doctor was still talking, "We have this new medicine that's called a 'sulfa drug.' I'd like to try it out on him, and if it works, we won't have to give him a shot. If it doesn't, we can use the needle for the next try. I'll be right back."

Dr. York went out to the Studebaker. When he came back, he was carrying a small, white cardboard box.

He tore off the cellophane and opened the box. What he took out looked like a flat, square piece of pink candy in a clear wrapper.

"This is it," he showed it to Mother, who looked like she didn't believe anything that looked like candy could be medicine. "All he has to do is to hold these in his mouth until they completely dissolve. Three times a day for nine days should do it. If it doesn't start to work in the first two or three days, I can always come back with the penicillin."

"It'll work," I thought, "I just know it will. Just give me a chance. I'll make it work."

Dr. York counted out twenty-seven of the pink squares, gave one to me, and handed the remainder to Mother. As I unwrapped the cellophane, he said, "I hear they don't taste very good, but this kid just could be the odd one who likes them."

I put the pink square in my mouth.

Never in my entire lifetime could I have possibly ever imagined that anything in all creation could taste that bad. The taste was like, but far worse than, the worst odor of long-rotted eggs. The only thing in the world which kept me from throwing up on the spot was the mental image of a huge, sharp needle full of thick, cold penicillin.

My eyes were watering when Dr. York said, "Now hold it in your mouth until it's all gone," as he walked back into the living room with Mother and Daddy.

"Shot or no shot," I thought, "I can't take this!" As soon as Daddy closed the door behind him, I jumped out of bed, took the pink, rotten sulfa square out of my mouth, and stuck it as far as I could reach between the mattress and box springs of the guest room bed.

The awful taste was still in my mouth, though. While Dr. York was still in the living room visiting with Mother and Daddy, I slipped through their bedroom, across the back porch, and into the kitchen.

Quietly and carefully I opened the kitchen cabinet beside the sink. If I could just find the sugar bowl in the dark, I knew that a spoonful of sugar would help to get rid of this terrible taste.

The sugar bowl wasn't there, but, in the dim light, I saw a big quart jar full of molasses. That would do just as well.

The lid was hard to unscrew, and sticky, too, but I got it off and treated myself to a big glob of molasses scooped up on my finger.

"Dr. York is right," I thought. "These molasses is the best medicine they is!" Especially if your illness is a bad taste you need to get out of your mouth.

Three times a day for the next nine days I repeated the same routine. Mother would bring me the pink sulfa square. She would watch me unwrap it and put it in my mouth. The happier I looked to get my medicine, the sooner she left the room. I was very gracious, and smiled.

As soon as she was gone, I was out of bed to make the

deposit. That terrible stuff went just where it belonged...under the mattress.

The first chance I had after that, I would slip into the kitchen for a heavy dose of molasses.

My first dose of medicine had been given me by Dr. York on Saturday night. By Monday I really was much better, and long before I finished all twenty-seven doses, I was really completely well. Mother made me take them all just the same.

"That sulfa certainly is a miracle drug," Mother announced.

"In this day and time," I added, "the world is full of miracle drugs." She looked at me like I was crazy.

"It sure is a good thing it worked," she said. "I was just sure it was going to take a big shot of penicillin. Daddy gave Dr. York an extra bucket of molasses for that medicine."

No one had any idea what had actually happened to the miracle drug.

The next spring when the weather warmed up, Mother decided it was time to give the house a good, thorough spring cleaning.

Organdy curtains were washed in the bathtub and dried on curtain stretchers in the sun in the back yard. Closets were cleaned out and winter clothes were packed in cedar chests with mothballs.

Mother announced, "It's time to turn the mattresses." I helped. The twin beds that Joe-brother and I slept on were easy to turn. More help was needed with the double beds.

We finally got Mother and Daddy's mattress turned. Then we followed Mother into the front bedroom, the guest bedroom.

I had not been in this room for months and had forgotten until this very moment what treasures lay hidden between the mattress and the box springs. The sight of the big bed brought it all back it me. I started to sweat.

"I don't think we need to bother with this one," I said. "Nobody ever sleeps in here."

"We didn't turn this one last year," Mother answered, and that was that.

"Oh, well," I thought. "I guess she has to find out sometime."

Both of us took hold of one side of the big mattress and pulled, trying to slide it toward us so that we could then lift our side and flip it over. The mattress wouldn't budge; it was stuck fast to the covering of the box springs.

After several tries, Mother said, "I don't know what's wrong. Let's just try to lift it up and flip it over right where it is."

We lifted, and as the mattress came up a faint ripping sound, like the sound of someone stripping wallpaper off a wall, came from under it. The mattress slid off the side of the bed and stood on its edge. There, in front of us, stuck partly to the box springs and partly to the bottom of the mattress, were the remains of twenty-seven barely-used doses of sulfa drug.

Mother had only one question. She could, as usual, figure out all the rest. "How did you get well?" she asked, then repeated, with amazement, "How did you get well?"

"A miracle drug did it," I answered. "I took Dr. York's special medicine."

"You did not. That expensive miracle drug is every bit right here," she pointed wildly to the mattress.

"That stuff's not expensive. You told me yourself that Daddy gave him two buckets of molasses for it. But, then, the doctor says, 'Them molasses is the best medicine they is.'"

We left it at that. She never did understand what any part of our conversation meant, but it all so confused and mystified her that she forgot all about the spanking I was sure would be coming next.

The next Wednesday afternoon we went, without hiding or complaining, to Miss Winnie's shot clinic, where I took my yearly typhoid shot quietly, without a whimper.

LS/MFT

WHEN I GOT TO THE SIXTH GRADE, we moved to town. Daddy borrowed Uncle Floyd's pick-up truck and we hauled load after load from the house on Richland Creek for nearly three miles all the way to the other side of Sulpher Springs. The new house was up in town, on a well-populated street named "East Street."

East Street ran downhill toward the center of town, finally crossing "Old Main" and ending at Railroad Street. The section where we lived was well over a mile from Main Street and near the top of the biggest downhill slope on the street's entire run into town.

From near our house, East Street sloped down and continued to slope down, almost straight, for over half a mile. Then it flattened out, made a ninety-degree turn to the right, and dropped downhill again.

The most wonderful thing about living on East Street, for a sixth-grade boy, was that no girls lived there. This fact of gender was not just true when our family moved there; it had always been true. For generations, as long as anyone could remember, no girls had ever been born into any families living on East Street hill.

People would say, "If you want to have a girl, you might as well move out of there. It'll never happen. But if you want to have a boy, just go buy you a house over on East Street—or at least spend the night over there once in a while. There's something in the water."

It was an obvious advantage to male sixth graders to live in an atmosphere totally devoid of female opinions, advice, or interference.

There was another advantage as well. Through past generations each group of older East Street boys had felt it their duty to educate younger East Street boys in the ways of the world. This had gone on for several generations before we moved there, and without benefit of feminine correction, we truly did know *everything.*

There were now, since our family had moved there, six of us boys living on East Street who were the same age and all in the same grade at Sulpher Springs School. Most of us were already old friends, since everybody in Sulpher Springs went to Sulpher Springs School. East Street School, where Mother still taught second grade was actually a county school, and none of us knew anybody who went to school there.

Among those I had long known were Red McElroy (who lived on a farm just out in the country, but close enough to walk to my new house) and Freddie Patton, both of Christmas Pageant fame. Our nearest sixth-grade neighbor was Charlie Summerow, whom I had seen at school but did not really get to know until now.

The six of us became inseparable. Since we were now holders of all knowledge in the human world plus all the wisdom of the ages, we knew everything there was to know about everything. (The only thing we didn't know was that, in this wise, we were no different from all other sixth graders in the world.)

And since there were six of us to protect one another, we weren't afraid to try anything. There was nobody in the world we were afraid of and nothing we could think of that we were afraid to do.

One of our favorite games was a game we called "Big Bird." Big Bird was a game which required several weeks of preparation time and our saving up just a bit of school lunch money to purchase equipment.

First, we'd walk to the dime store and buy a box of balloons. The best size for the game were the ones that would blow up to about the size of a grapefruit, if anyone ever wanted to blow them up. Next, we'd walk to Burgie Welch's store and buy baby food. No one ever questioned the jars of Gerber's we bought. There were always enough new baby boys on East Street to account for someone being sent to the store for baby food.

We chose our baby food by the color: bright yellow vegetables, dark green spinach, and always some of those terrible smelling, awful looking, chunky junior meats. Lamb and veal mixed were the worst.

Once back at one of our houses we would dump all the baby food into a mixing bowl and stir it up a bit. Then, with a big basting syringe (borrowed from the kitchen drawer), we would squirt about six or eight ounces of mixed baby food into each balloon, add six or eight ounces of water, tie the top of the balloon shut, and shake it up.

The longest stage in the preparation process was the waiting. We placed the loaded balloons in the sun and waited for them to ripen for about a week. When the skin of the balloon began to wrinkle like a prune, and when the balloon quivered and seemed to take on a pulse of its own, you were ready to play "Big Bird."

It was important that all six of us be present for this game. No one wanted to miss it.

Armed with a grocery bag containing our specially prepared bird missles, we'd climb up a big oak tree and out onto a limb over East Street. Once there, it was time to wait for a Buick.

Red McElroy had climbed higher up into the tree. He was the lookout. "Here comes one," Red hollered. "It just topped the hill at the Salleys' house. Looks like the Baptist preacher."

The Reverend N. N. Upchurch, longtime pastor of the Sulpher Springs Baptist Church (downtown), always drove a new Buick. He never washed the car because it never got dirty enough to wash. Each evening Reverend Upchurch dusted the Buick off in the garage, and he never took it out when there was rain or even chance of bad weather.

No one knew what the "N. N." stood for. He had kept it a secret from his wife and even from the deacons at the Baptist church. Everyone in town secretly called him "Preacher No-No," because that pretty well summed up his opinion about most subjects he had an opinion on.

Now the clean-and-identified Buick was coming down East Street hill.

We knew the exact crack in the street which the front bumper of the Buick had to cross when it was time to drop the bird missle. We were ready. The Buick crossed the crack and Freddie Patton, whose turn it was to be "Big Bird Bombardier," let loose.

It was a perfect shot. The ripe and well-loaded bomb centered the windshield and instantly covered almost the entire front of the shiny car.

The Buick slid sideways in the street and stopped with a thud against the curb as the door came open and Preacher No-No jumped out. Just as he stepped out of the car, his wife, just trying to help, reached over and switched on the windshield wipers. The big powerful Buick wipers threw the whole load of bird matter right up in his face.

We held onto the tree and tried to keep from laughing as we watched him trying to wipe his eyes out, at the same time insisting to his wife that he had spotted, flying away over the mountaintops, the "thing that had done it."

After the following Sunday morning, Charlie Summerow, who went with his family to the Baptist church, told us about the sermon. Preacher No-No had prophesied the coming end of the world. Among the signs cited were "prehistoric flying monsters hatching out and flying about everywhere." Charlie quoted him, even with gestures and emphasis, "Why, I myself was near victim to their crude and near-fatal droppings. The end of time is at hand!"

We continued to play Big Bird as scores of people all over Sulpher Springs began to prepare for the end, swear they too had seen the thing, and lived in fear of getting caught under it. The preacher's still unwashed Buick was the evidence. The thing was real.

One of our East Street neighbors was our old Sulpher Springs principal from elementary school, Mr. Lonnie Underhill. Now retired, Mr. Underhill spent his spare time gardening and raising prize bird dogs.

His dogs were friendly, long-haired dogs, brown and white, some speckled, some spotted. They loved to be petted and played with, and seemed to bounce as if their legs were made of rubber. As long as you kept petting or scratching their heads, you could do anything to or with them.

Mr. Underhill's prize dog was an especially friendly dog named "Susie." Susie was white with bigger brown spots than most of the other more-speckled dogs. During the panting heat of the summer, we East Street boys decided that poor Susie could really benefit from a haircut.

After slipping Daddy's haircut clippers out of his closet (he used them on us about once every two weeks to save sixty cents at the barber shop), we put them to their first good use.

We gave Susie what could only be described as a nice "high-low" haircut. We left all the brown spots "high," and we cut the white places as "low" as they would go.

Susie was a work of art! She looked wonderful, especially her tail, with small tufts of brown hair scattered here and there and the rest skinny and almost shaved white.

The traffic picked up on East Street as people drove through the neighborhood trying to get a look at that dog. "What kind of dog is that?" we heard strangers ask.

"It's a mixed-haired Pasture Terrier...special breed," we heard Red McElroy tell one curious enquirer.

Mr. Underhill used bad words—the kind he used to spank us for at school when he was the principal—about what he was going to do to "the one who had done it." He never found out.

In the wintertime, when the weather was cold, we would sometimes walk to Welch's Store with our saved-up lunch money, and buy sardines.

None of us ate sardines.

Sulpher Springs School was, however, an old building which had been built with the radiators set back into the walls to keep kids from messing with the control knobs. These recessed radiators were covered by sheet metal which had rows of little square holes across the top and bottom so the air could circulate and the heat could come out.

In the middle of cold weather, with the radiators at full steam, we would take a nice firm sardine, line it up in front of one of those little square holes, and—*thip*—the sardine was on the safely-enclosed radiator.

Load up several radiators with sardines, and school was out for a week while minor "remodelling" was done.

In spite of knowing everything, however, and even in spite of being nearly fearless, there was one person in the world that our little group of East Street boys was afraid of.

It was not Mr. Underhill, nor any schoolteacher, for that matter. It was not any of our parents. It was not even Preacher No-No Upchurch.

The one person in all the world we were afraid of was Terrell Tubbs.

Terrell lived with his mother in a big, white, two-story frame house which was located in the outside of the flat curve at the end of the long down-hill stretch of East Street hill. It was a huge old house, with blue shutters and a high front porch. The space underneath the porch was enclosed, as was common, with criss-cross lattice work.

The real truth is that we had never actually seen or met Terrell. We knew his name, and we had all heard him. He seemed to spend all of his time under the front porch of the white house, and anytime we got within a good hundred yards of the house we could hear him under there.

"UHH...*(wheeze)*UHH...*(wheeze)*UHHH...*(wheeze)*..." We could hear the awful sound coming from under the porch.

"I ain't getting close to anything that sounds like that," Freddie Patton volunteered for all of us. The safest way, we agreed, to deal with something which sounds like that is a good, safe distance or an extremely high rate of speed in passing by.

Passing by Terrell's house became a real preoccupation in

the coming year as the six of us became the proud owners of a bicycle.

It was a 1955 Columbia RX-5 Coaster Bike, and it had taken the six of us nearly two years to get it.

When we first saw one of the Columbia bikes, it had cost forty-nine dollars and ninety-five cents in the Sears-Roebuck catalogue of 1953. All six of us put together could not save up much more than the ninety-five cents, so there was to be no way for us to buy one. But there was another way: saving Blue Horses.

At school you could buy Blue Horse Notebook Paper at the little supply store in the office. On the wrapper of the paper was a horse's head coupon to be cut out. Save up enough of these coupons, and you could get anything.

The six of us went back to school almost every afternoon in search of an open window. Once one was found, we climbed in and searched all the trash cans for discarded Blue Horses. We pulled them loose from the old popsicle sticks, cut out the coupons, and saved them up.

In two years, we saved *fifty thousand* points in Blue Horse coupons. We could have gotten a black and white television set, but we wanted a bicycle. So off to the Montag company in Atlanta went the Blue Horses, and later, back on the Overnight Freight truck came our bicycle.

It was a wonderful machine. Two-tone with red and white paint, the bicycle had huge white-wall balloon tires front and back. We had saved enough money to buy a basket for the front and a set of multi-colored streamers which flapped from the hand-grips of the wide handlebars.

There was a light in the front which held two D-cell batteries until, at the first big bump, they bounced out. There was not one bar but two running from the seat to the stem, with what looked like a little motorcycle gas tank between your knees. On the back was a long luggage rack with three red reflector buttons on the very back.

The bicycle weighed eighty-four-pounds empty. We decided they called it a Coaster Bike because it was too heavy to pedal on level ground. All you could do was load up and coast down-hill on it. The real reason for the name, of course, was that the bike did not have hand-brakes but coaster brakes, the kind you back-pedal to put on. Slam back on the pedal, and you could lock the big back tire and make a long black mark on the pavement.

The RX-5 was not only the heaviest but also the strongest bicycle ever built. It would hold all six of us at one time without even mashing the tires flat.

We'd take it up to the top of East Street hill and load up—one of us in the basket on the front, two more on the bar between the seat and the stem, another on the seat to guide and pedal (and brake), and the last two on the luggage rack on the back. The last two passengers had an important job. They had to stick out their feet and keep us balanced until the bike built up enough speed to keep balanced on its own.

Once loaded, down the hill we'd come, as fast as we possibly could, straight toward Terrell's house.

The pedaller was in control. His main job was to start putting on the brakes in time to enable us to make the curve at the bottom of the hill. It was always done perfectly.

As we all leaned into the big curve, safely slowed just enough, we would all turn toward Terrell's porch and at exactly the right time yell, "L, S,...M, F, T...!" Then, zoom, we were gone down the next part of the hill.

You could read the slogan on billboards, on back-page maga-zine ads, or hear it on the radio: "L, S...M, F, T...Lucky Strike Means Fine Tobacco." Everyone knew that.

That is not, however, what we meant when we yelled it at Terrell's house. We meant "Lord Save Me From Terrell;" then, zoom, we were gone.

We would never, after that, walk straight back up the hill past Terrell's house. Instead we would walk way around, over to another street, and come out through the Salleys' yard near the top. Then we'd change places on the big bike and do it again.

One day, after half-dozen trips already down the big hill, we made our way back to the top for one more ride down. Just as we came out through the Salleys' yard, we spotted Mr. Jay Howard, the mailman.

Mr. Howard was fifty-three years old and walked eleven miles each day as he delivered the mail. We all knew this, because he told us every time he saw us. "Hello, boys," he would say, "I'm fifty-three years old and walk eleven miles a day." Then he would spit out his tobacco and start to bite off another chew.

Mr. Howard had a gray flat-top haircut and wore high-heeled, pointed-toed cowboy boots to deliver the mail. We all thought that anyone who could walk eleven miles in those things, and chew tobacco at the same time, must really be tough. We figured if you put PF Flyers on him, he could walk to California.

One of Mr. Howard's eleven miles was up and back down East Street hill. He didn't deliver the mail by going up one side of the street and back down the other, however. He went back and forth, back and forth, across the street as he went up. This, he explained, made his load lighter on the way up. "Very important," he said, "when the Sears-Roebuck catalogues come."

This method of delivery meant that most of his next mile was totally wasted as he had to walk straight back down the hill to get to his next undelivered street.

When we spotted Mr. Howard that day, he had just put the mail in the Salleys' box, the last box at the top of the hill, and was ready to start back down. All six of us had exactly the same idea at the same time. "I wonder," Red McElroy said it for us all, "if Mr. Howard would like a ride?"

"Save him almost a mile," I offered.

"Why, he'd get home early," Freddie Patton added.

We quickly drew straws to see who would offer Mr. Howard the ride. Red won, and the rest of us started walking down the hill as he pushed the red and white bike over to toward where Mr. Howard was standing.

The plan almost didn't work, as we could see Red talking to Mr. Howard and pointing to the bicycle, then watched Mr. Howard shake his head and point to his mail bag. We were about to give up on the whole plan until suddenly we saw them begin to load up.

By this time, we were trying to get way on down the hill to a point at which we could watch them go all the way to the bottom. We glanced back as we saw the big leather bag of the U.S. Mail go into the basket on the front of the bike, Red get on the seat to guide and pedal, and Mr. Howard climb on the luggage rack on the back, ready to hold on tight.

We could see his cowboy boots sticking out on either side of the bicycle as it started rolling, and I knew his gray flat-top haircut was soon going to lay back.

They started, slow and wobbly at first, then steady. We could see them coming.

As they really started down the hill toward us Freddie said, "Do we go that fast?" I was just wondering the same thing. I had never seen anything going that fast. They were absolutely flying. We never saw cars come down East Street that fast. We also noticed that sparks were flying up under the bicycle as they came. One of the straps on Mr. Howard's mail bag must be dragging, I thought to myself.

We all got right out in the street so we could get a good look as they passed. It didn't take long. They seemed to get faster and faster, until when they passed us in a blur, something went "ker-chunkkk," and fell off the bicycle into the street. All the sparks stopped. As the big bicycle flew on down the hill, we looked in the street and saw it: the broken sprocket chain.

Gradually we each began to realize why the bicycle was going so fast as we watched the U.S. Mail, a twelve-year-old boy (uselessly pedalling backwards as hard as he could), and a fifty-three-year-old mailman (hair flat on his head) on an eighty-four-pound bicycle without any brakes, headed straight toward Terrell Tubb's house.

We all knew there was no way they could make the curve at the bottom of the hill.

The five of us started running after them like there was something we could do about it, but really just trying to figure out which way they were going to go the get past the Tubbs' house.

On the left side of the house, the bank of the mountainside had been dug out to make enough room to build the house to begin with. They couldn't get past on that side.

Then there was the house itself, with the long porch all the way across the front. They couldn't go through it.

But at the right-hand side, at the end of the long porch, there was an open space about four feet wide, and then a big holly bush that went all the way up to the fence around the Gettys' yard.

It looked to us like their only chance was to try to hit that one four-foot-wide open space and hope for better luck in the back yard. As we chased them, it was evident that Red had the same idea. He seemed to be headed exactly toward it.

Mrs. Tubbs had flowers planted all along the street at the edge of the yard. The flowers were surrounded by a frail white picket fence. Freddie turned to me and said, "Those flowers are going to have to go." About that time they did, and the fence with them, as the big bicycle continued across the yard, full speed ahead.

Red's aim was perfect. They were going to make it.

Then, at the very last possible moment, "UHH... *(wheeze)*UHH...*(wheeze)*UHH...*(wheeze)*...," there came Terrell Tubbs, out from under the end of the porch, standing right up in the middle of that one four-foot-wide open space.

Red was left with no choice but to hit the holly bush.

In a matter of seconds the air was filled with pieces of shredded holly leaves, U.S. Mail was floating down out of the sky from Park Drive to Russell Avenue, about sixty pieces of red and white bicycle were still moving (each in its own direction), a twelve-year-old boy was lifting his face from the grass and spitting out dirt, and a fifty-three-year-old mailman was rolling over and over muttering, "What hit us...what hit us?"

All five of the rest of us came running up in the yard, where, joining Red, we now saw Terrell Tubbs for the first time in our lives, face to face.

He was not at all what we expected, not some fearsome creature at all. There he stood, still and gentle, nearly six-feet tall, a great big middle-aged child. He tightly held an old Teddy bear in his arms and chewed on the knuckle of his bent forefinger, looking, but not making a sound.

Mr. Howard began to understand what had happened. He looked up at Terrell and said, almost accusingly, "Terrell, why did you come out from under your porch?"

Terrell seemed to think long and hard, then he took his knuckle out of his mouth, and slowly said, "L,S...M,F,T..."

I almost fainted as I thought, "Oh, no! If he knows what that means, we've all had it!"

Mr. Howard asked the horrible question, "What does that mean, Terrell?"

This time Terrell didn't have to think to answer. "My momma says," he was smiling, "that when they yell that, it means, 'Let's Stop, Make Friends 'th Terrell.' I always knew someday you were coming."

The Haint

JOE-BROTHER AND I HAD BEEN spending time at Grandmother Wilson's house all of our lives. During the school year, our times to spend the night at the big log house were confined to weekends or sometimes to holidays. On those occasions, Mother and Daddy, or at least Mother, would be there with us.

In the summertime, though, after school was out for the year, we often went there and stayed, without parents, by ourselves, for days at a time.

As we grew up, those times at Grandmother's house were no less fascinating than they had been when we were small boys. For Southern mountain boys growing up into the 1950s, visiting Grandmother was a retreat to safety from the rapidly changing world being invaded by fast cars and television.

We were fascinated by the twentieth century we lived in, but also much afraid of it. Staying for a few days in the log house without electricity or running water reassured us of our basic ability to take care of ourselves in the real world, unaided by modern inventions. Those visits put us back in touch with the stability of the world-as-it-was-supposed-to-be.

The bigger we got, the more Grandaddy Wilson tried to put us to work. Now that Joe-brother was in the sixth grade and I was in the seventh, there was no end to the jobs he offered us.

The rocky ground of Cedar Fork Mountain seemed to breed field stone. One of our main and constant jobs was simply "picking up rocks."

"How about getting the rocks out of the garden today?" Grandaddy asked. "I'll get you some peppermint from Hoxie Gaddy's Store-on-Wheels if you do a good job."

Rocks had been being picked up from the garden for years, and still, each year, a new crop seemed to be there. So many rocks had been picked up over the years that an informal rock wall, almost four feet high now, had been built along the lower and back sides of the garden as the rocks were gradually piled there year after year.

We got an old wheelbarrow with a metal-rimmed wheel, brought it out from the barn, and started to work.

Since it was the middle of June, most of the garden was up and growing along quite well. The potatoes were so big that we couldn't push the wheelbarrow through the potato rows, so we skipped over that part of the field altogether.

We could, however, get through the corn and beans and easily through the okra and tomatoes.

Down a row we'd go. Joe-brother and I would pick up all the rocks we saw and pile them in the wheelbarrow. When it got so heavy I could barely pull it (I *never* could push it forward in the soft soil but always had to pull it backwards), each of us would get hold of a handle and drag it to the edge of the garden where we would add to the rock wall.

In a couple of hours we had given the garden a pretty good going over.

We went back to the house and reported to Grandaddy, who had spent most of this time sitting on the porch, rocking and watching us. "We're ready to get paid. When does Hoxie Gaddy's Store-on-Wheels get here?"

"Oh, he'll come along behind the mail man. Likes to catch people when they go to the road to get their mail," Grandaddy said. "It won't be too long now. Let's just walk on down to the highway and wait around for him."

Joe-brother, Grandaddy, and I walked from the big log house across his dirt road and followed the beaten trail that skirted the arrowhead field and ended at the mailbox beside the hard-surface highway below the field.

The arrowhead field was named by Joe-brother and me because we could look there in the spring of the year, after plowing time, and find flint arrowheads, especially after a good rain settled the loose dirt. Even though it was summertime now and the corn was so high that it wasn't even being cultivated anymore, I watched the ground as we skirted the field, just in case an overlooked arrowhead might be kicked up there.

Grandmother used to tell us that Indians must have once had a big camp or maybe even a whole village there, because arrowheads had been coming out of that field all of her life. Grandaddy Wilson had a good dozen cigar boxes full of them. He kept the boxes under his bed, but displayed the newest and best of his finds on the fireplace mantel before they ended up in another cigar box.

Joe-brother and I were fascinated by thinking about these Indians, surely ancient Cherokee, who had left us this sign of their life here.

Once we got to the hard-surface road with Grandaddy, we sat on a log beside the mailbox and waited for the mailman. It was easy for us to spot "Long-lip" Medford, the rural route mailman. He drove a 1948 Ford sedan which was painted such a bright orange color that Joe-brother and I called it his "pumpkin car."

The orange car topped Cedar Fork Gap and we could see Long-lip grinning with the prospect of someone to talk with as he slowed to stop at Grandaddy's mailbox.

Long-lip was so called partly because of his horse-faced appearance and partly because he could talk you to death. He talked, while everyone else had no choice but to listen, about the "damned Republican trying to get in the White House" and about "good old Truman," until finally Grandaddy told him that he better get going or he was going to be delivering after dark.

About the time the orange Ford disappeared, Hoxie Gaddy's Store-on-Wheels came over the top of the mountain where the road cut through the gap.

The Store-on-Wheels was in reality an old school bus. Built on an International Harvester truck chassis, the old bus had already spent a dozen years already hauling children to school in Nantahala County.

When the state replaced it with a new Ford, Hoxie bought

the old bus, rebuilt the engine, took out the seats, installed homemade shelves, and stocked it with, in his words, "just one or two of everything."

His main business was in candy, soft drinks—which he called "dopes"—and sundry items ranging from motor oil to sewing machine needles, all of which people ran out of and needed without wanting to make a trip to town to get. By following the mailman, he often caught people already at the roadside, who while they were there would sometimes buy a snack and remember something else they needed.

Grandaddy's favorite was soft-stick peppermint candy. It came loose, stacked in a cardboard box, like little rows of striped logs. Hoxie sold the loose sticks for a penny each. Joe-brother and I loved the peppermint as much as Grandaddy did. The soft sticks—"pure cane sugar," the box declared—would slowly melt in your mouth.

"Give me a dime's worth of peppermint, Hoxie," Grandaddy said. Hoxie took the dime, then motioned for Grandaddy to count out the ten sticks while he dug for some canning lids and tried to sell them to us to take to Grandmother.

"Not today, Hoxie. Too early to start canning anything. The peppermint's all we want," Grandaddy disappointed him. "Got to pay the boys for picking up a few rocks, don't you see?"

We stepped down out of the old bus as Grandaddy handed each of us a stick of the candy and broke a bite off his own stick as we started back to the house.

Joe-brother and I ate slowly and kicked at the dirt looking for arrowheads as we climbed the trail beside the cornfield. I didn't find anything, but Joe-brother did pick up a little broken tip of sharpened flint near the top of the field.

"I wonder," Joe-brother thought out loud, "if Grandmother still thinks she can see dead Indians?"

When we had been small boys, we had often heard Grandmother tell of seeing Indian ghosts—"haints" she called them—in and around the arrowhead field. She had, years ago when we were small, tried to get us to look out our bedroom window at night to see one. We had been afraid to look and later thought it was all a trick to keep us in our beds at night.

"I was just wondering the same thing," I confessed to Joe-brother. "Let's ask her tonight and see if she offers to show us one. I'm not scared to look anymore, are you?"

"Of course not," Joe-brother laughed. "I'm in the sixth grade, and next year I'll be in Junior High School."

We got back to the house and both finished our peppermint at about the same time. But when we went to find Grandaddy to get our next piece, all of the candy was gone. He had eaten eight pieces in the same time that Joe-brother and I had eaten our two.

"I'm not going to work for him anymore," Joe-brother whined, sounding much more his real age now than when he was declaring his lack of fear of ghosts.

That afternoon Joe-brother asked Grandmother if we could cook supper on the mountain. "Of course we can," she answered, knowing exactly what we had in mind.

She fed Grandaddy his supper early. He often ate by himself: left-over cornbread, mustard greens, and dried peas, with a couple of strips of fried fat-back. When he finished and Grandmother cleaned up his dishes, we were ready for our suppertime picnic.

In the kitchen with Grandmother, we gathered up everything we needed. Grandmother took an iron skillet off its nail on the wall. She wrapped a half-dozen sausage patties in waxed paper and gave them to Joe-brother to carry, along with some extra cornbread left from Grandaddy's supper. Then she handed me a little paper sack into which she had put a half-dozen brown eggs.

We said goodbye to Grandaddy and started out, heading up the mountainside above the log house.

For a good, long distance the whole mountainside between the log house and the top of the mountain was cleared and in use as pasture land. The three of us walked, not straight up the slope, but crisscrossing back and forth as we followed the worn-out paths made by the cattle as they followed their own more gentle routes across the slope.

Joe-brother and I were about out of breath, but Grandmother was still going strong, iron skillet and all, when we got to the edge of the trees at the top of the pasture land. This was our destination.

There was a big flat rock here, almost twenty feet across, which was to be our picnic site. The rock, ancient granite, had a big crack in it, narrow enough that you could set the frying pan across it, but wide enough to hold a fire plenty large for cooking.

We put all of our supplies together on the rock, then worked our way all along the edge of the woods looking for firewood.

There was a lot more firewood than we needed to cook with, but we used it all and built a big fire which the three of us watched until it slowly burned down to a bed of coals. Then we cooked our supper.

First, Grandmother fried the sausage, chopping it into small bits as it gradually browned in the frying pan until she was satisfied it was done. Then she broke the eggs into the pan, and scrambled the eggs together with the pieces of sausage until the eggs were all done.

With three spoons she had brought, we all ate out of the pan, sopping up the fragments with the cornbread. After eating, we all stretched out on our stomachs and drank cold water from the spring at the edge of the woods just above us.

With supper over, Joe-brother and I put more wood on the coals and sat on the rock with Grandmother as the sun set behind us. We watched the mountains across the valley as they were slowly shadowed by our mountain, changing and fading in color all the while, until finally we realized that without our knowing when it had happened, it was dark. It was so clear that the stars were out before all the last light actually drained from the sky.

Joe-brother brought the subject up.

Grandmother," he said, almost shyly, "Remember when we were little and used to come out here to your house to spend the night?"

"Of course I do," she laughed. "Why, that was just yesterday to me. Why?"

"Well...you used to tell us that you could see the ghosts of old Indians that used to live here. Did you really mean for us to believe that, or were you just making it up so we wouldn't get out of bed once you'd put us in there?"

"Of course I meant it." She sounded gently annoyed that we had even questioned what she had told us.

"Can you still see them?" I asked the question this time. "I mean, Joe-brother and I wouldn't be afraid to see one now the way we used to be."

"You can see them. Why, you can see one this very night if you want to."

"We can?" Joe-brother didn't sound as brave now.

"Every night, boys," she began, "there's an old Indian haint who comes right up through here just a little while after dark. He comes out of the woods just below what you boys call the arrowhead field and comes across the road just below the house. Then he comes right up through here to that spring where we were just drinking a while ago. After that, he goes back the same way he came and disappears into those woods. I've thought about it a lot. Seems like he's trying to get to the water or something. Your *Gran*daddy doesn't like for me to talk to *him* about it.

"We'll just wait here for a little while, and you can see him," she finished.

A shiver ran up my back, and I could see that Joe-brother looked absolutely scared to death. It was one thing to talk about ghosts in the daylight. It wasn't so bad to think about looking out the window from inside the house, but to be right out here in the open and have one of the things come close to us was more than either of us could think about.

It was, however, too late now. There was just no brave way we could get out of it.

Joe-brother had been thinking faster than I was. Perhaps greater fear had inspired his imagination. "Look, Grandmother," he said. "It's clouding up. We better get back to the house before it storms."

I had honestly not even noticed, but sure enough, the stars

were gone. Clouds had blown in from the west over the mountain top behind our heads. A storm was on the way, and fast!

"Well, boys, let's get on back down to the house. It *is* going to storm, and it's too early for that old haint to come out anyway. We can just look for him out the window from the dry of the house."

We gathered everything up and headed for the log house.

Hearing thunder rumbling now, we skipped the easy back-and-forth route of the cow trails and went straight down the slope toward the back of the house. The first big drops of rain were already beginning to fall before we stepped into the kitchen door and were safely inside.

Grandmother put the frying pan on the kitchen table. "I can wash that pan in the morning. Let's go upstairs to your bedroom and watch for that old haint."

It was really dark outside now and raining a good, steady rain. We went to an upstairs window on the front of the house to look out. Since the rain was blowing from the back of the house and away from the side where we were, Grandmother opened the window a little bit and propped it with a stick. There were no window screens, so we could see very well.

"Now," she instructed, "watch just right down there. At the edge of the woods by the corner of that field closest to the mailbox. That's where he comes out."

In the daytime, Joe-brother and I thought we could take anything. But now we were both scared to death to look, and at the same time more scared not to. Kneeling side-by-side on the wooden floor, we both clung to the window sill while we strained to look out through the rainy darkness.

Then we saw it! I felt Grandmother's hand touch my shoulder, and I knew that she saw it, too. I started to punch Joe-brother and show him, but when I heard his breath suck in, I knew he had seen it. The figure was like a brownish wisp, except that it had a regular and well-defined shape. It was the shape of a man, naked except for a cloth wrapped around his middle. The shape seemed to float just above the ground as it moved along the edge of the woods, up and beside the cornfield.

141

Then it came toward the road below the house.

It seemed we could see through the wispy figure, but it may have been the rain which made our vision less than clear.

"Do you see the arrow?" Grandmother asked. As soon as she spoke these words, I saw what she was talking about. Something which looked like the feathered shaft of an arrow protruded from the chest of the brownish figure.

"I do think it's an old Indian," Grandmother was talking softly but firmly. "I think he must have been killed around here somewhere and maybe never got buried the way he was supposed to, so he keeps wandering night after night. Every night that I look out he always comes. Now keep watching."

She did not have to tell us that. There was no way that Joe-brother and I could have done anything but watch.

When the Indian haint reached the edge of the road, he seemed to ignore the road completely. He walked right through the air so that he perfectly met the ground at the top of the bank on the other side of the dirt road.

"I think he's walking where the ground used to be," Grandmother explained. "This road would never have been here back when he was alive."

The figure continued up the hillside toward where we had earlier cooked our supper. I shuddered when I realized we would have been sitting out there in this thing's very path if it had not been for the saving rainstorm.

We left the front window and went into the other bedroom on the side of the house as the haint moved on up the mountainside. It went all the way up to near where the spring was, there in the edge of the woods above the big rock. Then it seemed to bend down and disappear.

"Keep watching," she ordered. "I think he's getting some water. I don't know if haints drink or not. Maybe just trying to get to it does something for him."

As surely as she had predicted, the figure appeared again and started back down through the pasture. As we watched, the thunder and lightning began to pick up. Joe-brother said, "You watch. Maybe the next time the lightning flashes, we'll really be able to see just what that thing is."

Almost before his words were out, a big flash of lightning illuminated the whole pasture. We looked intently, but in the brief light the Indian haint could not be seen at all! As soon as the darkness returned, there it was again, moving back down toward the arrowhead field. One of the many things I was thinking was that if this haint disappeared in the light, it could be right out there in the daytime, anywhere, and we wouldn't be able to see it at all. The three of us went back to the front window and kept watching until the brown figure disappeared into the trees below the arrowhead field.

Neither Joe-brother nor I slept at all that night. Our sleeplessness was as much from a sense of awe as it was from our meeting with our own fear. There was too much to think about to sleep just now.

The next day we went home.

Neither one of us ever said a word about the haint to Mother or Daddy. We didn't *decide* not to tell them; we didn't even talk about it with one another. It just somehow didn't seem to be the thing to do, for once back in Sulpher Springs, we had re-entered the modern world. It was a world of cars with AM radios, a world of newspapers and magazines with color pictures. There was just no room for unexplained Indian haints, even if we had both seen one with our own eyes. Once back in town, we weren't even completely sure of that anymore.

Labor Day was one of the few weekdays of the year when Daddy closed the hardware store. Since the fall of the year could already be felt in the September air, we were all aware that cold weather was making its own plans to come toward us in the months ahead. Long before it was even time to make molasses, Labor Day was always reserved to begin cutting firewood for the winter.

As soon as we got out of church on Sunday, we drove in the blue Dodge to Grandmother's house for Sunday dinner and to spend the night so that we could get an early start at cutting wood on Monday.

It was not thought permissible to cut wood on Sunday afternoon. This kind of work was strictly forbidden on Sundays. But it was perfectly fine to walk in the woods and pick out the trees we were going to cut the next day.

Grandaddy took good care of his hardwoods. If any oak or walnut or hickory trees had died or been blown down since last year, we would always cut them for firewood first. Occasionally an oak tree, hit by lightning and in the slow process of dying, would be cut.

We walked all over the farm on Sunday afternoon, hoping that the trees approved by Grandaddy would not be too far apart, so that at least the hauling of the wood would be somewhat easier.

By the end of the day, three trees had been picked for cutting. This would have been an impossible task in years past, but now that Daddy had brought two chain saws from the hardware store, the job could be done.

One of the trees to be cut was a blown-down walnut with a split trunk. "Not fit for a saw log," Grandaddy explained, as he knew we seldom burned walnut. It was too good for woodworking.

The second tree was a hickory. I didn't know why Grandaddy picked this one. There seemed to me to be nothing wrong with it. But it was straight, and hickory would be easy to split when the time came.

The third tree was the one we were going to start with. It was near the lower corner of the arrowhead field, an oak that had been hit by lightning during the spring and was still now in the process of dying. I couldn't help but realize that this first-to-be-cut tree was very close to the exact spot from which Joebrother and I had seen the Indian haint emerge from these very same woods.

Grandaddy had a new Ford tractor which had just this season replaced the aging workhorses. He drove the tractor down along the side of the arrowhead field and into the edge of the woods. Once the tree was down and all the limbs trimmed off, it would be cut in sections, and Grandaddy, with a big logging chain, would pull the sections out of the woods and up beside the road where they could be more easily cut up and split later. This plan helped lessen the job of carrying and kept us from having to move the wood twice just to get it home.

Daddy started one of the chain saws, a big yellow McCulloch, and cleared away a few sprouts to give him clear access to the tree trunk. From the upper side of the tree, he cut a big V-shaped wedge so the tree would fall that way when he later cut straight through from the other side.

Joe-brother held his ears and we both stood back to the side as the power saw threw a stream of wood-chips onto the ground and the smell of its exhaust mixed with the acidic smell of freshly cut oak.

The wedge fell from the tree trunk. The tree was ready now to fall uphill.

Daddy stepped back, let the saw idle for a few moments while he pumped the chain-oil plunger a few times. Then he stepped up to the lower side of the tree and began the long cut straight through, toward and a little above the center of the wedge he had cut from the upper side of the tree.

When he had cut about two-thirds of the way through, the big tree began to creak. He kept sawing until the oak visibly began its slow fall, then he quickly backed way off from the falling tree in case it kicked back from the stump as it fell.

With a great cracking of limbs and a huge earth-shaking bounce, the oak tree fell to the ground.

Now Grandaddy started the second saw, and for the next thirty minutes the two of them cut off all the limbs until they had isolated the trunk from the rest of the tree. Limbs of any size were cut up on the spot into burnable lengths of wood which Joe-brother and I would spend the rest of the day carrying to the edge of the arrowhead field from where they could later be hauled by sled back to the house behind the tractor.

Daddy and Grandaddy stopped the saws while they looked at the trunk of the tree. It was about forty-feet long and maybe eighteen inches thick at the base. Finally they decided to cut the trunk into three sections and drag them up to the road to work up later.

Grandaddy started the Ford tractor and backed it into the woods as close to the trunk of the tree as he could get. Daddy cut the trunk into the three parts they had decided on. During the time it took to cut the tree up, Grandaddy unwrapped the big log chain, looped one end around the first section of tree trunk, hooked it back on itself, and fastened the other end to the draw-bar on the back of the tractor.

All this time, Joe-brother and I were carrying arm-loads of the wood cut from limbs out to the edge of the field.

When Grandaddy started the tractor to pull, Joe-brother and I stopped what we were doing so we could watch. Daddy made sure we were standing above the log so it couldn't roll down on us. We watched as the tractor moved forward, hesitated while the log chain straightened, groaned and cracked, then slowly crawled forward, pulling the section of the tree-trunk behind it.

The log rolled over as it lined itself up to follow the tractor. The front end plowed a shallow furrow in the ground as Gran-daddy pushed up on the throttle lever, and the tractor sped up once clear of the woods.

"Look!" Joe-brother said, pointing to the path that the log had made on its way out of the woods. "What's that?"

We both saw something round and smooth protruding from the underbrush at the edge of the furrow cleared by the log.

Both of us ran toward it, already guessing what it was before we were really close enough to tell. Joe-brother poked at it with his shoe-toe, rolling it over.

It was a human skull, lower jaw missing, but with most of its upper teeth still in place. Together we hollered for Daddy.

The three of us were just standing there looking at it when Grandaddy returned on the tractor. He joined us. "Well, I'll swan!" he declared.

All four of us now began to clear aside limbs, brush, and leaves, and as we did, a scattering of ancient bones appeared, partially covered by the matting of decaying leaves on the ground. Some of the ribs and small bones had completely disappeared, but there were large thigh bones, the pelvis, and a wandering row of seemingly-intact vertebrae.

"Will you look at that!" Grandaddy said, pointing to the row of back bones. We were already looking as there we saw it: an arrowhead, embedded from the front, almost in the center of the row of vertebrae.

"Go get your Grandmother," was his order.

We ran to the house, and the four of us—Mother, Grandmother, Joe-brother, and I—ran back to where Daddy and Grandaddy waited. By the time we arrived, they had arranged all the bones they could find into a laid-out skeleton in the tree-furrow.

Grandmother spotted the bones. Grandaddy pointed to the arrowhead with a stick he had picked up. Grandmother nodded her head.

"It's him," she said, "the old Indian haint."

"Shouldn't we tell somebody?" Daddy asked.

"No," Grandmother quickly answered. "He's wandered long enough. We'll bury him proper so he can finally rest."

There was no questioning or arguing after that. Grandaddy got on the tractor and drove to the barn. Soon he came back with an assortment of shovels, a pick and a mattock. Grandmother had already picked the spot: at the edge of the woods next to the arrowhead field.

We all dug a shortened grave about three feet deep. "There, that should be far enough," she said.

Grandmother placed the bones in order. None of the rest of us dared interfere. Then all of us covered them and patted down the dirt on top when we had finished.

"Get some leaves and brush over here, boys," Grandaddy said. "Let's cover this up." In a short time Joe-brother and I had done such a good job that no one could tell the ground had even been disturbed.

The rest of the day passed with Grandaddy and Daddy sawing and splitting wood while Joe-brother and I stacked it up.

After supper we usually went straight home, but on this evening neither Mother nor Daddy made a move to leave. We were all waiting to see.

When it was dark we sat by the windows and watched until nearly ten o'clock. "He's always come and gone by now," Grandmother said. "I told you it was him. He's at rest now."

We went home.

No one talked about the Indian haint after that, except occasionally, when we were in the lower part of the arrowhead field, one of us would stop and look towards the woods. If Grandmother was with us, she would say, "No, he's never come back. He's with his own people now...where's he's supposed to be."

Wild Harry

I DO NOT REMEMBER HAVING TO learn to drive. Growing up in a rural county with tractors, Jeeps, and pickup trucks all used on the farms, a boy would no more wait for legal age to start driving than he would to ride a horse.

By the time I could reach the pedals, I was driving the blue Dodge up and down the mile-long dirt road which ran through the woods from the paved county road to Uncle Floyd's house.

At Grandaddy Wilson's house, Joe-brother and I learned to drive the Ford tractor. At Red McElroy's house (his dad was a dairy farmer like Uncle Floyd), we drove around on a green two-cylinder John Deere tractor which made a *putt-putt...putt-putt...* sound that no informed farm boy could fail to recognize anywhere. At the store near Uncle Floyd's, I once saw an orange Allis-Chalmers with a hand clutch, but they were rare in Nantahala County, and I never did get to drive one.

Our favorite vehicle was Uncle Floyd's old Jeep. A 1942 Willys, bought Army surplus after the war, the Jeep was still painted its original olive drab. It did have a white star on the side, but all of the military identification numbers had been painted over in black before Uncle Floyd bought it.

The Jeep had a row of bullet holes, German machine-gun we were sure, running at an angle across the tailgate. This made us all know that this Jeep would have quite a story to tell if we could just find out more about it.

Uncle Floyd had rigged the Jeep with a plow hitch and a power take-off wheel so that he could either plow with it, or, with a belt from the power take-off, run a little saw mill he had set up out beyond his big barn.

Whenever any of my friends and I visited his house, the Jeep was ours to drive all over the farm wherever we wanted to go.

We were fourteen years old now, and all in the eighth grade. The most exciting thing that Red, Freddie, Charlie, and I could do was to go to Uncle Floyd's on the weekend and drive the Jeep up onto the mountainside above the farm to have a big camping trip.

Before my Father's generation, there had been a number of short-term residents on the homeplace where Uncle Floyd now lived. They were mostly early settlers of Nantahala County who actually squatted for a while then migrated west in search of their own land.

One of those temporary families had been the family of a man remembered as Franklin Walsh. His abandoned log cabin still stood high on the Yunagusta Mountain above Uncle Floyd's house. It was the Franklin Walsh cabin which became our weekend camping place when we took off from Uncle Floyd's house in the old Jeep.

The cabin itself was not more than two miles up on the mountain, but with the old Jeep crawling through the woods in low-range four-wheel drive, it took us most of an hour to get there.

Built of poplar logs, the cabin had two rooms. There was a big front room that combined living and sleeping. It had a rock fireplace in one end. The fireplace was surrounded by a collection of mismatched cane-bottom chairs. In the other end of the room were three very mismatched double straw-tick beds, all so old that we slept on top of the cover in our own sleeping bags rather than take a chance on getting under the nasty covers.

We had named the three beds "the honeymoon special, the bug bench, and the valley of fatigue," and always drew straws to see who slept in each. The "honeymoon special" was everyone's favorite while the "bug bench" came in last.

On most any weekend, we would meet at my house after school on Friday and Mother would take us out to Uncle Floyd's to camp out for the weekend.

We would stop at Burnett's Store on the way to buy our food. We'd get eggs and bacon, canned beef stew or spaghetti, plenty of snack foods, and always a few "Swisher Sweets" cigars to smoke after supper.

We never touched cigarettes, but we did love to cough through a good, cheap cigar after supper. (These were a lot milder than the old Marsh-Wheelings.)

Mother would wait in the car while we went into the store and bought our groceries. That way she never knew anything about the cigars. The whole cabin was so smokey, and we all smelled so much like smoke when we got home from the trips, there was no noticable odor of *cigar* smoke to ever give us away.

Once at Uncle Floyd's, we loaded up the Jeep with our food and sleeping bags. All the pots, pans, and plates stayed at the cabin so we never needed to take those at all.

Then it was up the mountainside to the cabin.

We first checked out the water supply at the spring. There was a good spring of clear, cold water which came out of the base of the big rock behind the cabin. A wooden trough carried the water out from the rock to a little trail where you could get to it. We usually had to remove leaves and sticks from the spring and put the wooden trough back in place so it could run clear for a while before we could have good, clean water for the week-end.

After that, we spent a period of time gathering firewood. We always wanted a fire in the fireplace during most of the time that we were at the cabin. In winter we had to have it for heat, so we needed plenty of wood for that and to cook in the woodstove in the offset kitchen on the back of the big front room.

We would cook supper about the time it got dark and then smoke a cigar. After supper we often took flashlights or gas lanterns and walked to the top of the Yunagusta Mountain above the cabin. From there we could look down the back side and see all the lights back in town in Sulpher Springs.

The camping trips occupied almost all of our eighth-grade weekend time. During the week we had to go to school.

School was not so bad this year. Red, Freddie and I all had our first male teacher, Mr. Harry Wilde, who was about the best you could have if you were going to have to go to school between weekends.

Mr. Harry Wilde, who of course had been called "Wild Harry" by generations of students, was a bald, hook-nosed fifty-year-old giant who had spent most of his adult life as a public school teacher.

From the first day of the year he told us that his nose was so long that he had been "the only man in the US Army who could smoke a cigarette in the shower without getting it wet."

Then, for the first time, we heard the laugh which would forevermore identify Wild Harry to whoever heard it no matter where we were. "HA ha-ha-ha...HA ha-ha-ha..." he went, like some giant, baritone Woody Woodpecker. No one else in the entire world could possibly have a laugh like that.

"The eighth grade," he told us from the first day of school, "is your last chance to be educated before you have to go to High School. So, girls, (he called us all 'girls'), we have a lot to learn."

After our first weekly field trip, which was to the Sulpher Springs National Bank, Wild Harry taught us how to open and maintain a bank account, carefully checking to see that we all kept our checkbooks balanced.

Through the course of the year we learned to fill out income tax returns and to read every kind of map from road maps to topographical sheets. Red, Freddie, and I all used the Washington address he gave us to order "topo sheets" of all of Nantahala County so we could follow the detailed maps everywhere we went.

As the year progressed, we learned to play chess and backgammon, and finally the entire class learned to play contract bridge.

Wild Harry took us on field trips every week. They ranged from the Nantahala County Armory (a tank division) to the town dump, to visiting all the old mines and rock quarries in the area.

Along with eighth grade North Carolina history (required),

we learned the entire detailed history of Sulpher Springs and Nantahala County. He thought it was a waste to know about other places and be ignorant of our own home.

Wild Harry's literary love was Rudyard Kipling. On special occasions, which really meant whenever we could talk him into doing it, he would quote long Kipling poems for us from memory.

We loved it when, often right after lunch, he would throw his great head back and in a wonderful accent which sounded English enough to us, begin...

If you can keep your head when all about you,
Are losing theirs, and blaming it on you,
If you can trust yourself when all men doubt you,
But make allowance for their doubting, too...

...and so on and on through the whole of Kipling's "If."

Another favorite of ours was the "Requiem," with its wonderful scenery of "When Earth's last picture is painted, and the tubes all twisted and dried..."

Our real favorite of the dozens he knew, however, was "Gunga Din," that wonderful downtrodden waterboy caring for his English superior in India right down to his own suffering death. When Wild Harry quoted "Gunga Din," there was not a dry eye in the room by the time he quietly whispered those closing lines, which come just as Gunga Din is dying:

Though I've belted you and flayed you,
By the livin' Gawd that made you,
You're a better man than I am, Gunga Din!

In spite of his laugh, Wild Harry was *inspiring*.

The most wonderful thing about him, though, was that he drove a Jeep!

Wild Harry's Jeep was a bright red 1954 CJ-5, with a back seat and a full canvas top. The greatest delight of all came when one Saturday he took Red, Freddie, Charlie Summerow, and me up into the mountains above Sulpher Springs to find some old abandoned mica mines. The red CJ was a whole world better than Uncle Floyd's Willys.

While we were at the mica mines, Wild Harry began asking

153

us about our favorite hobbies and pastimes. We told him about going camping at Uncle Floyd's and began to wonder aloud whether he might like to come along sometime.

He really sounded interested as we told him about how to get to Uncle Floyd's cabin, how we drove the old Willys Jeep up to the cabin, and all the things we did when we spent our weekends there. We trusted Wild Harry so much that we even told him about the Swisher Sweets cigars.

After that, every time we planned to go to the cabin we invited him to go, and he always promised that someday he would.

Almost always four of us now went. Charlie Summerow had joined the regular group of Red, Freddie, and myself, but on rare occasions we might take an extra guest and sometimes something came up which kept one of the regulars from going.

It was a great disappointment on a Friday morning in November when I got to school and met Freddie with his bad news.

"I can't go this weekend," he told me. "We have to go over to Asheville to visit my grandparents for the weekend. I didn't find out until last night and it was too late even to call you. You all have a good time and smoke a cigar for me and I'll try to live until next weekend. OK?"

Red had come up by then. "Maybe Wild Harry will go with us," he said. I agreed that it would be worth a try.

"No," Freddie argued. "Don't ask him to go when I'm not going to be there." Finally he relented, though, when we convinced him that if Wild Harry would go with us once, he would probably keep on going.

At the morning recess we went to him. "We're going camping to the cabin tonight. Why don't you go with us?"

He looked at Freddie and asked, "All of you going?"

"Freddie's not," Red answered for him. "He has to go to his grandparents' house."

"I would love to go," said Wild Harry, "but I think I'll plan a time when you're all going. Ask me ahead of time so I can look forward to it...HA ha-ha-ha...OK?"

Every chance we had for the rest of the school day, we

shared little plans about the trip. When the bell finally rang in the afternoon, we were ready to go.

As we headed out the door, Wild Harry called to us. "Hey, girls. Wait a minute." Maybe he's changed his mind, we thought.

"I thought I ought to tell you. I was just up in the office and the radio was on. There was a news bulletin on the radio while I was in there. They said that a couple of convicts broke out of the prison camp at Mount Pleasant before daylight this morning. They tracked them with bloodhounds around toward Plott's Knob, but lost the trail when they walked up the creek there.

"You all better be careful on that camping trip. Do you ever take a gun with you?"

"Oh, no," I answered. "Uncle Floyd always says that the wrong people are the ones who get shot when guns are sitting around. He wouldn't ever let us take a gun camping with us."

"That's pretty smart," Wild Harry agreed. "Well, you-all just be careful."

When Mother picked us up in the car, I wanted to switch on the radio to see if there was any news about the convicts, but I was afraid that if she heard they were on the loose our whole camping trip would be called off on the spot. I left the radio turned off. We would just have to go on what Wild Harry had told us. Plott's Knob was still a long way off from the Yunagusta Mountain, anyway.

We packed our sleeping bags in the trunk of the blue Dodge, stopped by the store to buy food and our cigars, and arrived at Uncle Floyd's house.

We visited with him for a little bit, then loaded up the old Jeep, told Mother goodbye, and headed up the Yunagusta toward the log cabin.

On the roughest part of the "road," if you could call it that, we had to crawl the Jeep along in low-range four-wheel drive over big washed-out rocks. The old four-cylinder flat-head gave forth a pulsating *roar...roar...roar...* as it crawled and bumped along. We couldn't keep from remembering how quiet Wild Harry's red Jeep had been when we went up to the mica mines.

155

We all hoped that someday soon we would get to ride up here in it with him!

We got to the cabin, unloaded, cleaned out the spring, and gathered firewood until dark. The November night was going to be really cold, and we were going to need plenty of wood.

We built a big fire and cooked our supper of canned spaghetti and hot dogs—a combination we would *never* get at home—washed down with warm hot chocolate. Then we leaned back and smoked our Swisher Sweets cigars, including one we passed around for Freddie, as we thought about how miserable he must be visiting his grandparents instead of being here with us.

Charlie suggested that we walk to the top of the Yunagusta and look down at the lights, but Red was all against it.

"Those convicts," he reminded us. "What if they're out there somewhere in the dark and see our lights? They might be looking for hostages or a place just like this cabin to hide in."

This was the first thing anyone had said about the convicts, but I, for one, had not stopped thinking about them for a moment since we left home. We all decided to give up the walk and stick close to the cabin.

One of our favorite pastimes at the cabin was catching mice. So instead of walking to the mountain top, we decided to bait and set all the mouse traps we had collected there.

We had seven or eight spring-type mouse traps that stayed at the cabin. The place always seemed to be inhabited by plenty of field mice. In the deepest cold of midwinter, it would be so cold that a mouse caught in the night would be frozen stiff by morning, even inside the cabin.

Once the traps were baited—some with butter and some with bits of bacon to see which worked best—we placed them at prime-looking spots around the cabin, setting more in the offset kitchen than in the front room.

"I wonder where all of these mice come from?" Charlie asked. "Do you think they come in here just to get warm?"

"I think they come in for food," I offered.

"They won't get much from us!" Red said.

"Not our food," I answered. "They come in to get into Uncle Floyd's dog food. You know he keeps dry dog food in that barrel in the corner for when he brings his dogs up here in the summer to go fox hunting. I'll bet they've got a nest right there in that barrel."

"Let's look," Red said.

He took a Coleman lantern off its nail from the rafter in the center of the room and carried it to the far end of the room where the big barrel was. We followed.

The steel drum was covered by a loose metal lid which we lifted off.

When we looked inside by lantern light, we saw more than one mouse. There were several big, fat mice that had gone down into the nearly-empty barrel to eat dog food. We couldn't tell whether they couldn't climb back out of the steel barrel, or whether they had a hole in the bottom but just couldn't find it because of the blinding lantern light.

At any rate, three of them were madly running in circles around the bottom of the barrel.

"I'm going to squash them," Red chuckled. "One of you get me a stick of firewood." Charlie handed him one.

Holding the lantern in his left hand and the stick of wood in his right, he leaned over the barrel and started poking the firewood at the three mice.

"Squash! Squash! Squash!" Red hollered as he jabbed at the mice, missing every time.

Next time he jabbed at the mice, one of them saw the stick of firewood as a free ride out of the barrel. The mouse jumped on the firewood stick and ran up it, running right up the sleeve of Red's jacket when the stick ran out.

"WHoooaa!" Red screamed as he slung both arms straight back over his head at once.

The firewood hit the wall at the other end of the cabin. The lantern hit the ceiling and clattered to the floor, mantle broken, still hissing gas in the dark. No one knew where the mouse had gone, but at least Red had slung it out of his sleeve.

"Get the lantern...get the lantern," Charlie hollered over

and over. "Turn off the gas before it blows us all up!"

Red dived for the hissing sound, blistered his fingers on the hot glass, but did get it turned off.

Finally we settled down into laughing, found a flashlight, and worked at putting a new mantle on the lantern.

"I thought I was going to have a heart attack!" Red sighed, as he relighted the repaired lantern and we had light again. We all rolled with laughter.

"I've got to go outside and pee after that," Charlie said.

"Me, too," I agreed.

We went outside and watered the yard in the dark.

"Let's go to the spring and get a drink," Red said. He already had the lantern, so he led the way while we followed along the short trail around the house to the cold water.

We were almost there when several things happened so fast that it was all over before I could even begin to sort it out.

As the light of the lantern Red carried moved down the trail, I saw clearly illuminated a pair of legs clad in striped pants. They were sticking out into the trail from behind a big oak tree.

"Oh Lord God!" I thought, "Those damned rats made us forget all about the convicts!"

By this time, Red had already slung the lantern way over his head just the way he had when the mouse ran up his arm, and it went out somewhere in the woods behind us.

Before the lantern had even hit the ground, we were all screaming and running blindly in different directions through the woods, falling over anything and everything that happened to be in our way.

Just as I tripped over a root or a rock, I could not tell which, and was down, to be caught and murdered for sure, I heard that unmistakable laugh.

"HA ha-ha-ha...HA ha-ha-ha..."

Only one person in the entire world sounded like that, and he wasn't an escaped convict! We all turned around to see Wild Harry and Freddie Patton, flashlights in hand, as they stepped out from behind the big oak tree, laughing all the time.

I was so relieved that I couldn't even get mad.

When they got close, we could see that they were wearing plain, dark clothes, with stripes made of white adhesive tape.

"We made the whole thing up," Freddie laughed. "I didn't have to go to see my grandparents at all. We slipped up here in Mr. Wilde's Jeep. We didn't even have to worry about being heard. You-all were making so much noise back there inside when the light went off that you wouldn't have heard anything. What was all that screaming inside the cabin about?"

We just looked at one another, embarrassed, as Wild Harry continued the story. "What we were going to do was throw firecrackers on the porch and stand out in the edge of the woods where you could see our convict's stripes.

"Just as we got ready, you came out to pee. We were actually trying to hide and wait for you to go back inside, and we didn't realize that we were hiding almost right in the trail to the spring. We're here to spend the night."

We went inside. They had brought popcorn and some soft drinks. We all had a big old time on our first camping trip with Wild Harry. It was not our last, however. He went with us about once a month for the rest of the year.

We kept camping all through high school. Even after we could legally drive on the highways, there was nothing as much fun as driving the old Jeep all over the Yunagusta Mountain and camping there.

Late in the spring of the tenth grade, we were talking about camping while at school one day. Jean-ette Carlson, a beautiful red-haired girl Freddie seemed to talk about a lot, and Lori Deaver came over to us.

"We go camping, too," they said together.

Lori, a short, round blonde, bounced as she told us about it.

"We started with the Girl Scouts, but now we go on our own almost every Friday in the woods below my house."

"Who goes?" Red asked.

"Jean-ette, Mary Thomas, Carrie Boyd and yours truly!" Lori bounced more as she talked. "Why don't you come with us sometime?"

As the weeks passed we began talking with these girls more and more about the idea of all going camping together. We never noticed that *they* always brought the subject up.

On several Monday mornings, we discovered that we had gone to the cabin on our own and that the girls had camped in the woods below Lori's house on the same weekend.

"We missed a good chance this weekend," Lori said. "My parents were gone for the whole weekend and no one would have ever known."

"You mean you go camping up there even when your parents aren't home?" Red asked.

"Sure we do. My big sister, Marie, is always at home if anything goes wrong. Her boyfriend comes over, and after that she doesn't care what we do," Lori explained how the whole plan worked.

"When are they going to be gone again?" I asked. (This just might possibly work, I thought.)

"Not this weekend, but the next. They're supposed to go to Atlanta for some kind of market meeting or something like that. My daddy has to go to them all the time."

"Let's do it!" Red suggested.

The decision was made to go camping together not in the woods below Lori's house but at Uncle Floyd's cabin. All the girls had been told about it and that's where they all wanted to go.

Since the plan was two weeks away, it didn't seem real, but as the days gradually passed, we all came to realize that unless we backed out this thing was actually going to happen. The plan was carefully worked out down to the last detail.

"After school on Friday, the girls and I will all meet at my house," Lori offered. "You-all can pick us up there."

We had to do all this very carefully so as not to get caught. It was going to be somewhat easier in now that Red and I were driving (Freddie was still only fifteen), and we took ourselves to Uncle Floyd's instead of being driven there by Mother.

"I know what we'll do," said Red. "I'll borrow Daddy's old Ford pickup. Then we'll get a big tarpaulin. We can put the girls and all of their stuff in the back of the truck and cover them up with the tarp until they're out of sight."

"That's great," I agreed. "Uncle Floyd's always milking when we get there. I'll just go in the barn and tell him we're driving the truck as far as we can because we're hauling a lot of stuff. Then we'll beat it and get on our way."

The plan was made. We'd go over things at lunchtime in the cafeteria at school each day. This kind of stuff just wasn't safe to talk about on the phone. We all thought that Friday would never come, but finally the great day arrived.

We were nervous all day at school. All of us boys went home with Red when school was out. After loading our stuff into the Ford pickup, we headed to Lori's house.

All the girls were there except Mary. Lori told us she had chickened out, but had promised not to tell anybody else about what we were doing. Lori's sister, Marie, was eager to cover up for us in order to get the house all to herself for the weekend.

The girls loaded their stuff into the truck bed. Then they climbed in, and we covered them up with the tarp.

All the way to Uncle Floyd's house, we kept looking back to be sure that the tarp didn't blow off. They must have been hanging onto the edges because it stayed right in place the whole way.

Sure enough, Uncle Floyd was in the dairy barn milking when we drove up. Red stopped the pickup in the road and I went inside.

"Well," Uncle Floyd drawled, "I thought maybe you-all weren't coming."

"No, we're here," I answered, trying not to let my voice tremble too much.

"I thought I might just go with you," he said. My heart almost stopped. Then he continued, "I haven't been up to the cabin for a long time. Don't think I will, though. It looks like it's going to start raining anytime now and I'd rather be at home and in the dry when it does."

I sighed with relief. "We're not taking the Jeep," I filled him in. "We've got a lot of stuff to take with us and we're taking Red's truck as far as we can. (If he only knew what kind of stuff I was talking about!)

"What kind of stuff?" he asked, and my heart stopped for sure this time.

Before I could try to make something up, the cow in the first milking stall jumped and kicked loose two of her pneumatic milkers. Uncle Floyd hurried to reattach the milkers and, having forgotten his own question, said, "Well, have a good time."

I trotted out to the truck, yelled "Hit it!" to Red, and we started off up the mountain, our cargo of girls safely out of sight in the back of the truck.

About the time I got out to open the gate at the near end of the lower pasture, the rain started to hit. It began with big, heavy drops as the waiting storm jumped across the mountain as though it had us personally in mind.

By the time we got to the next gate at the upper side of the same pasture, it was pouring, and we still had a good, slow half-hour mile to go. We knew, tarpaulin or not, that the girls had to be getting wet since all the rain that had fallen had to collect in the floor of the truck bed, not to mention soaking all the sleeping bags and sacks of food.

About two hundred yards up in the woods above the gate we had just come through was an old winter feed barn. It had an overhang on the side that you could drive under and a big loft where Uncle Floyd stored hay from the higher fields for hard months in the winter.

"We'd better pull in at the hay barn," I said. "You can drive right under it."

Red turned the Ford truck off the dirt road, dipped through the rocky ford of a little creek, and drove under the dry overhang of the old barn.

We jumped out. Freddie pulled back the tarp to uncover the girls. They were sitting, soaked, in what looked like a good inch of water accumulated in the truck bed.

"I am drowned," Carrie Boyd wailed.

"We're going to freeze to death." Tears were running down Jean-ette's cheeks.

"Oh, shut up!" Lori yelled at both of them. "This whole thing was your idea."

Red took over. "Let's unload everything into the barn loft and see what's wet and what's dry."

We did. Everything was dripping wet, especially the girls.

"I'm not staying," Jean-ette cried.

"Me, neither," Carrie agreed.

"Oh shut up!" Lori yelled.

After arguing for a while it began to get dark—and cold. We couldn't build a fire in the barn, and it was still pouring rain outside. After what seemed like hours of listening to the girls cry, we decided that the best thing to do was to try, somehow, to leave.

We would just leave all the wet sleeping bags and food here and come back and get them tomorrow or Sunday. For now, the most important thing was to get those girls out of here.

"Let's go," Red said.

"We're not riding in the back anymore," Carrie declared, so Red and all three of the girls piled in the front seat while Freddie and I got under the wet tarp and tried to invent some way to stay dry in the back. Red started the engine.

He had to back out from the barn to the dirt road, and of course the old Ford had no back-up lights. I held a flashlight out from under the tarp and tried to tell him which way to back. We made it OK back to the ford in the creek, then saw that it was so swollen by the rain that we couldn't tell which way to cross.

"Come straight on back," I tried to guide him. The truck backed into the swirling water, then seemed to shift downstream to the side and settled at a crazy angle with one corner of the bed wedged into the creekbank on the far side. I knew that we were impossibly stuck.

"Pull up," I said, as if that would fix anything. Red put the truck in low gear, and when he let out the clutch the lower wheel turned, free in the water, without even touching the bottom.

We sent the girls back into the barn and for what seemed

like hours, we spent the next twenty minutes trying to get the truck unstuck. No luck.

Now, completely soaked and with even shoes full of water, we returned to the barn loft to admit defeat.

Carrie and Jean-ette were huddled together crying with a wet sleeping bag draped around their shoulders. Lori stood off to the side yelling, "Oh shut up!" every time one of them let out a wail.

"We're stuck for the night," Freddie said it all.

We were hungry, wet, cold, and in the dark. Freddie lighted a gas lantern and we began to try to figure out some kind of arrangement to get ourselves through the night. We were sure we could get the truck unstuck in the light of day.

The rain had slacked off some and suddenly we heard the roaring sound of a Jeep engine, crawling in four-wheel drive up the road through the woods.

"Now we're caught, too!" Red said it aloud as we all thought the same thing.

Uncle Floyd must have decided to come up anyway. Maybe he was worried because of the storm. Whatever, the whole show was about to come to its awful end.

"We might as well go out to the road and meet him and get it over with," I suggested. "That way we can at least tell our version first."

We left the girls and the three of us made our way by flashlight to the creek, waded the knee-deep water, and got up into the road. The Jeep lights came around the curve in the road and hit us. We waved our arms. The Jeep stopped about twenty yards from us, the engine died, and the lights cut off.

"HA ha-ha-ha...HA ha-ha-ha...!"

The sound cut the darkness. It wasn't Uncle Floyd's Jeep at all. It was Wild Harry.

We ran to him, and he actually hugged all three of us boys at once. He laughed again, then said, "You're saved! Where have you got the girls?"

We waded the creek back to the barn as the story unfolded. The storm had been even worse in town than here, and Lori's sister Marie had gotten scared. Lightning had hit a big tree outside the Deavers' house, and Marie got so scared that she had called Wild Harry (he had once been her teacher, too) and, crying, spilled the whole story to him. He had come looking for us.

"I'll take the girls back to Lori's house." He talked and we just listened. "You boys can make it here and get yourselves on back tomorrow. I know you can do it." We knew it, too.

We told the girls goodbye, knowing that not one of them would ever dare say a word. Carrie and Jean-ette cried, and Lori said, "Oh, shut up!" and they left.

The next morning we walked down to Uncle Floyd's and borrowed his old Willys Jeep. It worked very well to pull the Ford pickup out of the creek, and we were on our way home.

When we happened to see Wild Harry at school on Monday, all he said was, "It sure was a stormy weekend, wasn't it, girls?"

Experience

HIGH SCHOOL AT LAST! RED, Freddie, Charlie, and I were all now in the ninth grade. While the entire seventh-through-twelfth grade classes at Sulpher Springs School shared the same buildings, there was a vast psychological and social difference between being in the eighth grade and being in the ninth grade. Eighth graders were junior high school *children.* Ninth graders were High School Students.

After eight years of public school education in Sulpher Springs, we were all experienced at dealing with teachers. We were ready and eager for the ninth grade. It took us some time to come to realize that the ninth grade was also ready for us.

One of the first things we noticed about the ninth grade was that all of the teachers were old. The oldest teacher we had ever had up to now had been Miss Daisy Rose Boring, back there in the fourth grade. Here in the ninth grade, all of the teachers looked as old as Miss Daisy had ever looked, and this entire old bunch seemed to be tough.

English was taught by Mrs. Amelia Harrison. Her class consisted of sentence diagramming, vocabulary drills, and manners lessons. Manners were very important to Mrs. Amelia, and every third day, alternating regularly with her other two priorities, we had manners lessons.

Each day of the world, she stood by the door as we entered the classroom. As we filed past her imposing presence, she held out a brown paper bag and sang a little song about "please leave your chewing gum and razors at the door," which she thought was very cute.

We were all supposed to drop our gum into that bag, though

no one ever exactly figured out the part about the razors.

Every week we had a "chewing gum check," an examination of the underside of our desk tops, to see if anyone with "bad manners" had actually slipped in with chewing gum and, horror of horrors, stuck it on the underside of his or her desk top.

One of the boys in our room was Billy "Bad Boy" Barker. Bad Boy happened to live down on Cold Ridge, and also, my Mother said, was Leon Conner's first cousin. "He can't help it," she tried to explain, "their mothers just happened to be sisters."

Bad Boy, called this all his life by friend and foe alike, had what the teachers at school, after going to a workshop, began to call a "personality problem."

About seventeen years old now, Bad Boy would have quit school by now except that his mother, a real brute of a woman, didn't want his "personality problem" at home all day. So she made him stay in school.

Bad Boy was a long-time tobacco chewer, but he had been suspended from school for spitting in the floor and had learned to put his wad out when he got off the bus at school in the morning. His oral dependency was so strong, however, that he spent the rest of the day with a big wad of Juicy Fruit chewing gum in his mouth.

Mrs. Amelia should have been happy to get rid of the tobacco and let well enough alone, but she didn't. On the day of the first desk check, she found a half-dozen big wads of Juicy Fruit on the bottom of Bad Boy's desk.

"Why did you do it?" was her only question.

"The flavor give out in that Juicy Fruit, and I had to get rid of it," Bad Boy answered.

"That's not what I mean, and you know it!" she fired back. "Why did you dare come in my classroom with chewing gum in your mouth to start with?"

"Aw!" said Bad Boy. That was mostly all he *ever* had to say when he was asked a question.

She watched him like a hawk after that, doing everything but poking around in his mouth as he came into the room each day.

Bad Boy was lacking in many ways, but he was persistent. Even if he came in the door of the classroom empty-mouthed, it was not long until he had slipped a stick of Juicy Fruit into his mouth. He could sit, jaw slack and motionless, for minutes at a time—then chomp real fast whenever Mrs. Amelia turned to write on the board.

It had been so much trouble to have to chip and scrape the gum off his desk the first time he was caught that Bad Boy came up with a new solution for stale Juicy Fruit. Now when the flavor ran out, he just added a fresh stick to the wad and kept the whole thing in his mouth. His taste buds were so toughened by tobacco juice that he was often chewing a whole pack of Juicy Fruit by the time class was out.

As the year rolled on, Bad Boy grew bolder and bolder. Everyone in the room except Mrs. Amelia knew exactly what he was doing, and after a while the big seventeen-year-old ninth grader thought that even *she* probably knew but was just afraid to say or do anything about it.

The big day finally came. One day during vocabulary drill, the word under discussion by Mrs. Amelia was *hubris*. We couldn't find the word in the dictionary.

Mrs. Amelia said that didn't matter, because we needed to learn it anyway...especially in the ninth grade. She began to describe and define *hubris* as "fatal pride. The kind of pride which makes you truly believe that you are not like everyone else...the kind of pride which makes you feel that none of the normal laws of life apply to you...the kind of pride which brings you to a great fall in the end."

No one ever figured out what Bad Boy was thinking about on that day, but as Mrs. Amelia talked on about hubris, he very slowly began to chew, right there in front of her, what had to be a full five-stick wad of Juicy Fruit chewing gum.

Suddenly we realized that Mrs. Amelia, still talking, was looking straight at Bad Boy, unblinking, eyes open widely and set in a focussed stare as she talked.

"Hubris is like," she went on, searching for an example, "it's like...it's like...well, it's like thinking"—she was on her feet now, and moving toward Bad Boy's desk—"you can chew gum out in the open in Mrs. Amelia Harrison's room and somehow get away with it."

Now she was face to face with Bad Boy. She held out her hand and with authority unmistakable even to a seventeen-year-old ninth grader, she said, "Spit it out...NOW!"

What happened next was so fast that it took a few seconds for all of us in the room to actually realize what had just taken place. Bad Boy did spit the huge wad of gum into Mrs. Amelia's outstretched hand. She, in one smooth move, stuck it right on the top of his head where, using the dictionary in her other hand, she smashed the whole, huge wad down into his hair.

"Those who live by hubris," she kept talking as she walked back to her desk, "always get stuck in the end."

Mrs. Amelia had experience.

One of the bigger new things about High School was that we now had a chance to take a real foreign language. There was no choice about what to take. The one foreign language taught at Sulpher Springs High School was Latin. It was taught by Miss Vergilius Darwin, who had taught first-and-second year Latin for forty-six years.

We all called her "Miss V.D." behind her back.

Some days Miss Vergilius would tell us that she had started teaching Latin when it was still a living language. This was her joke, and she did not seem to think it funny at all when Charlie Summerow once asked her if she had ever had a date with Julius Caesar.

Miss V.D. was barely five feet tall and could have weighed no more than ninety-five pounds fully dressed. The main strength and power of at least ninety-four of her ninety-five pounds resided in the bent knuckle of the middle finger of her right hand.

She could grab a two-hundred-pound football player by the shirt, lift him out of his seat, sink that crooked knuckle into his chest and seem to stop his heart for twenty minutes. They rolled in the floor in pain.

One day during a grammar drill, Miss V.D. called on Big Tater McCracken to "conjugate 'carry,' present indicative, all three persons, singular and plural."

Big Tater was not only the first of the Rabbit Creek McCrackens ever to take Latin, but if he made it, he would be the first in his entire family to ever graduate from high school. He worked at Latin seriously and had just spent the entire weekend memorizing the very verb endings he was now being asked for. He was prepared.

There was only one problem. The model verb for this conjugation was the verb "to love," *amo,* and through the long weekend of Latin study, Big Tater had, a thousand times, repeated the conjugations to that verb: *"Amo, amas, amat...amamus, amatis, amant..."* He had it cold.

At this moment, however, an awful truth emerged. While all the verb endings had been memorized to perfection, Big Tater had forgotten to learn the new vocabulary words, one of which was the word *porto,* which meant "to carry."

Miss V.D. repeated the order. "Big Tater, I'm talking to you...conjugate 'to carry,' present indicative, all three persons, singular and plural."

Determined to get it right, especially since he knew all the verb endings, Big Tater sought desperately for the right word. Out of the corner of his mouth he whispered to Red McElroy, "What is it?...what is it?"

Red was the last person who wanted to get in trouble with Miss V.D. He shushed Big Tater, and then finally whispered back to him, "Damn if I know!"

That clue was all Big Tater needed, and he cut loose on the prize conjugation of the year: "To carry: *damifino, damifinas, damifinat...damifinamus, damifinatis, damifinant!"* He was proud to the end that he had done it.

"Whoooo!" Red threw his head back and hollered. "Damn-If-I-Knooow! HA, HA, HA, HA!"

Miss Virgilius Darwin was on him in a flash, had him by the shirt and up in the air, then down onto the floor while she twisted that bent-auger finger into his chest.

All the breath went out of Red as Miss Darwin looked around the room and said, "Damn-if-you-better-try-that-again with Old V.D.!"

She had experience.

We all knew very soon, however, that experience was much more than a combination of old age and long tenure at school. This was obvious when we realized that our high school principal, in spite of his being principal for thirty-four years, was not a person of experience.

Before becoming principal, Mr. Walter Farlow had been the basketball coach, and as such had produced winning teams for several years. At some point along the way, the School Board decided that Coach Farlow would be a natural at being school principal, and so when old Mr. Wiggins retired, they put Coach Farlow in the office.

The mistake was soon realized, but it was too late, for his father-in-law was also chairman of the School Board.

No one was sure whether it was having to clean up and wear a suit and tie that did it, or realizing you just couldn't make teachers run laps around the gym if they didn't do what you wanted them to do. Whatever, the new job just didn't work. Maybe he just couldn't function without his whistle.

When at our first assembly program Mr. Farlow gave us the school rules, we were slow to catch on. He began his recitation of each rule with the words, "I'd better not catch you..." and then went on to tell us what was prohibited.

It took us nearly a week to discover that that is exactly what he meant. He didn't say "don't do it"; he said "I'd better not catch you," for he had absolutely no idea what he was going to do with any of us if he did catch us in some awful violation.

At every social activity, from sock hops to football games to real dances, Coach Farlow (as he was called forever) could be seen wandering the perimeter with a long, six-cell flashlight. The flashlight was not so he could see what we were doing, but so *we* could see him coming in time to stop so he wouldn't be forced to catch us.

Some of the teachers were heard to say, "He had ten good years of experience coaching basketball, but he's just been principal one year, thirty-four times!"

Coach Farlow did not have experience.

Back on the other end of the scale, the tenure and experience champion of all time at Sulpher Springs High School was Mrs. Ellen Birch Bryan.

Mrs. Birch Bryan, as she preferred to be called, since it "honored her dead father as well as her dead husband," was a huge, towering woman. Six feet tall, with big bones and broad shoulders, she wore her hair in a big gray pile on top of her head, which all went together to make her appear even taller.

Mrs. Birch Bryan was seventy-two years old and had taught typing, shorthand, business, and bookkeeping for fifty-one years.

"I'm not about to retire," she would say, which was no surprise to anyone at all at the time. With almost no retirement benefits and no mandatory retirement age, many teachers stayed in "for life."

"Why," she would say, "I've taught the principal. Not just this one, but the last three. I've taught the superintendent, I've taught every single member of the School Board, and I'm not afraid of the Supreme Court! Why should I stop teaching?"

Freddie, Red, Big Tater, Charlie, and I had Mrs. Birch Bryan for first-year typing during the last period of the day each day.

Every day, class began the same way it had for the past fifty years. We began with our finger exercises. "Now, boys and girls, hold up your hands and extend your fingers. Now, stretch, relax, stre-etch, rela-ax, stre-e-etch, rela-a-ax..."

After a few rounds of such digital calesthenics, we would all insert a sheet of paper, set our margins, and place our fingers on the home keys of the blank Underwood manual keyboards.

"It is now time for letter-by-letter dictation. Are you all ready? F...D...S...A...J...K...L...semi." Over and over again, we repeated that pattern until we all had it perfectly and as fast as Mrs. Birch Bryan could reel them off, first in order and then mixed up.

As the weeks went by, we added a letter at a time, gradually getting to "G," then "H," and finally on to the exotic fringes of the keyboard including "P" and "Q" and "Z." We could do the entire alphabet now.

Once each week, there was a sacred time in Mrs. Birch Bryan's class. It came at the same time each week, as regularly as church came on Sunday mornings. It was the weekly "timed writing."

For the last ten minutes of the period on Fridays, we would type as fast as we could, copying a measured timed-writing selection, to determine our speed and grade for the week. Divide the total words typed by ten, and you got your words-per-minute weekly score.

Every mistake a person made subtracted one word per minute from the score, so that it was possible—several of us proved it—to come up scores like "minus seven words-per-minute," or once even "minus eleven-words-per-minute." Sometimes after that I thought of just sitting still and not typing at all. At least I would end up even.

"Nothing, boys and girls, and I do mean absolutely *nothing,* must interfere with a timed writing. This is your grade, you are to stop typing for no reason until I tell you." This was the rule and the final word on timed writings.

We typed selections, old and yellowed, printed years earlier as advertising by typewriter companies who always pictured their newest machines at the top of the pages.

Some of these advertisements featured champion typists. Mrs. Birch Bryan's personal favorite was Mr. George Hossafield. He was pictured at the top of several of the timed-writing selections, pictured seated at a now-ancient-looking glass-sided manual typewriter. He wore an eyeshade, and his sleeves were pushed up and held in place by elastic sleeve-holders.

The legend under the picture proclaimed that Mr. George Hossafield had attained his world championship status by averaging one hundred and forty-three words-per-minute over a period of time of one hour.

Mrs. Birch Bryan would hold up the sheet with his picture on it, tell us again what we already knew about his record-setting time, and say, "Aspire, students! Aspire! Some of you only have about a hundred and thirty words-per-minute to go and you'll catch him."

The selections to be typed were all about events which had been current in their time. Now, however, they were history. We typed about such things as Woodrow Wilson and the League of Nations, and even about Mrs. Coolidge redecorating the White House.

Mrs. Birch Bryan had a track clock with red and green stop and go buttons on the top of it. It was bigger and better than any timing device Coach Farlow had ever had when he was in the coaching business. This time clock was used solely for the purpose of timing the timed writings.

When we were all ready, she carefully wound the track clock. Then, as always, she left us with that last important admonition: "Remember, boys and girls, nothing...nothing must interfere with a timed writing. Are you ready? BEGIN!"

With that she punched the green start button on the track clock, and for the next ten minutes we all typed just as fast as we possibly could.

To be sure that we learned to type through any kind of interference, Mrs. Birch Bryan would actually try to interrupt us while we typed. She would sneeze or cough loudly, blow her nose, open and close file cabinets, pop balloons, slam the door, and finally one day she smashed a water glass in the sink. If anyone paused to glance up at her, she would pronounce loudly, "Nothing must interfere...nothing must interfere with your timed writing."

Within a few weeks, all of us could have typed through anything from a tornado to a train wreck.

By the end of the first six-weeks grading period, I was really beginning to become a typist, in *spite* of the discouraging scores on my timed writings. I actually thought about typing a paper for Mrs. Harrison's English class.

That thought vanished when report cards came out.

All of my grades were pretty much what I expected until it came to typing. Instead of a letter grade, there appeared the word "incomplete."

I didn't understand. There had not been a single day when I had missed school or typing class, the usual reason for "incompletes." I went to see Mrs. Birch Bryan to try to find out why I didn't get a real grade. She was ready for me.

"You are going to have to improve," she told me in her most formidable voice as she towered above me. She trembled as she spoke. "You are going to have to improve before I can give you an F. Yes, it would be an insult to the good, hard-working students who are *earning* good, solid, high Fs just to *give* you one for the kind of work you are doing. You must improve... you'll never catch Mr. Hossafield at this rate."

I was destroyed only briefly, however, as I very quickly learned that Red and Freddie also were going to have to improve in order to get an F.

On the next Friday, when it was time for the timed writing, I had an entirely new thought when, after the usual ritual, Mrs. Birch Bryan gave us the sacred reminder: "Remember, students, nothing must interfere with a timed writing."

Inspired by the realization that when you're already below F you don't have much to lose, I began to wonder—did I really think that *nothing* could interfere with Mrs. Birch Bryan herself during one of those timed writings?

After class, I raised the possibility with Red and Freddie and found out that they had been thinking about almost the same thing.

"Next Friday we'll find out," Red suggested.

On the next Thursday afternoon, we sneaked back to school and climbed in a window (we had taped it unlocked) of Mrs. Birch Bryan's room armed with a big roll of mason's twine.

The room was in an old building with tall windows. Each window had two shades mounted about halfway up the windowframe. The top shade pulled up by a cord which ran through a roller at the top of the window. The bottom shade pulled down

175

normally. Mrs. Birch Bryan never touched the shades. They were supposed to be fixed in a precise and unchangeable way: top shades all the way up, bottom shades one-third of the way down.

With the big ball of twine, we began tying on string to extend all the shade-pulls until we had a string from each coming around various heating pipes and meeting behind a radiator at the back of the room. After the ends were all tied together, enough tension was put on the cords to release the spring-locks of the shade rollers; then, by one string, the whole window-shade network was tied to the radiator pipe.

We were nervous all the next day about whether Mrs. Birch Bryan would discover the strings or not. She didn't.

Class opened as it usually did, from finger exercises through dictation and even some form-letter practice. Finally, after much instruction and preparation, we began the timed writing.

After waiting for about three minutes, Freddie Patton cut the main string.

There was a great noise all along the back of the room as sixteen window shades all rolled up so fast that most of them popped out of their brackets and fell on the students in the back row, unrolling all over everything.

Mrs. Birch Bryan simply bellowed, "Don't stop!" as if she had planned it that way. After school that day, she took the rest of the shades down and put them in the closet, and for the rest of the year we sat there in the afternoon sun, burning up.

"Let's try again," Freddie said a couple of weeks later. "I've got an idea."

Jean-ette Carlson was in our typing class—the same Jean-ette who almost spent the night with us on the camping trip. Jean-ette had cultivated a special talent. She could hold her breath until she fainted. We had seen her do it at school dances and picnics, and even once right behind the visiting team's bench at a basketball game. We each saved up a dollar, and we offered Jean-ette three dollars to faint during the next timed writing.

As soon as we started typing, Jean-ette began to hold her

breath. It seemed like it took her five minutes until, beet-red, she fell out of her chair and into the floor right in front of Mrs. Birch Bryan.

Mrs. Birch Bryan simply folded her arms and looked the other way. "Nothing interferes," she whispered to herself. Jeanette had to come back to life all on her own without any help! We could not ever get her to faint again after that.

We were beginning to realize that it was not going to be as easy to "interfere" with Mrs. Birch Bryan as we had first thought. Almost every day we spent some time trying to come up with a plan that might work.

Bad Boy Barker had study hall in the library while we were in typing class, which really meant that he could usually wander all over the school wherever he wanted to during that hour.

We saved three more dollars, plus an extra dollar for what Bad Boy called "expenses," and paid him to acquire a cherry bomb (he seemed to have sources for such things) and to throw it into the room during a timed writing.

He did.

The only result was that before the next Friday came around, Mrs. Birch Bryan had installed a padlock and hasp on the inside of the door, and now, as part of getting ready for our timed writing, she locked us in! This really was going to be hard.

It was a very simple trick which finally did produce results. Without even planning anything in advance, Red happened to come to school the next Friday with a coil of transparent fishing line in his pocket.

While Mrs. Birch Bryan was shooing students out of the hall at class change time, he casually tied one end of the fishing line to a leg of her big oak teacher's chair. From there he ran the line through a drawer pull on the file cabinet at the end of the room and back under the front row of typing tables and tied it to his desk.

She never saw it at all.

We had class as usual: finger exercises, then F...D...S...A, all the way up to Q by now, a long series of form-letters to type, and then, at last, the timed writing.

Mrs. Birch Bryan passed out the yellowed sheets. Today's selection was entitled "President Harding dies in California." She told us again about George Hossafield's record and admonished us to aspire. She wound up the track clock, and then she said it: "Remember students, nothing interferes with a timed writing! Are you ready? BEGIN!"

When Mrs. Birch Bryan pushed the green button on the track clock, Red McElroy pulled on his end of the fishing line.

The entire class was trying to type about poor President Harding's mysterious death while at the same time every eye in the room was watching Mrs. Birch Bryan as she slowly sat down toward a chair which wasn't there. Red had not, however, pulled the string quite far enough, and about four inches of Mrs. Birch Bryan's broadest self tried to sit on a four-inch side edge of the almost-absent chair.

Suddenly the chair popped sideways out from under her like a giant tiddly-wink, flew through the air, and crashed into the file cabinet, while Mrs. Birch Bryan hit the floor not once, but twice.

She sat smack on the floor, hard, bounced, straightened out, then landed flat on her back with her head making a loud *cra-a-ck* against the floor.

The entire room was silent, every typewriter dead still. We thought we had killed her! Sweat broke out in my armpits until they ached, and I could see Red's face flushing.

Then we heard a sound. It started like a groan or a whisper, but then, siren-like, it raised itself to fill the room.

"Don't stop!...Don't stop..." It was Mrs. Birch Bryan, flat on her back and bellowing at the ceiling. "Nothing must interfere with a timed writing."

We gave up on trying after that. Though some future typist might indeed catch Mr. Hossafield, Mrs. Birch Bryan, with a fifty-one-year head start, was clearly out of our class.

Daff-knee Garlic and the Great Drive-In Fire

.

WHEN I FIRST MET DAFF-KNEE Garlic, I thought he had been given a girl's name as some grotesque commentary by his mother, who had, after all, "married a Garlic." It was much later that I discovered that his real name was not "Daphne" at all, but rather "Clarence." Daff-knee was a nickname shortened from the term "Daffy Knees," a term that he himself used to describe a peculiar but interesting defect of birth with which he had spent his entire life.

"I was born without kneecaps," Daff-knee described himself, "so my knees will bend one way just as far and just as fast as they bend the other way. Why, I can run *backwards* as fast as I can run forwards."

It was true—the running part, that is. None of us in Sulpher Springs ever did have any medical understanding of exactly whether Daff-knee actually did have knee caps or not, but we knew that they did bend both ways and that he could run backwards just as fast as most people could run forwards.

"It is a great advantage," he would say, "to be able to look at what you're running from while you do it."

Daff-knee Garlic was the owner, operator, and sole proprietor of the premier educational institution for teenagers in all of Nantahala County, the Sulpher Springs Big-Screen Drive-In Theatre.

The Big-Screen was the first and only drive-in theatre in the county. Built in an already-natural amphitheatre on the outskirts of Sulpher Springs, the theatre had opened after World War II as

179

drive-in movies followed the love of the automobile across the country.

The first version of a drive-in theatre to be built on this spot had been only half as large as this one. When he bought it in 1950, Daff-knee doubled the number of cars the field would hold and more than doubled the size of the screen, hence the new name, "The Big-Screen." You could still see the outline of the smaller original screen within the new and larger one, but with it painted over in white, you really couldn't tell the difference when it was dark and the movie came on.

The field of the theatre held sixteen rows of cars. The rows curved and the entire field sloped slightly from back to front. The front row only held about twenty cars, but the long, curving back row held at least twice that number.

In the mowed grassy area in front of the screen, there was a playground for children, to encourage families to "come early and get a good spot...your children can play in safety while you wait for the feature to begin," or so the radio commercials went.

In the more remote cars on the back row, more "adult" adolescent education took place.

Daff-knee operated the theatre "all by himself," as he liked to tell everyone. This statement overlooked his employment of four to six teen-age boys to do most of the work while he ran the projector and became as absorbed in the movies as any paying customer ever did.

During the summer after our junior year in Sulpher Springs High School, Freddie, Red, Charlie, and I got our first real summer jobs working for Daff-knee at the drive-in.

We all went to work about two hours before dark each day, as there was a lot of getting ready to be done long before any customers arrived.

Daff-knee spent this time in the projection booth, which was right in the middle of the field in the same low building as the concession stand. While he was setting up the reels and the two big carbon-arc projectors, we popped and boxed dozens of boxes of popcorn for the evening. About half of these were taken to the ticket booth at the entrance so they could be sold to cars as they came in. The remainder gave us a head start on the big business in the concession stand.

About six o'clock, with no daylight savings time, and depending on what the movie was and how early cars started to line up, we opened up the box office at the entrance. It was a small, triangular building with the entrance drive coming in on both sides. Normally only one person sold tickets, but if there was a real hot movie we would have to open two ticket lines, one on each side of the booth, to keep the cars moving in from Raccoon Road so they wouldn't back up into a jam on the main highway.

Admission was one dollar for adults and fifty cents for children. On Friday nights, the price was two dollars for a car load, no matter how many that was.

Three sets of movies were shown each week. Each night was a double feature. One set showed on Sunday, Monday, and Tuesday. These were usually Westerns. The next set showed Wednesday and Thursday. The third set showed on Friday and Saturday. There were five extra cartoons before the show on Friday to try to attract more families.

Once the movie started, except for the person whose turn it was to run the ticket booth, our main job was to operate the concession stand. Daff-knee called it the "confession stand." When we asked him why, he replied, "'cause all the guilty ones come walkin' in here with a grin on their faces and stuffing their shirts in their britches. They also go wash their hands before they buy anything to eat. If hand-washing ain't confession, then I don't know what is!"

During the early parts of the evening, the food business was pretty slow, so we often left only one person in the concession stand, and the other two of us went out to try to catch "slip-ins." If the film was running smoothly, Daff-knee loved nothing better than to join us for a few minutes. He loved catching a "slip-in."

"Slip-ins" were, of course, people who slipped in to the drive-in without paying, usually planning to get into the car of a paying friend who was already inside.

There was a chain-link fence which ran all the way around

181

the field. It had barbed wire on top, which should have discouraged climbers, and it did. The problem was that Daff-knee, obsessed with the idea that people could watch without paying, had planted three rows of white-pine trees just outside the fence to block the view of anyone trying to look in from outside. They did block the view, but the pine trees had now grown until their long limbs, many of which went straight over the barbed-wire of the chain-link fence, made it very easy for determined people to climb out on a limb and drop down on the inside. Our job was to catch them.

All kinds of interesting things were sure to happen when catching slip-ins. The best method was to hide in the darkness behind the back row, wait until a slip-in got way out on the limb, then scare them so badly that they'd fall off.

Once we startled Miles Chambers, and he started to try to climb back up the limb so that he could run for it. The pine limb broke and Miles landed astraddle of the barbed wire. He never tried to slip in again.

When we caught someone, we were supposed to bring the culprit to the concession stand and turn them over to Daff-knee. He delighted in scaring them to death.

"Don't you know that this is exactly the same thing as stealing?" he would rant and rave. "Every time you come over that fence without paying, it's like reaching in my pocket and taking money out, money that I have to use to buy groceries for my little girls. Why, I think I'll just call the police and have them come right out here with their sirens on and their red lights flashing and haul you-all up to jail."

To most teenagers, especially girls, his threat was, "I'm going to call your daddy right now. I'll bet he thinks you're at church or choir practice, anyway, and not here trying to steal from me by sneaking in at the drive-in theatre. What do you think of that?"

Since he enjoyed the yelling, Daff-knee never did any of the things he threatened to do, and the slip-ins kept doing it again and again, climbing the trees, hiding in the trunks of cars, only to be caught again and again.

The really busy time each night was the fifteen-minute intermission between the two features. While a short advertisement for food and drinks showed on the screen, we all worked like wild serving hot dogs, hamburgers, cold drinks, candy, and other treats to the droves of people who came to the concession stand to load up for the second show. Much of the evening was spent in cooking up for this ahead of time, serving as fast as we possibly could, then cleaning up after intermission. We earned our pay based on the success of these fifteen minutes.

During the second show, we were paid for working in an entirely different way.

Once the second show was well under way and the concession stand cleared out, Daff-knee would make an announcement over the speaker system to be heard in all cars: "If you wish to be served in your cars, please turn on your parking lights." Then it was time to "get the lights."

Out we would go to cars with their parking lights on to take food orders which we filled, curb service style, on small window trays.

"Getting the lights" was the educational part of our whole job, for next to every car which had its parking lights turned on there were cars in which the show was much better than anything going on on the movie screen. Who could possibly help it if on the way to and from these cars-to-be-waited-on we happened to pass by and even casually notice the strange happenings in other cars—in which the occupants did not need to be waited on in any way whatsoever.

We knew exactly who in all of Sulpher Springs, and indeed in most of Nantahala County, was doing what, and exactly with whom. We would have worked all night free just for the educational value of being able to "get the lights."

Working at the Big-Screen was not just a night job, though. There was work that had to be done during the daylight hours. This involved mowing the grass and "picking up the field."

"Picking up the field" was a nasty job that had to be done every morning. We met Daff-knee at ten o'clock and started to work gathering up everything people had thrown out the windows of their cars the night before. This was another educational experience.

Each of us had a trash can on wheels and a stick with a spike on the end of it. We also wore work gloves. "Don't pick this stuff up with your bare hands," Daff-knee would always warn us. "You're liable to get gonorrhea of the galoshes, or a whole lot worse. Don't step in anything, and use your spike."

From what we picked up each morning we gradually came to name each row of the theatre parking field. The front rows were called "Candyland," because about all which was thrown out there were children's candy wrappers. The parents seemed to keep even the popcorn and drink cups off the ground—or more likely, they just didn't buy any.

Farther back in the field was an undistinguished area simply known as "Popcorn Alley," where every kind of discarded food trash abounded. These were the rows inhabited by serious moviegoers who worked at eating their way through both features, some coming three and four nights a week.

Way in the back came the more educational area. On the high side of the back was what we called "Budweiser Boulevard," an area close to the gate where all the serious beer drinkers seemed to congregate. It was also an area that looked like the whole town had somehow conspired to empty their ash trays there.

On the low side at the far back, in the row next to the fence and partially overhung by white pine tree limbs, was the area we called "Condom Canyon." Daff-knee said, "You've got to be especially careful where you step back there, even with your shoes on."

A few specific spots had names from unusual finds, such as "Brassiere Beach" and "Panty Place." If we could only remember who had parked where on the night before, the amount of useful information we were able to gather could easily double.

One of our biggest daytime duties was mowing the grass. While the driving lane between each row of speaker posts was graveled, the spaces where the cars actually parked and a large area around the perimeter of the entire outdoor theatre was grass. We took turns working at the job of mowing with two Yazoo High Wheel Mowers.

Made in Yazoo City, Mississippi, the High Wheel Mowers had small wheels on the front and large, bicycle-type tires on the back. There was no safety guard of any kind around the whirring rotary blade, which often slung rocks at tremendous velocity in totally random directions. There were actually several holes in the big-screen itself which had come from Yazoo-thrown rocks.

Daff-knee took his turn in the grass-mowing as well. "You boys don't know how to do nothing," he would say, then proceed to run the mower into rocks and even mow into wires of fallen speakers on occasion.

When we worked outside, Daff-knee wore worn-out tennis shoes. They were worn out on the top rather than on the bottom. Not only were his knees multi-directional, his big toes turned up at a harsh angle. The constant rubbing of these upturned toes wore through the tops of the tennis shoes, and he walked along with his big toes sticking straight up, toenails never cut, poking out of the tops of the shoes.

"Why doesn't he cut those awful toenails?" my Mother once asked, after stopping by as we mowed and seeing Daff-knee's apparel.

"He says," I answered, telling her what I had already heard him tell everyone, "that the way his toes stick up, his shoes would hurt his feet worse than ever if he didn't have those toenails to protect him."

"I can't stand to even look at those things," she went on. "They're enough to make a dog sick."

No matter what anyone said, Daff-knee continued to wear his toes, and toenails, out the top of his tennis shoes.

One day Red, Freddie, Charlie and I were all taking turns mowing. We had picked up the field and were now just getting a really good start on the mowing job when Daff-knee arrived.

"You boys don't know what you're doing," he began. "Give me one of those high wheelers." We did.

He started prancing around with the big lawnmower, throwing gravel every which way and constantly commenting on how slow and sorry we all were, or we would be long finished by now. We were, at the time, mowing along the fence at the back of the field behind what we called "Condom Canyon," and Daff-knee kept running the blade of the Yazoo mower again and again into the chain-link fence. "CLIIINNNKKK-K-k-k-kkk" it would go every time he did it. All of a sudden Daff-knee let loose of the mower handles and slapped at his neck. Then with his other hand he slapped his leg three times. We could see yellow jackets everywhere and knew that he had mowed into a nest. Yellow jackets were simply all over and still pouring out of the cut-open nest in the bottom of the fence.

Daff-knee grabbed the high wheel mower and began to run backwards, letting go to slap at a new sting with every step. Running backwards as he was, he didn't see a speaker pole and ran straight into it. He stopped dead cold, but the big mower kept coming and rolled over his right foot.

Before Daff-knee even felt what had happened, he looked down and his right toe no longer stuck up out of his tennis shoe. We looked up just in time to see the big toe, all in one piece, flying through the air over Budweiser Boulevard, across the fence and out of the drive-in theatre field.

Still not feeling pain, Daff-knee hollered, "There goes my toe," and, running forward this time, he took off in the direction in which it had gone. The four of us were right on his heels.

We got to the fence in time to see the big toe land on the roof of Rufus Stamey's tool shed. The tool shed was behind the Stamey house next to the drive-in. As if in slow motion, the toe, toenail visible and intact, rolled off the edge of the roof and was caught in mid-air by Towser, Rufus Stamey's big cross-breed German shepherd/boxer. In one great gulp, Towser swallowed Daff-knee's lost toe! Daff-knee sat down and cried. It was not the pain. It was the insult of the entire event. He cried and muttered, "Ignorant teen-age incompetents...damned yeller jackets...half-breed mongrel..." the same lament over and over again.

Red got Daff-knee's Oldsmobile and, incompetent and ignorant or not, Daff-knee was glad to have us drive him to Dr. York's clinic.

Dr. York cleaned up where the toe had been, gave him a tetanus shot, and stitched him all back together again.

On the way to take Daff-knee home, he wanted to go by the drive-in and get his check book which he had left there. As we drove in past Rufus Stamey's house, there in the yard stood old Towser, gagging for all he was worth. We watched as, with a great retch, Towser vomited the intact toe onto the ground.

"Whooo, look, Daff-knee," I shouted. "Mama always said that your toenails are enough to make a dog sick. You ought to pick that thing up and trim the toenail right now."

Daff-knee didn't think it was funny. He also did not want the toe anymore. Later, with the help of a long stick, the four of us boys reclaimed it from Towser's lot. We respectfully buried it under the pine trees behind Condom Canyon and erected a small wooden cross over the grave-site. We were certain that the cross caused much confusion to those moviegoers who chose to park there afterwards.

Daff-knee never helped us with the mowing again.

The first thing all of us wanted to do once we had an income from working at the Big Screen was save up to buy a car.

Red didn't need a car. His father had given him the old Ford pick-up truck we had already driven so much. It was his sixteenth-birthday present, and he spent his money buying all kinds of junk to fix up his truck.

The Ford was a 1951 model with a flat-head V-8 engine. One of Red's first improvement projects was to put on big chrome-plated dual exhaust pipes which ran exposed back along both sides of the truck and ended with a flare just in front of the back fenders.

Later improvements included spinner hubcaps, ripple bumpers front and rear, half-chromed headlights, and an eight-ball gear shift knob. The truck didn't run any better than it had when we got it stuck at Uncle Floyd's, but it looked better, and it sure did make a lot of noise.

Red loved to "race" the Ford truck around the outside track of the drive-in field, pretending that the gravel perimeter drive was a dirt stock-car track and sliding around all the curves at what was something close to thirty miles-an-hour. All of us knew that Wendell Sutton and some of the big guys who really did have their own cars drag-raced them out toward Yunagusta Mountain, but we wouldn't dare enter into this real world of racing on the highway.

After saving up for the first six weeks of the summer, Freddie, Charlie, and I had accumulated a total of one-hundred-and-sixty-one dollars in our automobile fund. It was time to go shopping.

"Larry Hendricks' Used Car Heaven" was the biggest and best place in Nantahala County for "pre-owned", as he called it, transportation.

"Look at it this way," Larry himself said on his own radio commercials, "somebody else has already had all the problems and paid to have them fixed. All you've got to do now is 'Buy from Larry, and ROLL!'"

It was early on a Saturday morning in July when we went, money in Charlie's pocket, to deal with Larry Hendricks.

It looked like he had two hundred cars on his big lot right in the middle of Sulpher Springs. Most of the Fords, Chevys and Plymouths on the front row had prices of twelve to fifteen hundred dollars on the windshields. We passed them by and went straight in and asked to speak to Larry himself.

After we told him what we were looking for, and he had managed to find out, down to the last cent, exactly how much money we had between the three of us, he said, "What you boys need is a good, solid, fisherman's special." Since none of us particularly liked to go fishing, we didn't quite get what he was talking about, but we followed him back to the very back row of the lot.

"Here's your choice boys," Larry said, pointing down the back row, "Not a lemon on the tree. You can have any car of your own choosing on this row for one-hundred-and-fifty-dollars. See, you'll have eleven dollars left over after you deal with Old Larry."

We walked down the row. There was a 1948 DeSoto with fluid drive, which I knew to stay away from. Next came a 1950 Pontiac Super-Chieftain with a straight-eight engine and an amber head of Chief Pontiac which lighted up at night as a hood ornament. The Pontiac had a big, oval shaped pool of oil under it, so we kept on walking.

Next was a '38 Ford roadster, with no top and, we noticed, no engine either. Then we saw our car.

There it was, at the end of the row. A baby-blue 1949 Hudson Hornet which looked like a big, beautiful upside-down bathtub with wheels under it. It was gorgeous!

The big Hudson had a sun visor which wrapped all the way around the windshield. There was plenty of room in the front and back seats to haul six or eight people without even crowding them in. And the trunk—the trunk would hold enough junk to camp out for a week.

We quickly began to talk about how easy it might be for us to make a trip all the way across the country in a car like this. Why, by the next summer, we would surely be planning to go all the way to California.

We paid Larry the hundred-and-fifty dollars. He jump-started the Hudson, and we drove it away.

We couldn't wait to get it to my house where we could really go over it and shine it up. We drove straight there and started by washing the car and drying it all over. There was a little leak which went from the base of the back window into the trunk, but we thought a person shouldn't really put anything in the trunk of a car that shouldn't get wet anyway. Before we were finished, we waxed the baby-blue car and shined it all over.

Finally we lifted the huge engine hood. Freddie began looking for the dip-stick to check the oil. He located it and pulled it out with a jerk. To our dismay, the dipstick was broken off. Only enough of it was left to hold the handle in place, and this fragment was not nearly long enough to check the oil.

We went in the house and called Larry back at the used-car lot.

"Don't worry boys," Larry assured us. "That Hudson is a precision machine. It burns exactly one quart of motor oil to each tank of gas. Put in a quart of thirty-weight every time you fill up, and you won't have a thing to worry about."

Right now we were beginning to worry about what we had done with our hundred-and-fifty dollars.

Actually the Hudson ran pretty well. The engine hummed and the car rode great. It was heavy and the shocks were pretty well shot, so that it rode like a big boat. In fact we called it the "Blue Boat," and it became a favorite vehicle for many of our friends for riding around in through the course of the summer...for a while.

One day, while mowing at the Big-Screen, Red McElroy said, "You-all think that Hudson's so great? Why it couldn't outrun my Ford pick-up around this field if I gave you a half-a-lap head start."

The challenge was so ridiculous that we couldn't resist.

Red walked about half-way around the field and tied his handkerchief to a speaker post. "When you pass that post, I'll start after you. My guess is that I'll pass you before you come all the way around and back to here. Give me room across in front of the screen. That's where I plan to pass you up. Go on ahead and start when you want to."

Freddie was going to drive. Charlie Summerow and I would be spectators and judges of a sort.

Freddie said, "Holler 'go' and I'm off!"

The Hudson revved up. We hollered "GO!" Freddie took off. The Hudson was especially slow on the takeoff. Red knew that, and it was the reason for the head start. Otherwise there would be no race at all. Freddie got it in second gear and planned to stay there all the way around. He was probably going thirty or thirty-five in second gear when he passed the handkerchief.

At this point Red popped the clutch on the Ford, and in a shower of gravel and a cloud of dust, started right then to overtake the Hudson. It looked like a scene out of an old silent movie meant to be accompanied by tinny piano music: a blue Hudson Hornet, roaring in second gear at thirty-five miles an hour, leading an old red Ford pick-up truck, complete with spinner hubcaps and chrome exhaust pipes. Charlie and I laughed until we could hardly stand up.

The Hudson won! When they came past us at the finish line, Freddie had the gas on the floor and the Hudson was still thirty or forty yards ahead.

He was so excited by the victory that he forgot about the Condom Canyon Curve on the back side of the Big-Screen field. He had just been getting started when he rounded this sharp corner on the first lap, and now he was going into it at more than thirty miles an hour.

We watched with mixed fascination, amusement, and horror as the big Hudson entered the turn, worn-out shock absorbers giving way completely on the outside, and the huge, blue bath-tub of a car went down on one side, then rolled all the way over on its top and slid to a stop against the chain-link fence under the white pine trees. Freddie crawled straight out, dusty but unhurt.

By now Red had stopped the truck and was wondering with the rest of us: "What the hell are we going to do next?"

Daddy had paid for the insurance on the Hudson even though he really didn't think we should have bought the old car. Along with this payment went a threat: "I don't go for this car business. You just better see that you don't get into any kind of trouble with it. Owning an automobile is an adult responsibility."

How in the world were we going to convince him that this was an unavoidable "accident," and that we weren't really what Daff-knee Garlic always called us—"Durn immature teenagers!"

"I've got a plan," Freddie stopped us all. He explained his brainstorm to us, and we set to work putting it into action.

With all the ropes we could find, we used a combination of poles, jacks, and the Ford pick-up truck to finally turn the Hudson back onto its wheels. It hit the ground with a great dusty bounce, leaving as bare evidence of what had happened a big spot where all the motor oil had run out.

"Looks like it might still run," Charlie said. Only the roof itself was mashed in. Not even a window glass was broken.

"It's out of oil for sure," said Freddie. "We'd better roll it."

Roll it we did, behind the screen of the Big-Screen, after which we got a big tarp from Red's father's barn and covered the blue wreck up with it. It was completely out of sight. Now all that was left to do was to rake the gravel back in order and cover up the big oil leak. We did that, and there was nothing to be seen at all.

"It's out of sight," said Charlie. "What do we do to explain why the car's gone?

"Wait until after dark and I'll show you," Freddie answered.

We couldn't do anything as soon as it got dark, though, because that was movie time and we all had to work as usual. All through the evening, we waitied until the seond feature was finally over and the cars had all left for the night. We got in Red's truck and rode around a little while to give Daff-knee a chance to go on home before we returned to the scene of the crime.

Now, in complete darkness, we drove the Ford truck behind the screen and backed it up to the Hudson. Charlie and I pulled the tarp off, folded it, and put it into the bed of the truck.

Next we tied the Hudson to the back of the truck with a big rope. Red got in to drive and Freddie rode in the Hudson to steer it.

There was no traffic on Raccoon Road as we pulled the wrecked car out the back gate of the Big Screen and headed out into Raccoon Cove. In complete darkness we drove to the first big curve where the road crossed a culvert over a nearly dried up offshoot of Raccoon Creek. Red pulled to the side of the road.

Reaching behind the seat of the truck, Red pulled out his daddy's twelve-gauge shotgun, loaded a shell, and walked around the Hudson. He got as close as he dared, aimed the shotgun at the right front tire, and pulled the trigger.

"BLAM!" the shotgun roared.

"Blowout!" Red laughed.

We untied the rope, then the four of us pushed the crippled Hudson off the bank so that it rolled over on its top for the second time in less than twenty-four hours and landed upside down in the dry bed of Raccoon Creek.

At that point, Red told us good night and drove off and left us there. Freddie, Charlie, and I started walking for Charlie's house. It was the closest. We got there in about twenty minutes.

"The car blew a tire and we slid off the road," Charlie told his mother. "It turned over in Raccoon Creek, but we're OK."

"Oh, you poor babies," she wailed. "It's just a miracle under heaven that you weren't all killed."

We then called all our parents and went home.

It was too late that night to do anything about the Hudson, so we waited until the next day. Daddy drove us to where the ruined Hornet lay and looked it over with us.

The blown out tire was obvious. "Lucky you came out alive. One of you did a good job not to hit some other car." He never knew that there wasn't another car within a good two miles at the time.

"Let's try to roll it over and pull it up out of there."

We drove to Red's house and told his father what had happened. Red hadn't said a word about it at all. Then Daddy asked if he could borrow Mr. McElroy's tractor to help us pull the Hudson out of the creek.

Back at the wreck, we rolled the Hudson over with ropes, again for the second time in a day, and pulled it back up into the road with the tractor. We put on the spare, then towed the Blue Bathtub back to Charlie's house behind the borrowed tractor.

The right side was pushed in some, having rolled over that way twice already, but the doors worked, and somehow, still no glass was broken.

The top was pushed down, but Daddy got inside, laid down on the front seat and pushed his feet against the top of the car. Up it popped into almost the same shape it had had to begin with, though a great deal of paint was scraped off and there was a definite wrinkle all the way around the perimeter.

"For a hundred-and-fifty dollar car, I believe you can sand that top and repaint it with a brush and you won't be much worse off." Then he took a plumber's friend and popped some of the dents out of both doors on the right side of the car.

193

"Let's see if she'll start."

We quickly suggested that some oil might have run out into the creek and, with Daddy's help, we borrowed the dipstick from the Dodge and tried to check it. That didn't help much at all. We had to add four quarts of oil just to get it to show up on the Dodge stick, which may not have been right at all, but at least we knew we had some oil in the engine.

The Hudson cranked and ran perfectly on the very first try.

During the coming weeks, we did sand the top and painted it, with a brush and paint from Daddy's hardware store, a dark blue color. We tried to paint the doors a color to match the original baby blue, but it never did quite match. I have, in years since, continued to see that now-two-tone Hudson still roaming the roads of Nantahala County, through a succession of mostly teenage owners.

The Big Screen Drive-In stayed open through the month of September each year, then closed down until the first of May, when the weather warmed up enough for people to sit in their cars through the movies. The high point at the end of the season was the week-long run of a special double-feature sure to please everyone.

This year the first-run special feature was to be "The Guns of Navarrone," followed by an all-time favorite, "The Robe." The incongruity of these two features seemed to occur to no one and the combination was to be a sure pleaser, as they ran one after another for the final week of September.

At the very end of the summer, Red had added the ultimate custom modification to the red Ford pick-up. Near the end ports of both giant chrome exhaust pipes he had installed spark plugs, wired through a dashboard switch to the ignition coil.

Now he could pour on the gas and flip the dash switch causing the spark plugs to ignite the unburned gas coming out of the exhaust pipes just as it reached the oxygen of the outside air. Roaring flames would shoot at least ten feet out of each side of the pick-up truck.

It was an awesome sight and sound to behold.

During the last big week at the Big-Screen, Red drove the pick-up to work each night and parked it beside the concession stand. During the big climax scene of the "Guns of Navarrone," he would crank up the Ford and shoot flames each time one of the huge guns went off on the screen. We were never sure if the movie-goers ever figured out what was happening, but they sure did pour into the concession stand to buy cold drinks at intermission. "Was that movie in 3-D?" one thirsty customer asked.

On Friday night, Freddie was selling tickets and he called to the concession stand on the intercom to report: "Miles Chambers and Lori Deaver on the back row." This was sure to be an "action car" we'd want to be on the lookout for later on in the evening.

About half-way through the "Guns of Navarrone," Red came up with an idea. "Let's give Miles and Lori a big thrill for their money," he said.

"What do you mean?" we all asked.

"Let's go back and park the truck in front of them and toast them a little bit when the big-gun scene goes off."

It sounded like a wonderful idea to all of us.

There was no business in the concession stand during the big climax scene, so we all got in the pick-up and moved it around to just in front of where Miles and Lori were parked. They didn't see us. In fact, they didn't seem to be seeing anything that was happening on the outside of the car.

As we worked the truck into perfect position, Charlie noticed Miles's car windows were down and he had his shirt hanging out the window. "That show-off!" he commented. "I wouldn't be surprised if he hung his pants out next."

The big shooting scene was already starting on the screen. Red had the truck running so that he was ready. "The Guns of Navarrone" were being blasted away and the whole mountainside was being blown apart. "It's almost time," said Red as he revved up the engine.

The screen seemed to blast apart as Red shoved down on the accelerator and flipped the switch on the dashboard. The truck felt as if it lunged forward, and the night was lighted up by two huge flames rushing backwards, seeming to engulf Miles Chambers' Chevy.

Everything happened fast. Miles's shirt caught fire and fell inside the Chevy. When it did, he and Lori jumped out opposite sides of the car and ran, trying desperately to pull various articles of clothing back into more decent positions.

As all of this happened, we realized that the flame-throwing exhaust pipes had set fire to the matted pine needles that had built up over the years from the white pine trees all around the perimeter of the entire parking field. In the dry and windy September night, the pine needles blazed up quickly, and the fire spread to the trees themselves in no time.

Car engines leaped to life all over the drive-in as the circle of flames crept around the triple row of pine trees and threatened to shut everyone in. There was a race to the exit gate that put the great Hudson race to shame as the whole field of moviegoers decided they had seen enough.

Inside the projection room, Daff-knee knew that something was going wrong outside. "The Guns of Navarrone" wasn't over yet and "The Robe" was still to go, but he could tell there were a large number of cars moving about outside.

He came running through the empty concession stand just as Miles Chambers's Chevy, long since abandoned by Miles and Lori (who stood, now clothed, except for Miles's burned shirt, by the back of the concession stand), exploded as the burning pine needles swept under the gasoline tank.

"Hell's bells!" Daff-knee hollered. "What the hell have you-all done now?" Just then, the flames from the circle of pine trees reached the Big-Screen, and it burst into flame, the creosoted framework burning with great intensity and adding to the climactic elegance of "The Guns of Navarrone."

The last thing we saw before we, too, jumped into Red's truck, taking Lori and Miles with us, and sped for the exit gate, was Daff-knee. He was running full speed backwards, headed down Raccoon Road and watching his own Big-Screen Drive-In Theatre go up in flames.

As he disappeared from sight, the second camera automatically kicked in and began to project the intermission commercial onto the flame-covered screen.

"Do you call the fire department to put out a fire at a drive-in theatre?" Miles asked?

All Lori said was, "Oh, shut up!"

Each time I drive down Raccoon Road, I remember—the old blue Hudson, Condom Canyon, the Yazoo High Wheel Mowers. I see the vines and grass year by year hide all evidence that the Sulpher Springs Big-Screen Drive-In Theatre was ever there.

I did, though, walk up one day and look through what was left of the rusty chain-link fence, and there I saw, still in place, the faded wooden cross marking the final resting place of Daff-knee (his real name was "Clarence," you know) Garlic's big toe.

"Big-Screen," I thought reverently, "rest in peace."

Winning and Losing...Again

CARRIE BOYD WAS STILL AROUND. Our life together, beginning with that awful first day of school, had been one of hate, and at times, almost love.

I hated her with a passion that first day of school when her cry of "That little boy wet his pants" echoed through the halls of Sulpher Springs Elementary School. In the second grade, I hated her with a *vengeance* when I wet my pants a second time, she announced it to the entire class, and I knocked her front tooth out. My vengeance was made complete by her own father when he paid me five dollars for getting rid of the tooth. She hated me back, and I loved it!

Years later, we both thought we were going to love it when we slipped off on the big camping trip to Uncle Floyd's cabin, but as things turned out—or *washed* out, I should say—we ended up not speaking at all for months afterward.

All through the summer when Red, Freddie, Charlie, and I worked at the Big-Screen Drive-In, I jealously tormented Carrie anytime I knew she was parked in a car with a date other than me. At the same time, I totally refused to get closely enough involved with her to make any kind of exclusive go of her potential affections.

At the bottom of it all, I knew that it was Carrie's mother who was in love with me. Not me specifically, in any perverse way for herself, but the *idea* of me as the perfect mate for her own daughter and only child.

I enjoyed this special relationship because it meant that Mrs. Boyd cultivated social events to place Carrie and me together, and the events themselves were always fun, whether or not I could bring myself to admit that being with Carrie might actually be fun after all. I was becoming her socially cultivated and acceptable "date."

Through the autumn of our senior year at Sulpher Springs High School, Carrie and I seemed to fall together into a kind of unspoken understanding based not so much on passion as on a cross between convenience and marginally-comfortable acceptance of one another. It was finally assumed we would end up together at all of those events that our community of peers was a part of.

Still, as far as passion was concerned, there remained a fence between us that neither was willing to cross.

Winter seemed to come early in the mountains this particular year. The first big snow fell on Thanksgiving Day—unusually early, as most of our snows usually came from January to March. When a second big snow fell about the tenth of December, school closed, and Freddie, Red, and I spent our days sledding and partying. We would go much farther to a good party at night than we would ever dare go to get to school in such dangerous weather.

About the third day school was out, Charlie Summerow called to invite everyone to come to his house for a big sledding party.

Charlie's father owned an apple orchard which began behind their house on East Street and went on for acres up the mountain on the opposite side of Sulpher Springs from Yunagusta. Charlie had made plans for us to use the apple orchard to build sled runs.

We all went to his house about lunch time and found that he had invited half of our class from school, had built a bonfire at the bottom of the biggest hill, and was waiting for everyone to get there. His mother had fixed lots of sandwiches and hot chocolate for everyone.

Carrie Boyd was there, along with Lori Deaver, Mary Thomas, Jean-ette Carlson, and about a dozen of our friends in all. We were really set up for an afternoon of fun.

The apple orchard made a wonderful place to sled. The hillsides were terraced for the apple trees. The trees ran in rows around the hillsides and a grassy road was cut around the hill between each row of trees for spraying, pruning, and picking during apple season. This system of terraces made each sled run a series of jumps, one after another, from level to level, down the long hill.

We would go up to the top and come down, often several on a sled at a time, building up speed as the sleds left the ground each time we crossed one of the terraced roads.

After we had the hills all packed down and really slick, we heard Charlie yell, "Hey, look at this!"

When we looked, we saw him emerge from his father's barn with a huge blown-up inner tube from a tractor tire. "I'll bet this thing will hold almost all of us!"

We pulled the giant inner tube to the top of the orchard hill and began to try to figure out how to get on it. On the first few tries, everyone ended up falling off in no time, so that we ended up on the ground watching the big inner tube fly, all by itself, playing carom off the apple trees, to the bottom of the hill. Then we had walk to the bottom and pull it back to the top.

On about the fourth try, we figured it out. We must all sit on the sides of the inner tube, put our feet into the hole in the middle, and hold hands so as not to fall off. This worked pretty well, except that the unsteerable inner tube kept hitting apple trees, which turned out to be especially hard on the person nearest the tree.

A new plan was in order. This time we all sat on the inner tube with our backs to the middle and our feet on the outside. We interlocked arms and cut loose down the hill, leaning back against one another. Whenever we came near a tree, the nearest person could give a big kick and propel us away and on down the hill. It was something like being inside a pin ball machine and riding on the pin ball as we bounced off trees all the way down the orchard hill.

When we got the hang of things, we could go faster and faster, now with the entire tube bouncing off the ground each time we went across a terraced road with enough speed. It was great fun.

On one expecially violent trip, we missed most of the trees and built up a terrific head of steam. As the inner tube bounced into the air crossing one of the roads, all of us seemed to leave our seats, and for a moment, we flew through the air.

I came down first. No one ever figured out why. And instead of our landing evenly back-to-back, my rear end dropped entirely through the hole in the inner tube and everyone else landed in a tangle on top of me.

The inner tube did not know that it should, at this point, have stopped. It continued full speed down the terraced hill.

Each time we crossed a road, the entire contraption would fly into the air again, and then come down—again—with my rear end hitting the frozen ground before anything else did. I could not even begin to scream loud enough to tell the world about the horrible death I knew I was in the slow process of dying.

Finally we got to the bottom of the hill and ran out of speed. The whole load stopped. I lay on the ground, writhing in pain, unable to move and not at all beginning to get up.

When I opened my eyes, Carrie Boyd was standing over me smiling. She gently took my hand, brushed the snow from my face, looked me straight in the eyes, and said, "Would you like to go with me to a New Year's Eve party?"

I was too hurt to say "No," and so the date was made.

A brief moment of vengeance occured later in the day when we built a fake jump by the creek at the bottom of the hill, brushed our tracks away, and convinced Carrie and Lori to take a sled "across the jump...we've all done it...it's fun!" It was fun. Fun for those who were watching, as the two of them landed precisely in the middle of the half-frozen creek. Still, Carrie and I were going to the New Year's Eve party.

A few days later, when I could walk and talk again, I saw Carrie and she told me all about the upcoming party.

"It's really an adult party," she told me. "Every year my parents go to a big Elder's Club party at the Biltmore Hotel in

Asheville. This year they told me I was old enough to invite someone and go, too. We don't even have to ride to Asheville with them if you want to borrow your parent's car or something. I don't think that Hudson will make it to Asheville and back. Does that thing have any heat in the wintertime?"

"Of course that 'thing' has heat." I thought to myself, "More heat than you do, for sure," but I politely kept my mouth shut. After all, this sounded like a party that would be pretty good to go to, and I didn't want to get un-invited.

All through the Christmas holidays, Red, Freddie, and Charlie were jealous of my being invited to an "adult" party. They gave me quite a time about what kind of "adult" things I thought might go on at an Elder's Club New Year's Eve party.

Most of my Christmas presents this year were from the clothing department, as I was being outfitted by Mother to go away to college next year. A few of the things I got, I actually wanted: a camel's hair sport coat, Bass Weejuns, a blue and a yellow Gant shirt (complete with loops on the back), and a half-dozen pairs of Gold Cup socks. Many of the things I got were not my choice at all.

Heading the list of gifts I never would have chosen was a long, heavy, black wool overcoat.

The overcoat seemed to be two sizes too large to begin with. It was so heavy and so black that I couldn't imagine why anyone would actually buy something like this for himself and then wear it on purpose. I envisaged an entire textile industry built around the manufacture of giant, heavy overcoats designed to be bought by the mothers of college-bound high school seniors.

"I'll never wear this thing," I argued, only to be overcome by the parent speech about working-my-fingers-to-the-bone-to-give-you-what-I-never-had. I gave up and cut the long speech short by agreeing to wear the thing.

My new tactic was to wear the overcoat all the time and everywhere I went in hopes that Mother would get so sick of seeing it she would tell me to take it off. I was determined she would only tell me once.

At last New Year's eve came.

We had a new two-tone blue-and-white push-button trans-mission Dodge. Daddy had bought it as a year-end left-over when the new models came out in the fall and had gotten a good deal on it. As I had asked way ahead of time to use it for the big trip to Asheville, I spent the morning hand-washing the Dodge inside the garage (to keep from freezing to death) and carefully cleaning every part of the already-clean and new insides. The new Dodge had beautiful dark blue brocade upholstery, which Mother thought made it the "prettiest car I have ever seen."

When the Dodge passed my inspection, I drove it to War-ren's Blossom Shop to pick up Carrie's corsage: two pink carna-tions made into a wrist corsage for the pink spaghetti-strap dress her mother had taken great care to tell my mother she would be wearing. Then I drove to the dry cleaners to pick up my Sunday suit, which I had to wear because Mother insisted that the party would be "too formal for that new sport coat."

Too much of the afternoon was spent in bathing and dress-ing. I had gotten my hair cut the day before, to give it a day to grow back out a little. Everything was in order.

I got out of the bathtub and dried off only to find that Mother had picked and laid out my underwear while I was bathing. "I can at least pick out my own underpants!" I yelled at her for her effort.

"You never can tell when you might end up in the hospital," she yelled back. "It would be awfully embarrassing to wake up in the emergency room and hearing all the nurses talk about your hole-y underwear."

I got all dressed, right down to my Ipana tooth-paste and English Leather cologne, then had to wait over an hour before it was anything like time to go to Carrie's house.

The plan was for Carrie and me to follow the Boyds to Asheville. We were going to stop and eat supper somewhere on Tunnel Road. After that, we'd follow them on to the party, and then we were on our own for the rest of the night. Neither set of parents had set any time limits on our being home.

Arriving at the Boyds' house in my clean suit, clean car, and new black overcoat, I gathered Carrie's corsage from the seat beside me and marched up to the front door.

Mr. Boyd greeted me. "The girls aren't quite ready yet," he said with a wink and an invitation to sit down in the living room.

Soon Carrie and Mrs. Boyd came down the stairs. Both were lovely, I had to admit. I gave Carrie the carnation corsage, she "oohed," and we headed for the cars.

As it was more than an hour's drive to Asheville, we had to come up with a lot to talk about on the way to the party. We covered every topic we could think of—who was where and with whom tonight, what everyone we knew was planning to do after graduation, what everyone we knew had gotten for Christmas, along with evaluations of all our preferences ranging from dogs to cars to perfume. Long before we got to supper, we were talked out.

I followed Mr. Boyd as he turned into the Mountaineer Steak House, where we all had supper together. I tried to pay for my own, but of course, he insisted. (Mother had told me "Just be gracious.")

Now it was up to the Biltmore Hotel and the Elder's Club party.

Mr. Boyd took us in the door, and then we were really on our own.

"I want to see how Carrie can handle the adult social life before she goes off to school on her own next year," he told us.

"Oh, we can both handle this," I replied, "I've been to some parties in my time."

The Elder's Club New Year's Eve party was actually a quite simple affair, organizationally speaking. There was nothing to it but a big ballroom with a band in one end and a bar in the other. Liquor sale by the drink was illegal at this time, but this was a private party, all the booze belonged to the club, and all the drinks were free.

Being at the party was actually much easier than the ride over to Asheville in the car had been. The music, provided by a band with the unbelievable name of "Georgie Bowling and His Nine Pins," was loud enough to provide us with an excuse for not talking. We were both determined to dance every dance because neither one of us could think of anything else to talk about.

Since Nantahala County was publicly dry, I had never actually seen a bar in my life, let alone one at which anyone including myself could walk right up to and order a free drink.

We spent the evening trying to act informed, as again and again we took breaks from the dance floor to visit the bar.

Just before midnight, someone came in from outside to report that it had started snowing. Everyone rushed to the balcony at the side of the ballroom to see the beautiful, gigantic flakes filling the air and already covering the ground and the bushes outside.

By the time the band played and we sang "Auld Lang Syng," the whole world was as white as could be.

The party started to run down about one in the morning. It had snowed so much that Mr. Boyd suggested perhaps we follow him home, in spite of what he had said earlier about our being on our own. "It's just for the sake of safety."

We brushed the snow off both cars, started and warmed them, and began the long drive home.

It was slow going in the snow, and slower because Mr. Boyd was always watching to see that I was behind him.

"It's going to take us a couple of hours to get home, for sure," Carrie commented. As she said it, she slid way over in the seat of the Dodge until she was right next to me and draped her arm around my neck. I could smell what I thought was Jack Daniels and orange juice on her breath as she kissed me smack on the mouth!

At this rate I wasn't going to mind at all if it took several hours to make the long trip home. Mr. Boyd could slow down all he wanted to without ever knowing what he was causing to take place in the car behind him.

She did have enough sense to be careful not to make me run off the road. It was an evening to remember, and I was not very sure that Carrie (courtesy of Jack Daniels) was going to remember all of it.

About halfway home, I suddenly remembered that I had

gone to the bathroom the last thing before we had left the party. I remembered now because I was thinking that I might soon need to go again, and in spite of Carrie's new-found aggression, I was not about to admit to her that I was hearing a more acute call of nature than even *she* was sending.

For about fifteen minutes, I managed to avoid thinking about the inevitable. Then a growing pain started telling me that I would *have* to pay attention, one way or another. I did.

"I'm getting a little bit warm," I said. "Could you scoot over a little bit so we could get some air?"

"If it's air you want, you can certainly have it," she answered, with a definite sound of rejection in her voice, as she scooted away.

"No, come on back," I reassured her, and she did, again draping her arm around my neck.

It was a battle between two elemental forces of nature for the next half-hour as I alternated between delighting in Carrie's warm presence and trying to keep from wetting my pants. All the suppressed memories of first- and second-grade embarrassment came flooding back into my mind and flourished there.

Gradually one force won out over the other, and I began to groan and hold my breath as I tried to convince my bladder to hang on for another fifteen minutes until we might make it home. Carrie mistook the moaning and heavy breathing for excitement on my part, and she increased her attention accordingly.

I was in a real mess.

As we came into Sulpher Springs from the main highway, I knew I would never make it to Carrie's house in time unless every single traffic light was green. At this hour of the night, it seemed to me they should be turned off, but when I saw the first one turning red, I knew they were not.

As I lifted my foot to put on the brake to stop for the cursed red light, my bladder lost its grip on reality, and my newly pressed Sunday suit, the black wool overcoat (which I had kept on through thick and thin), and the beautiful blue brocade seats of the new Dodge all suffered from every trip I had made to the Elder's Club free bar.

It was the first day of school all over again as I thought, "If you're going to lose, do it big and get it all over with." I did it right!

Suddenly it seemed we had arrived at Carrie's house. Her mother came back to the Dodge as Carrie quickly scooted over to her side of the car.

"Why don't you come on inside and I'll fix breakfast for all of us?"

"I can't," was my quick reply. "I've got to get home. I think we're going to my grandmother's house to spend New Year's Day."

Quickly I took Carrie to the door, cut short her goodbye kiss, jumped in the Dodge, and took off.

On the way home I stopped at the first snowbank I came to. I took off the black, wool overcoat and stuffed it, soaking wet, into a culvert under the road by the snowbank. Then I found some newspapers in the trunk and spread them on the seat for the rest of the ride home.

Everyone was asleep at home. I discarded the newspapers (the seat was not very wet after all), hung my suit in the very back of the closet, changed into the underwear I would have chosen myself to begin with, and slipped into bed.

"I have finally done it!" I thought as I drifted off to sleep. "Eighteen years of trying...but tonight, I finally managed to wet my pants in front of Carrie Boyd without her ever finding out about it! Maybe I'm ready to grow up after all."

I lost touch with Carrie Boyd soon after high school, but every now and then, even to this very day, when I see someone who reminds me of her...I start looking for the bathroom.

A Different Drummer

RED MCELROY'S MOTHER DIED WHEN we were all in the seventh grade. She had been sick as long as I could remember, though I never really saw her much until I started going out to Red's house after we moved to East Street.

"Twelve years," Mr. McElroy said, "Twelve years she spent dying...ever since she found that hard lump in her breast when Red was just a baby."

Every time I had ever been to Red's house she was in bed, except for one warm summer afternoon when she was bundled up, even in the heat, and stretched on a lounger on the back porch.

She was a thin, wispy, ashen woman who called us into her room to speak to us when we were there. Once in a while she would ask me to stay and spend the night with Red, but when I called Mother to ask for permission she always said, "No, you bring Red over here to stay with us...that's too hard on Marie."

It came as no real surprise one day when Red didn't come to school, and Mrs. Evans, our seventh grade teacher at Sulpher Springs Junior High, announced to us that his mother had "finally died."

The night after that, I went with Daddy to Sprinkle's Funeral Home (Mother never did such things), to pay respects to Red and his father. It was then that I saw my first dead body.

There she was, Red's mother, stretched out on her back in a white-lined coffin and wearing a light blue night-gown. She looked almost as alive as she had at home, and about as able to get up as she ever had. I almost spoke to her without realizing what I was doing.

We stood in line and spoke to Mr. McElroy and to Red, though I didn't know what to say. Through the course of the evening, I heard several people say the same kinds of things to one another in conversations off in the corners of the crowded funeral home: "First Little Wally and now Marie...that leaves Wallace and Red all alone now..."

When we got back in the blue Dodge to go home, I told Daddy what I had heard and asked, "Who's Little Wally?"

"He was Red's brother who got killed," he answered straightforwardly.

I was left nearly breathless as here in one night I had both seen my first dead body and heard that Red, my best friend in all the world, had a dead brother I had never even heard of.

I looked at Daddy, wanting so badly to be told the whole story, but not daring to ask. He saw my look and began to tell me the story.

"Wally was thirteen years older than Red," Daddy began talking as I listened with the fascination of one who could not believe he had never heard this story before. "But I better start way back at the beginning so you'll get the whole picture.

"Wallace and Marie got married about 1930. I remember it because it was right in the hardest part of the depression and was six or seven years before your Mother and I got married. Marie was from South Carolina—I'm not sure how they met— and Wallace went down there to live and work on her daddy's farm.

"He loved airplanes and learned to fly while hanging out with a bunch of crop-dusters he got to know down there. I remember him flying up here once and landing in that same field of Burgie Welch's they used to fly out of later. I think that's what gave some of the younger boys the idea of using it after the war. Wallace was a real barnstormer.

"When the Second World War came around, Wallace joined the Army Air Corps and signed on as a pilot. Little Wally would have been ten or eleven years old by now, because he was born pretty soon after they were married. The Army decided that Wallace was too old for combat, but since he was an experienced pilot, they made an instructor out of him. He spent the whole war as a frustrated hero, training group after group of young boys whom he watched go off to the war he never got to go to.

"Right in the middle of the Second World War, when Little Wally was thirteen years old, Red was born...kind of a surprise a lot of people thought...Do you know that his real name is 'Horace?' "

My mind was moving as fast as it could trying to take in and put some kind of order into what I was hearing. It was a mixture of fascination and uncertain belief. I had never heard *any* of this. At the same time, I wanted Daddy to get on with what happened to Wally.

"What happened, Daddy?" I asked. "I mean, what happened to Little Wally?"

"That came in Korea," he answered, and I began my listening again.

"Little Wally graduated from Sulpher Springs High School and went down to State College to study agriculture. The Korean War broke out and Wallace, his daddy, got real excited. He was too old now even to be a trainer, but he wanted Little Wally to sign up. The boy joined the Navy and became a pilot like his daddy wanted him to be. Pretty soon he went off to Korea and was flying missions off an aircraft carrier. Wallace was tickled to death."

We were almost home now, and I was afraid time would run out before I found out what had happened. "What happened to him? I mean, in the end?" I asked almost desperately.

We turned into the driveway at home, and Daddy simply switched off the engine of the Dodge. We sat there in the dark as he told me the rest of the story.

"One day," Daddy went on, with deliberate slowness, "Little Wally got shot up pretty badly on a mission and was trying to get back to the carrier. Part of a wing-tip was shredded and his radio was dead, and everyone on the carrier thought he would ditch the plane in the sea and get pulled out. But he didn't. He tried to bring it in on deck and at the last minute stalled and hit the end of the carrier...there wasn't even anything left of him to send home.

"Haven't you ever seen his picture on the mantel at Red's house?"

I had often seen the picture he was now telling me about. It was an old, browning photograph of a young man in a uniform. "I thought that was Mr. McElroy's picture," I said.

Now I knew the story, and it was true, like the corner whisperers at the funeral home had said, "now there is only Wallace and Red." Everyone else was sadly gone.

With no mother, Red became every mother's child, and the time he spent at our house was so regular that he really was just another member of the family. He was also one of the very strangest people you could ever want to meet.

No matter where we went, Red was always the last one to get there. Movie, band practice, church, or camping trip—he never got to where he was going within thirty minutes of when he was supposed to be there.

My mother would ask, "Where have you been?"

"I was putting on my socks," he would answer.

I discovered he was telling the truth when he'd come spend the night at our house. I'd call him to breakfast and find him sitting on the edge of the bed trying to decide which sock to put on first—for thirty minutes at a time.

Red loved being in Wild Harry's class in the eighth grade. They both seemed to abhor the discipline of having to always be "on task," as teachers would later call it. It was very important to Red to know that it was important to Mr. Wilde that we learn as much about playing chess as about North Carolina history. "It's good for your mind," they both agreed.

Red really learned from Wild Harry. They were two of a kind, except for one thing. Red never had the patience or the subtlety to "stick with Mr. Goren's experience" (as Wild Harry described it) when we played eighth-grade contract bridge.

Freddie and Charlie and I loved to play bridge, even if we had to play with Red. The hard part was being his partner. In spite of everything Wild Harry had taught us about point counting and careful bidding, Red always insisted on opening with exactly what he thought he could make! Out of the clear blue, he would open with bids like "four hearts" or "five no-trump," never having heard even an opening offer from his partner.

One night we were at Lori Deaver's house playing bridge with Lori and her mother. Red's partner was Mrs. Deaver. When, on the first hand dealt, he opened with "five spades," Mrs. Deaver screamed, turned over backwards in her chair, and kicked a tray with cokes and potato chips all over the carpet. The evening was over before it started.

In junior high school, Red, along with all the rest of us, joined the band. He was going to be a drummer, and he was a natural.

Soon he was running the entire percussion section. No one ever knew what sounds would come from there next.

Red began to assemble for himself a huge, home-made trap-drum set. It was composed not only of second-hand drums of various sizes, but also of hub-cap cymbals, various tin drums and cans, and even a long board on which he had mounted eight car horns salvaged from Zimmer's Junkyard, and all wired to a series of buttons. He could play an entire out-of-tune octave on the car horns if his battery were charged up.

During marching band season, Red played snare drum and marched beside Freddie Patton's bass drum. He always fastened something (it might be a cow bell or a home-made cymbal) to the bottom of Freddie's bass drum. No one ever knew what to expect.

Right in the middle of wonderful old military cadences like "Hell on the Wabash" or "The Downfall of Paris," we'd hear adornments, paradiddles and strange sounds no one had ever imagined before. Mr. Lowe, the band director, said it was the first time in his career that people had been more interested in the drum cadences than in the marches the entire band played.

By now, Red was the owner of his father's old pick-up truck. Though we also had the blue Hudson, the truck was often the vehicle of choice when either off-road driving or heavy hauling were our priorities. With its spinner hub-caps and chrome exhaust pipes, Red decided it also needed a new paint job.

We bought a gallon of red enamel, taped all the chrome and covered the glass with newspapers, and painted it with a fly-sprayer. Some of the paint ran a bit, but overall, the red truck was as pretty as the Hudson.

The only problem with the Ford truck was that Red kept losing the keys. We would go bowling or to a movie, and when it was all over the keys were nowhere to be found. We'd end up having to walk all the way home, get the spare keys Mr. McElroy kept on a nail in the kitchen, and go to Daddy's hardware to have a new set made before we could drive again.

"It sure would be nice," Red said, "if you didn't have to keep up with the keys to drive this truck."

When we got into electronics class at school that year, we came up with a solution to lost keys—a keyless ignition.

We removed the ash tray and sawed off half the metal slide on one side. Then we removed the track in the dash that the ash tray slid into and cut it in two pieces.

The rest was easy: insulate both pieces, connect one ignition wire to each, then push the ash tray all the way in, and—*click*—you could hear the ignition come on. The starter was even easier. It was made by installing a cigarette lighter, wired so that when you punched in the lighter, the starter turned over.

Now all we had to do was push in the ash tray and punch the cigarette lighter, and we were on our way! We never told a soul about our invention.

During our senior year at Sulpher Springs High School, our English teacher was Red's nearest neighbor, Mrs. Amelia Harrison. Mrs. Amelia, who loved to take walks in the woods and read poetry aloud to herself as she walked, was absolutely in love with Henry David Thoreau. She even had a small farm pond in the back of the woods beyond Red's house which she named "Walden Pond." It was a place she went and meditated for hours.

"I wonder what she thinks about, all the time she spends out there?" I had once thought aloud.

213

"Probably about where her husband went!" my mother said, reminding me of the story we had all heard of how he just up and left a few weeks after their marriage, decades ago, and had never been seen or heard of again. "He probably got tired of sleeping with Thoreau," she commented, but I really didn't get it.

Mrs. Amelia still loved Thoreau, and one fine day in the spring of the school year, she was "taking us on an imaginary walk in the woods around Walden Pond" during English class. She had been doing this with deadly seriousness for all of the thirty-nine years she had been teaching English. This year was different.

The high moment was supposed to come as she read to us from Thoreau's "wonderful conclusion," which blessed the lives of those who were somewhat unique in this world as being persons who "hear a different drummer."

It was important to her to correct the way Mr. Thoreau had been most often misquoted as blessing those who "*march* to the beat of a different drummer."

"That's not what he said at all. That implies that we all *hear* the different drummer, but only a few choose to march to the sound. What he *does* say is that it is only the rare few who ever hear the different drummer, and once they have heard, they cannot keep from following."

It was a warm enough day that the heat should have been off, but all through her reading there was some sort of percussive accompaniment coming from the radiators in the back of the classroom. Everyone but Mrs. Amelia knew it was an arrangement of two yardsticks that ran from Red McElroy's feet through his desk and under the back radiator which made this music possible.

Never in all her years of teaching had Mr. Thoreau's conclusion evoked laughter. But this year, with Red McElroy in the back row of her English class, and soft rhythms coming from the radiator, it did. After all, Red was a most different drummer, and all of us had heard him.

After that day, all the kids in the band called him "Thoreau" McElroy.

We graduated from high school and went off to college. It was the early 1960s, and sending your kid to college was the thing every successful parent hoped to do. Few of our parents had been to college, and every parent's goal was to send us where they had never been. So off we went.

Red, not knowing what he really wanted to do with his life, followed his dead brother's example and went to State College to study agriculture. "I can always come home to the farm if nothing else turns up," he reasoned.

When we had graduated from Sulpher Springs High School, not one single one of us had ever heard of a place called Viet Nam.

But two years later, John Kennedy was dead, Lyndon Johnson was in the White House, and we watched as college seniors, without even having to apply for it, went straight from graduation to Saigon instead of to law or graduate school. We were all scared to death. We didn't understand what Viet Nam was all about.

Mr. McElroy was thrilled. He had been long worried, it seemed, that there would be no war for Red. Viet Nam was the answer to his prayers.

The conversations started on Red's next trip home, and continued, almost unchanged, all through his third year at State, where he was now an engineering student.

"You ought to drop out of school and join the service," Red's father argued. "Son, you've got the chance to be a hero that I never had and that your brother lost. This little war won't go on forever, so you had better come on home now and join up before it's too late."

"Not now," Red argued. "I'm in engineering now, and this stuff we're learning is so complicated that I'm afraid if I drop out I won't ever be able to catch back up. Let me get one more year out of the way, and then we'll see...OK, Dad?"

It was *not* OK, and the argument went on—Thanksgiving, Christmas holidays, semester break, spring holidays—until one weekend near the end of the year when we were all home at the same time.

"I've figured it out," Red said when we were together. "I don't know why I didn't think of this before. This will take care of me *and* satisfy everybody else at the same time."

"What are you talking about?" we all asked.

"I'm going to join the Army Band. That way I'll be in the service for Dad, and I'll also be doing something that I don't mind doing. I've already been to see the recruiter, and everything is taken care of."

So, after his junior year at State College, Red McElroy dropped out and joined the Army with a recruiter's promise that the band was waiting for him.

I saw him just before he left for basic training. "Everybody has to go through basic training," he told me uncertainly, "even those of us who are going to be in the band."

The fall semester began before Red got to come home from basic, so I had gone back to college without ever getting to see him on his first leave. When I did come home for a weekend later in the fall, Mother dropped the news casually during breakfast one morning. "Red didn't get in the band," was all she said.

"Is he home then?" I asked.

"Of course he's not home...you don't just get out of the Army." Her answer seemed charged with more feeling than she usually let herself express.

"What is he going to do, then?"

"They're going to send him to school to become a medic," she answered.

I was relieved. That's not so bad, I thought to myself. He can just work in some hospital somewhere.

When Red did come home for Christmas, the awful truth came out. He was being trained as a helicopter med-evac medic for immediate deployment to Viet Nam. He was to ride rescue missions to airlift wounded combat troops from battle areas.

We didn't talk much during those holidays. Even playing bridge seemed sadly tense.

The last day before going back to school, Red called me. "How about coming over," he said. "I want to put the truck away for safekeeping while I'm gone."

At his house we washed the truck and cleaned the inside. He topped the tank with gasoline so no moisture would condense in a half-empty tank. We topped up all the fluids. Then we backed the truck into an usused tractor shed on the side of the barn behind Red's house. We tied a tarp over it and closed the shed doors.

"I'll bet it starts first try when I get back."

"Yeah, if you haven't lost the keys."

Red managed a short laugh, and we said goodbye.

Almost as soon as Red got to Viet Nam, the letters started to arrive.

The very idea of Red McElroy writing letters was strange enough to begin with. He had never done that before, to anyone, not even to Jean-ette Carlson as far as anybody knew. Now, however, the letters seemed never to stop, as though his writing to all of us was a way of breathing enough real air to stay alive.

"It's exciting to be here," the first letter began, followed by long descriptions of strange people and stranger food.

Soon, though, it sounded like Red was riding some sort of wild emotional see-saw, or like his letters were coming from two different people. On one page a letter might sound patriotic and all "eager to win," while by the next page he was asking, "Why are we here? Why can't we all just come home?"

There were hints of his work, references to death and a few grisly jokes about body parts, but the letters were mostly political, even philosophical, in their tone.

We had seen in newspapers and on television that different groups of people were divided over this war. But Red was clearly divided within himself, as totally as if he were two completely different people. He sounded more and more terribly torn in two, and his letters led us all to realize that some people may be certain about this thing called war, but that sometimes there may be no such things as winning or losing. I felt torn with him.

I remember very well the night the phone call came. It was Mother calling, but she didn't say, "It's Mother," or "How are you?" or even "Hello." When I picked up the telephone, the first words she spoke were "Red's missing..." She finally went on. "The helicopter he was on was shot down. It crashed where they couldn't get to it or anything. Mr. McElroy says that's why they're just saying that everybody's 'missing'."

We all lived silently with that information for most of the coming year. Then, with an offensive which changed territorial lines a new message came. The wreckage had now been found, identified, and excavated. No one seemed to be sure about what was found at the crash site, but now Red was officially declared dead.

We all went home for the memorial service. It was held by an Army chaplain who never knew him, assisted by our minister, the same one who had buried Wally and Red's mother. Red was gone.

Mr. McElroy would not believe his son was dead.

"He can't be dead," he insisted. "He's going to be a hero. He can't be dead. And besides that, they didn't send his body home." Neighbors shook their heads in a sad way and tried to convince him to accept what had happened.

Several months after the memorial service, Mr. McElroy had a visitor. The stranger, who had asked for directions around Sulpher Springs and then showed up at the McElroy farm, introduced himself as Harold Bryan. We had heard of him, as Red had mentioned him in several letters.

Harold Bryan and Red had become close friends in Viet Nam and now home from his own tour, Harold had come to visit Mr. McElroy. The real purpose for his coming was not just for a visit. He had brought a package.

From inside his coat pocket, Harold Bryan produced a brown envelope, which he said nothing about as he handed it to Red's father. The envelope was sealed and on the front were printed the words "LAST WILL AND TESTAMENT." In the blank space below them was printed "Horace L. McElroy."

"I carried this for Red until I came home," he explained. "He wanted to be sure you got it exactly the way he prepared it for you. He didn't want it mailed. I promised to carry it here to you. I'm sorry, Mr. McElroy." Then Harold Bryan left.

Red's father would not open the will. He placed it on the mantel, next to Wally's picture, and refused to open it. "If I open it, he'll be dead. He's not dead...I know he's not...he's going to be a hero...I won't open it or he'll be dead."

Mr. McElroy closed Red's room up and kept it exactly as it had been left. There was even an odd dirty sock on the floor next to the dusty trap-drum set and the silent car horns. The shade was pulled down tight and the door was locked.

We learned to live with his absence.

The most insulting thing of all happened the next summer.

Someone stole Red's pickup truck. Mr. McElroy was in tears as he told us about hearing a noise in the night but not looking until morning when he saw the tractor-shed door standing open. The thief had even taken the tarp that covered the truck.

Still the room waited. And the unopened "LAST WILL AND TESTAMENT" remained sealed on the mantel.

Mr. McElroy lived alone for twelve years. His days were filled with working on the farm. No one even dared imagine how he lived through twelve years of nights all alone.

At last he suffered a stroke, and after a blessedly brief hospitalization, he died as he had lived those last years—alone.

There were no relatives at all. The farm had been left to the church as a possible site for a retirement home.

It was Mrs. Amelia Harrison, the nearest neighbor and our old senior English teacher, who gathered a few neighbors and went over to clean the house before out-of-town church officials arrived to look over their new property.

While they were cleaning, Mrs. Amelia picked up the brown envelope on the mantel. It seemed worn, as it it had been handled often through the years, but it had clearly never been opened. All of the neighbors looked at her, and unflinching, she looked back at them. "Would it do any harm?" was all she asked. No one said a word.

Slowly she tore open the brown envelope, while everyone else watched.

It was a standard printed form for simple wills, with blank spaces for names and dates to be filled in. She scanned the first page, all in order, then turned to the next.

On the back side of the first page there was writing scrawled by hand. Mrs. Amelia turned the paper over and began to read the handwriting only she, of those gathered there, could truly recognize as Red's. His last message home:

"I am not dead," she read quietly. "I am having Howard bring this to you so that it will surely get to you.

"I cannot take it here anymore…I must get out. Some of us have a plan. Every time a chopper goes out, a few of us sign on who don't go. We send dog-tags and boots and uniforms, but WE don't go. If the chopper doesn't come back, the extras disappear.

"There are a dozen ways out of here—Thailand, Cambodia, on to Japan—Sweden and Canada. I do not know if you will ever want to see me again after this or not. Because I cannot be the kind of hero you wanted.

"If I get all the way out, I will somehow come and get my truck. If you want to see me again, leave the light on in my room for a few days after the truck disappears. If not, I won't embarass you anymore. No matter what—Dad, I love you."

Mrs. Amelia quietly folded the page and it disappeared, probably forever, into the deep pocket of her old dress.

"Wherever Red is," she said, "we all know he hears a different drummer."